The Samaritan Treasure

The Samaritan Treasure

STORIES BY MARIANNE LUBAN

COFFEE HOUSE PRESS :: MINNEAPOLIS :: 1990

"Tomorrow You'll Forget" first appeared in *Stiller's Pond*, an anthology of fiction published by New Rivers Press.

Cover painting by Shlomo Marni.

Back cover photo by Michael Siluk.

The publisher thanks the following organizations whose support helped make this book possible: The National Endowment for the Arts, a federal agency; Dayton Hudson Foundation; Cowles Media/Star Tribune; Jerome Foundation; and Northwest Area Foundation.

Coffee House Press books are distributed to trade by Consortium Book Sales and Distribution, 287 East Sixth Street, Suite 365, Saint Paul, Minnesota 55101. Our books are also available through all major library distributors and jobbers, and through most small press distributors, including Bookpeople, Bookslinger, Inland, Pacific Pipeline, and Small Press Distribution. For personal orders, catalogs or other information, write to:
COFFEE HOUSE PRESS
27 NORTH FOURTH STREET, SUITE 400, MINNEAPOLIS, MN 55401.

Library of Congress Cataloging in Publication Data
Luban, Marianne, 1946-
    The Samaritan treasure : stories / by Marianne Luban.
        p. cm.
    Contents: Tomorrow you'll forget—Professor Mondshane—
The Jew of Bath—The Samaritan treasure—The Last of Rafaela.
    ISBN 0-918273-79-X   : $9.95
    I.   Jews—History—Fiction.   I.Title.
PS3562.U218S36   1990   90-2690
813'.54—dc20   CIP

Contents

Tomorrow You'll Forget

NEAR WHAT USED TO BE the Five-and-Dime but is now the Salvation Army, you will find a little cafeteria where I used to eat my lunch every day. I write copy in a small-scale ad agency for my living and write short stories in my spare time. But this is not my story. I prefer to write pleasant, amusing tales.

As I really didn't spend much time there, it didn't matter to me that the cafeteria was hot in the summer, or that during the winter, the big window facing the street was always clouded over from the steam. This little eatery was perfectly homely and typical in every respect. Squares of jello quivered on shreds of romaine and nobody ever asked for a breakdown of the content of the hot dishes. In these places ignorance is the better part of contentment.

When you have only a half-hour for lunch, there is not much time for socializing with your fellow diners. The patrons are mostly regulars; you come to accept them as part of the atmosphere, the daily routine. I liked sitting near the window in summer in order to watch the world go by, but sometimes I was forced to squeeze into a corner where the Woman always sat.

The most reliable of regulars, she never took a place near the window, caring perhaps neither to watch nor be observed. She was an elderly woman, thin and used up, who looked as if she had a thankless exhausting job somewhere. Not an office job, surely; her clothes were too tacky and worn for that. She made no effort whatever to be in fashion. In all seasons she wore the same stretched-out cardigan over her other garments. Since I had never seen the Woman wearing a coat, I assumed that she, too, worked nearby.

It seemed she cared about her hair. Oddly enough, she kept it dyed a delicate shade of blonde, and it was always neatly arranged. Sometimes I stared at the Woman and briefly glimpsed the ghost of a long-lost beauty. Yet, the next moment, I was convinced that she was ugly and had always been so. Those burnt-out eyes of hers seemed fixed on some point beyond the cafeteria, the zombie gaze of someone who just doesn't give a damn anymore. She still frequents the cafeteria, of that I am positive. But I cannot go back.

Once in a while there were disturbances in the cafeteria— people would laugh too loudly at some joke or the cook would burn something in the back, releasing a mighty oath. Small but jarring things like that happened about once every lunchtime, but the Woman never paid any attention. If someone threw a bomb through the window, I believe the Woman would refuse to give up her place, ignoring the shower of glass and catsup.

Somehow I had always managed to avoid sitting next to her. To tell the truth, I was afraid. Perhaps I thought she wasn't playing with a full deck. I possess that fear of the unbalanced that is within us all, a dread of latent, unexpected violence. Most of us keep our hostilities in check and are wary of those who might not have the same inhibitions. It is unfair to say that the Woman appeared violent, however. It's just that I had the sense that someday she would break into a scream that might never stop. When that happened, I didn't want to be too near.

But it was inevitable—one day there were simply no other vacant seats. The Woman never even glanced at me as I lowered my tray. She merely kept on eating in a painstakingly deliberate manner that I hate. It bothers me when a person's fork takes an age to reach his lips and each mouthful is chewed a hundred times at least.

But then I noticed her arm and forgot about her eating habits. What is it about a tattoo that makes it so startling? Most of them are plain silly: hearts, girls in grass skirts. Yet somehow they all suggest mutilation, and so we stare. The Woman's tattoo was the worst kind.

Being a Jew, myself, I like to believe, as does every Jew, that I can spot one of my own. But my neighbor had struck me as being absolutely non-Jewish in every way. Not so much her face; faces can fool you. It's just that she was so damn unanimated, so bland. But that was before I had seen those blue numbers right there on her forearm.

Flustered at the moment of my discovery, I upset my coke. The ice cubes flew across the table like dice out of a tumbler, and some of the liquid sloshed over onto the Woman's tray. I mumbled something and went to the counter to get a rag. When I had cleaned up the mess, I resumed my seat and began to eat. The Woman, for her part, had never interrupted her own meal and seemed oblivious to the embarrassing incident. Once my wariness had disappeared, an overwhelming curiosity took its place.

"I'm sorry," I said. I meant that I was sorry about having spilled coke on her tray, but, since my eyes were on those numbers, I think she understood that I was offering my belated condolences. I suppose I surprised her. Anyway, she noticed me for the first time in two years.

The Woman looked down at her arm and then at me.

"What can you do?" she shrugged.

I couldn't help smiling. With one gesture, a Jew materializes before your eyes. "I would guess that you're from Poland," I ventured. "Am I right?"

A line formed between the Woman's eyebrows and she looked at me with either suspicion or amusement.

"You're a smart young man," she drawled. "I am from there. I was born in Warsaw. This," she said, tapping her tattoo, "is my diploma. It means I am a graduate of Auschwitz, summa cum lucky. I was in another camp, too, after that. You are Jewish?"

"Yes," I replied, "of course."

"Of course? So what do you know about Warszawa—Warsaw?"

"Nothing, actually. Except that it was heavily bombed during the war."

Her blue eyes were fastened on me now. Yes, I was certain of it. She had been attractive once. Perhaps even a beauty. How could I ever have thought otherwise? Her English was very good—there was even a hint of something British in her voice—or so I imagined.

"The old Warsaw no longer exists," said the Woman, "but, in my dreams, nothing has changed. When I wake up all I want is to be back there again, in spite of all that happened."

"Have you ever thought of actually going back?" I asked naively.

The Woman sipped her coffee, holding it up carefully with both hands. "Go back to what? It's over now. The beautiful times are gone. A young man like you would have liked being there. Oh, yes, it was not dull. It was wonderful to be young and to look good. It was unthinkable not to be able to dance. When the music stopped, we scarcely knew what to do." She chuckled but it came out more like a gasp. "Well, of course, we soon learned to dance to a different tune."

"But you survived," I said. "That implies a great deal. I mean, it must have taken a lot of—"

"Courage?" she supplied, eyebrows lifted.

"Well, yes, naturally."

"Those with courage were killed off almost immediately. Brave people are not survivors. Don't forget it."

"But surely . . . "

"No," she interrupted curtly. "The ones with courage went to the ovens with their babies. The ones still living left theirs on street corners in rucksacks."

I was taken aback. "It's really impossible to judge people under those conditions, isn't it? A madness took over. Even good people weren't themselves. At least that's how I understand it."

"You weren't there, young man. I was, and even I don't try to understand. But I know one thing. People don't really change no matter what happens to them. Do you want to know how I came to survive?"

"Well, sure, but something tells me you weren't capable of giving up your babies to save your own life."

She stared at me as though she wasn't sure I was for real.

"I had no babies. I was a *kurveh* . . . a whore."

Stuck for a response, I suddenly noticed that I had automatically polished off my food. I glanced down at my watch. My half-hour was up and then some.

"I have to go back," I moaned. "It's been nice meeting you, but I really have to go to work. I'm already late."

Idiotically, I showed her the time. She acknowledged it with a nod. I was horribly embarrassed to be leaving her just like that after what she had told me. But she showed no sign of sharing my discomfort, nor of taking pity on me. She continued eating, apparently in no hurry to return to work.

On the following day I fell all over myself in order to get a place near the Polish woman. She was there before me, as usual, wearing that awful sweater that had been washed to the consistency of limp cotton. It occurred to me that perhaps she had been saving that vacant seat, knowing that I would return to hear the rest of her story.

"Do you mind?" I asked her. "May I sit?"

"Why not?"

I was resolved there would be no mishaps that day and set my lunch down as if I were dining on live grenades.

"By the way, my name is Bob Samuels."

"Halina," she answered simply.

"Look, Halina," I began, but she had no patience with my fumbling diplomacy.

"Concerning," she broke in, "concerning what I revealed to you about myself yesterday, I want you to know that I was not doing that before the war. I was innocent in those days, too stupid for words. I exist today only because in nature's lottery I drew a pretty face. I know it's difficult to believe now, but it's the truth. I'm not a survivor in any real sense. Even my face did not survive." Halina smiled at me in a wry fashion. "I was very young when the war began, younger even than you. My father had a shop and I worked for him. I helped customers try on gloves and hats. I was barely out of the gymnasium. I was seventeen.

"One day, a man came into the shop and asked for assistance in selecting a tie. He was old, perhaps even forty, but as magnificent as a prince. Yes, a Jewish prince. While I showed him the ties, he asked me a lot of questions about myself: what I did for amusement, what my favorite perfume was. I replied with the name of the most expensive fragrance that I knew of, but in truth, I seldom wore perfume. But he did, my customer—a wonderful scent that, together with his presence, addled my senses and left me nearly speechless. Finally he said, 'I can't decide. These silks look pale next to you. You are the most beautiful girl I have ever seen.'

"I don't remember what he bought that day, if anything. He was so charming and genteel. I forgave him his advanced years, as he seemed more handsome than anyone I knew. He could have been a film star."

"No doubt he thought the same of you," I said.

Halina twisted her mouth. "Very likely he was already laughing at me. A foolish girl, I must have seemed to him, a little sacrifice with neck exposed for the knife. Immediately after meeting him, I received, in the post, a bottle of the perfume I had mentioned. Tied to the flask was a little card asking me to meet the sender at such and such a place at a given time. There was no signature, of course."

"So you went, right? If you hadn't, there would be no story."

"Maybe not—in any event the story would have been different," she admitted. "His name was Adam Feder. I suppose he was a well-to-do man—money flowed from him. He was in some kind of business but never wanted to discuss it with me. Perhaps he was protecting himself from the day when an irate Halina would storm into his place looking for him. When I asked him to tell me what he did for a living, he would say that it was demeaning for lovers to speak of crass matters. I could not reply because it occurred to me that all I knew about were dull and commonplace things. One could scarcely speak to a man like Feder about one's schoolgirl adventures. But I got along by listening and making admiring remarks, which seemed to satisfy Feder. He constantly expressed his delight and good fortune in having found me, while taking me to fancy places in parts of the city where he was not likely to be recognized. Sometimes I pretended that being recognized did not actually worry him—he appeared so free of anxiety. He was witty, affectionate and a complete gentleman. I loved him to distraction. But one day I could contain myself no longer and I asked Feder if he loved me as well. His answer was, 'A silly question. How could I fail to love you? Next to you I am nothing more than a poor old fellow.'

"When I began to sleep with him, we made love in a little flat he was keeping especially for that purpose. Nowadays, I might have moved myself into that flat, but in 1939, unmarried girls lived with their parents until they stood under the wedding canopy. And, needless to say, they did not sleep with married men. I was under constant pressure to invent new and convincing alibis to explain my absences to my mother and father. It hurt me to deceive them, but my love for Adam Feder overruled everything. It seems to me I would have committed murder for him I adored him so. I cannot tell you how deeply I cared; such things are beyond words. My only happiness was to be with my Adam, who in reality, was the Adam of another woman. When we were together, the world, Warsaw, the troubles brewing for Poland didn't exist for me. I had no patience to actually sit down and read a newspaper. I did listen to the radio, but the news flashes had nothing more than a fleeting effect on me. When one is young and silly and in love, one doesn't contemplate catastrophes. A major upheaval is when one's love is late for a rendezvous, and should he not come at all, only then does the world come to an end.

"If I were oblivious to the events of 1939, you can imagine Mrs. Sarah Feder didn't give me any sleepless nights, either. I was not even curious about her. Feder had told me that they were of an age, and that made her old, not to be taken seriously as a rival. I had never seen her and did not wish to see her. True, I did begrudge her the time Adam 'had' to spend with her, but I was basically a very proper girl at that stage and believed that a wife had priority over a mistress. You see how it was? The minute one finds oneself in a socially unacceptable role, one usually stops fighting for one's basic needs. One becomes undeserving in one's own eyes. It is really too unnecessary, too sad." Halina patted my arm. "I must stop or nothing will stop me. Eat, eat. Your lunchtime will be over soon."

"No, don't stop now," I told her. "I plan to stay here until you're finished. The office can run very well without me. I'll make up some excuse."

Halina smiled. She and I were close friends now. We had known each other forever.

"I'll be here tomorrow. You know that."

I said, "I don't care about tomorrow. I am in the year 1939 and a beautiful girl named Halina is eating her heart out over a man with a wife who both exists and doesn't exist. Tomorrow doesn't count for me any more than it does for her. Please go on with your story—oh, how selfish of me—you have to go back yourself."

"I have gone back," said Halina. It was true. The years had fallen from her. Her eyes were luminous and her skin flushed. Her lovely hair color was now in harmony with the rest of her appearance. She was charming; how could I have ever thought otherwise? Even the sweater seemed a piquant affectation. For the past two years I had been observing another woman.

Halina stirred some more sugar into her coffee, too much sugar, as if to counteract the bitterness of what she was about to say.

"Don't worry about me," she told me with a kind of sigh. "I am in no hurry at all. Can you say of your own life that those you loved the most gave the least of themselves in return? Of course you can. It's an endless and universal lament. A perverse law of nature. As you've already guessed, my affair with Feder came to an abrupt end. Perhaps the inconvenience of it had become too much for him. For me, it had become relatively easy—my parents were so caught up in the worsening situation in Europe and the rumors of impending war that they hardly noticed my comings and goings anymore. If they suspected I might have a secret boyfriend, they figured the war was likely to take him away in any case. I don't believe it occurred to them I might not be seeing a fellow my own age.

"In August of 1939, Adam Feder took me to a restaurant that had a terrific orchestra. Naturally, I wanted to dance. The tango was very popular and nearly every hit song, happy or sad, was set to the tango rhythm. But Feder didn't feel up to dancing. I suggested we order something to eat, but Adam stared at me in a strange way. 'Have a drink, Halina,' he said. 'Have one yourself,' I laughed. 'Maybe it will put you in a better mood.'

"Feder placed his hand on mine. 'Halina, this is the last time we shall see one another like this. My wife knows about us. Don't ask me how she found out. She may have her own spies, for all I know. You understand there is nothing I can do, Halina.'

"In the background, the singer was performing a tune called 'Wanda,' which is about a man who would have done anything for the girl he adored. It was one of my favorites. I would never hear that song again, would never want to hear it.

"'No,' I told Feder, 'I don't understand. I love you and I know you love me in spite of what you are saying. I'll never let you go.'

"'I beg of you not to make this difficult, Halina.'

"Although I was fully aware that what Feder was saying to me was a lie and an evasion, he had never looked more beautiful to me than in that sickening moment. I saw him as a fallen angel and not the devil he was, to so ruthlessly tear the heart out of a young girl. He had not many gray hairs yet, but somehow they held a tremendous poignancy for me. I should have hit him over the head with the wine bottle, but I only wanted to throw myself into his arms and plead with him to take back his rejection of me.

"'Halina, you're not going to cry, are you? You must go outside if you're going to cry. You'll be so ashamed if you make a spectacle of yourself.'

"Cry—I was too stunned to cry. I could scarcely breathe. I felt as though my heart were being squeezed like a sponge and that I would momentarily suffocate.

"Feder added, 'Halina, darling, you knew I wasn't a free man.' He pressed my hand reassuringly as though *he* were forgiving *me* for something I had done. I snatched my hand away as though it had been burned. I left that restaurant with all those dancing people and the baritone singing a Krukowski hit entitled 'Tomorrow You'll Forget.' But I never forgot. And I never danced again. I might have. I might have met another man and gotten Feder out of my system. I might have had the chance to be happy once more, but as it turned out, the heartbreak of that evening was only the beginning of a long nightmare for me. As you know, Germany invaded Poland and Poland fell. Then came the black night that lasted for what seemed a century."

The cafeteria had nearly emptied. There were only a few persons left, watching us furtively, wondering, no doubt, what a middle-aged woman could be saying so earnestly and at such length to a man of my years.

"How long was it before you were taken away?" I asked, but my voice sounded odd to me, too American, like an interviewer.

"Oh, years passed. Not that time meant anything to me, particularly. I was physically ill for months after Adam left me. I ate haphazardly and seldom went out. I heard talk about the campaign against the Jews, but as I was considering suicide anyway, I was un-

moved by the danger. I no longer worked in my father's shop because I couldn't concentrate and made too many mistakes. Soon
there was no more shop. Who could afford my father's expensive
hats and ties any longer? My father was crushed by the loss of his business. How we ate didn't concern me. I was 100 percent self-centered
in my grief.

"By 1940 all Jews who didn't already live there had to move into
the Warsaw Ghetto, while all the Gentiles who were living there
had to get out. My family had to leave our nice apartment in an
upper-class part of town and were installed in a crowded, squalid
building. Our neighbors were desperate people wearing white
armbands with blue Stars of David, all of them hungry and scaveng-
ing for food. But food was scarce and the starving died literally in
their tracks. A corpse in the street was no more unexpected in the
Warsaw Ghetto than a crumpled cigarette package is here. Typhus
raged and this illness became more feared than the Nazis. By 1942,
100,000 Jews had perished in the ghetto.

"In that same year the Germans began to intensify their terroriz-
ing *Aktions*—dragging Jews out of their homes and murdering them
in view of everybody. But it was rumored that if able-bodied men
and women voluntarily reported to an area called the *Umschlagplatz*,
they would be deported to 'the East' to work. Well, anything
seemed more tolerable than the ghetto, so my parents decided that
we ought to go there and take our chances. We had heard all kinds of
stories about this 'selection place.' Sometimes everyone who
showed up was immediately taken away by train and, at other times,
the SS was fussy. They formed two groups, a right and a left. The
only ones that were chosen for the right side on those occasions
were persons who looked strong and capable or those who might
prove useful for some purpose or another. Very pretty girls were
always motioned to the right. Pretty boys, too, sometimes. When
this method of selection became common knowledge, people took
pains to make themselves appear younger, or older if they were not
quite adult.

"My parents, however, did nothing to themselves. They were
both over fifty and knew they weren't fooling anyone. But my
mother, thinking I would have a good chance, made me put on my

best clothes and do a full makeup. And I obeyed like an automaton. I felt exhausted and without hope. It seemed incredible to me at that time that anyone, much less a German, would find justification for my continued existence. How could it be, when someone I had loved more than my own life had no use for me?

"Have you ever seen a Hieronymus Bosch painting? What he would have made of that selection place! It was something from the netherworld, the wailing and pleading rising as from out of hell, itself. The SS tried to keep things moving in an orderly fashion, but how can there be order when families are torn apart, loved ones shoved to the left, marked for extermination? Of course, we all denied the possibility, while at the same time our very bones ached with the certainty of it.

"When I heard the sentence 'Links' pronounced on first my father and then my mother, my legs turned to water. I now realized the odds were good that I might be sent to the right group, and I grew frightened of being separated from my parents. I only wanted to be near them, come what may. I kept my eyes glued on my mother, desperately trying not to lose sight of her as she and my father were being pushed back into the crowd.

"Suddenly I felt my head being jerked around and found myself looking into the face of a German. I remember that it was not a face to inspire terror. His were ordinary features, even kindly ones if one can go that far.

"'You don't look Jewish at all, Fräulein,' I heard him say to me. 'Are you sure that you belong here?'

"I replied that it was my parents he had just sent to the left.

"'Perhaps they are not your true parents. If you are adopted, you don't have to be here. Could you have been adopted?'

"Before I could answer, his superior officer came over to see what was holding up the process.

"'Was ist los hier?' he demanded of the other German.

"'Sir, is it not amazing? Here is a perfect Aryan type. I thought she might have been adopted by the Jews.'

"The officer scrutinized me from beneath his black visor. I could not see his eyes; only the death's head on his cap leered at me.

"'A beautiful girl. But we can't be sure, can we? Anyone can claim she is adopted. We haven't the time to investigate these things. Send all the Aryan-looking young women to the right, whether they have children or not. Understand?'

"As he motioned me to the right, the lower-ranking SS man actually said 'Mach's gut,' which is German for 'Take it easy.'"

Halina paused. I wanted to ask her if there was a chance she actually might have been adopted, her parents having been so much older than herself, but instead I said, "Did you ever see your parents again?"

"Never. I can't even say whether we were sent away on the same transport."

"So you found yourself completely alone in the world. How old were you then?"

"Twenty. But I wasn't alone for long. The fact is, I was actually adopted by another person. This is what happened: When the train stopped and the boxcars were opened, those of us trapped inside more or less fell out onto a large platform where other Jews were already waiting. For what? Even the best informed of us could only guess. The unbelievable stench on the train left the ones who could still breathe gasping for air when we were let out. I stretched on the platform. Tightly packed in with other bodies, I had not been able to lie down for what seemed an eternity. My legs were in excruciating pain, and I smelled from vomit and excrement.

"Confusion was still the order of the day. People were frantic to know where they were and what was to become of them. Some, of course, didn't care; they became sleepwalkers, their mental balance having collapsed beneath the enormity of the cruelty and suffering.

"When my legs ached less, I got up. It was then that I received another shock. Not more than a few feet away from where I stood were Adam Feder and his wife. She was clinging to his arm and shaking her head to and fro in a way that said she simply couldn't go on. He was patting her shoulder in a detached manner, not looking at her at all. It seemed a century since I had accidentally run into them in a store after our split-up. Adam had looked through me as though I were transparent. And I had said nothing. There had been nothing to say.

"But now I burst into tears and rushed over to Feder, throwing my arms about his neck. I don't believe I actually expected him to comfort me, but I did think he would acknowledge me, perhaps even keep an eye on me for old times' sake. The games that we had played in Warsaw seemed too stupid and of no avail whatsoever in view of our predicament.

"But Feder had played those games too long. He pried my arms off of him. 'You've made a mistake, young woman.'

"'Adam, for God's sake!' I shrieked.

"'Young lady, this is no way to behave. You're upsetting my wife.'

"In Yiddish there is a saying—'It went dark before my eyes.' Well, that is what happened. I went berserk. I clawed at my former lover's face and called him names that had never passed my lips before. 'I'll show you how to behave,' I sobbed over and over. 'I'll kill you, you lying bastard!'

"A German finally dragged me away, laughing. He found me a great joke, as did some of the Jews. I had created a diversion, something to take their minds off their own suffering. Finally, a couple of kind women took charge of me and calmed me down.

"'Listen, doll-face,' one of them said to me, 'if he's got anything coming to him, he'll get it all too soon.'

"Then bedlam broke out in earnest. Men and women were being divided into two groups by gender, couples literally torn apart. I didn't much care about myself—I had no one left to lose—but I couldn't bear the shrieks and tears of the women. I say I couldn't bear it, but the truth is I took it pretty well. I had cried myself out over the months . . . there was simply nothing left. My sobbing over Feder's coldness moments before had been the last of it. My poor battered heart turned to stone that day on the platform. I felt the actual weight of it in my chest.

"As I was being herded away with the rest of the women, I felt a hand on my arm and heard my name spoken. Sarah Feder was trying to get my attention. I took it for granted that she wanted to dress me down, so I made an effort to avoid her. But I couldn't shake her off. There were too many women crushing against us. How did she know my name? Had Feder let it slip out when he was fighting me off, or had she known it all along?

"At that moment the guard came over and shoved me away from Sarah. Sarah had already collapsed on the floor. The guard was furious with *me*, as though *I* were responsible for everything.

"'Your mother has typhus!' the guard raged. 'You've been covering up for her, you little shit! Now her lice will be all over the rest of us!'

"'She hasn't got lice!' I snapped. 'She's got influenza. She'll be over it in a day or two. The buttons are being cut. Use your eyes! Look at them all!'

"She looked at them all right—she grabbed two handfuls and threw them in my face. Then she began to beat me with her club. I only threw up my arms to shield my head, even though those scissors were stuck to my hand. I thought if she took it out on me, she would maybe forget about Sarah and let her live another day, but I failed to reckon with Adam Feder's wife. Maybe it was the fever, the delirium that made her do it, but she jumped up like a tigress and stabbed that guard in the throat with *her* scissors. This was the act of a woman who had once been too fine a lady to put her hand in cold water.

"The guard didn't die, but that was the end of my so-called adopted mother, and nearly the end of me. I was a hardened specimen at that point, but fate had it in store for me to grieve first for the husband and then for the wife.

"On the other hand, fate somehow snatched me out of the fire. I knew that as soon as the Brunhilde felt better, she would make my life miserable or even send me to my death. When it came time to eat the scraps that were called our evening meal, I went to the yard. I had still not been able to pull off the scissors, which had raised a painful blister on my hand. I was hoping to find a woman Sarah and I had befriended to ask her to help me remove them, but I didn't see her. If I didn't get back quickly, someone else would finish off my soup. I was resigned to eating with my left hand when I saw a man, an SS officer, staring at me on the other side of the barbed wire.

"'Grosse Problëme, Schönes Fräulein?' he asked in a pleasant tone.

"I placed the voice right away. It was the top official from the selection place in Warsaw. He still thought me beautiful, as he had on that day, even after what I'd been through. True, my hair had grown back and I no longer had a bald, shaved skull, but I felt that I had grown ugly beyond recognition. There were no mirrors in the women's barracks, but I later discovered that I had not changed much. I was one of those freakish people who simply continued to bloom, no matter how severe the drought.

"From that moment on, I became a whore for the Nazis or, I should say, the private whore of one whom I shall call Martin Lentz. His true name has been eradicated—may it be blotted out forever—and is not for me to pronounce. And yes, I was once again the mistress of a married man.

"It was actually against the laws of the Third Reich for Aryans to have sexual relations with members of so-called inferior races, especially Jews. But quite a bit of it went on . . . the Germans just pretended it didn't happen. At that time a great many things were taking place that the world refused to acknowledge, so you can imagine a little thing like a Jewish concubine was easy to sweep under the carpet, especially if she happened to look more Germanic than most Germans. No one in the camp where Lentz was in command suspected what my background was and Lentz passed me off as a real Pole. As soon as I began to feel safe, I regretted everything, knowing I had become a despicable creature, but there was no going back.

"I lived well from then on and lacked for nothing. Lentz wanted me to call him Martin, but I avoided calling him by any name as much as possible. I didn't object when he had me sterilized so I couldn't get pregnant. I never expected to live to be thirty, much less have children. I didn't hate Lentz at all, for that matter, and even having sex with him ceased to be a trauma after a while. That is not to imply that I cared for him in any sense of the word. I cared for no one. Not for the Jews, not even for myself. Psychologically, I had removed myself from the atrocities, and spent hours just daydreaming about my life in Warsaw before evil had come into its own in the world.

"But finally what is most bizarre about this situation was that Martin Lentz truly loved me. What had been denied me by Adam Feder, this member of the Master Race, Lentz, lavished upon me without reservation. His greatest fear was that the Nazis would win the war soon and he would be forced to go home to his wife. I think he missed his children, though, this man who was untroubled by millions of children going up in smoke.

"Yes, Lentz often thought of the children. He loved to play with my hair, braid it, comb it, as he spoke to me of them. Only his little Hansi at home and I had hair like real gold, he said. To this day it refuses to turn gray, as if by Lentz's everlasting order. I looked more like little Hansi's mother than Lentz's own wife, he claimed. What a laugh that was. But I had lost my sense of humor.

"Were you wondering what had become of Adam Feder, or have you forgotten him? I still thought of him quite often, but I never dreamed he was still alive. How that fastidious, dandified character managed to bear life in the camp I'll never understand, but there he was one day in the yard with the others. Feder was the merest ghost of himself, but I would have recognized that face anywhere. I made sure he saw me right away, but this time there were rows of electrified wire between us. Feder looked as though he'd been struck by a bolt of lightning. When he assembled his wits, he rushed over to the fence, coming as close as he dared.

"'My God, it's Halina! Halina, don't you remember me? My beautiful darling, you don't know how happy I am to see you!'

"Then it must have dawned on him that I looked too well, that my dress was too fine, for he backed off a little.

"'But, Halina, what are you doing here?'

"'Working, Adam,' I said, 'working hard.'

"He didn't pursue it. 'Well, at least you're alive and well. Will we see each other, Halina?'

"I assured him that we would. 'Adam, aren't you going to ask me what became of your wife, Sarah? She was with me at Auschwitz.'

"'She's dead.'

"'How did you find out?' I wanted to know.

"'I never thought she'd make it. She wasn't the type to survive, poor Sarah.'

"'Maybe not,' I replied, 'but one thing is certain.'

"'What is that, Halina?' Feder said, coming nearer again. He was smiling in the way that used to make me melt. I believe he thought that I was going to tell him that I still loved him. He seemed to want to reach through the fence to touch me.

"'Watch out. You'll electrocute yourself,' I cautioned. 'The fact is now, Adam, that you are a free man. How does it feel to be a free man at last?' With those words I turned away.

"From that day forward I lived only to torment Adam Feder. No, you mustn't imagine I did him any physical harm. I told Lentz he was a relative of mine and that I would be grateful to have him unmolested. Lentz was anxious that Feder might spill the beans about me being Jewish, but I told him that one warning from me would seal Feder's lips on the subject. This, you may be certain, put Feder in a most uncomfortable position—he could never be sure when I might decide to be rid of him. After all, he had the goods on me, especially if the Allies were victorious. There might be plenty of persons who would take the position that I should have died rather than sleep for three years with a murderer of my own people. If and when we were liberated, the inmates of the camp might decide to strangle me themselves. So not a day went by that I didn't pass casually by Feder and murmur, 'Don't make things difficult, Adam. You've got to go on pretending you don't know me, or I don't know what I'll do with you.' It got so he was afraid to speak to anyone for fear that I'd think he was informing on me.

"So now what do you think of me, young man—Bob Samuels? Are you sorry you spent this time listening to me? Do I disgust you now?"

I toyed with my fork. The noonday light had long left the cafeteria. Halina and I were the only patrons left in the place.

"I think," I said, making sure to look her in the eye, "that you saved a man's life and nearly that of his wife. You may have spared people misery whom you never mentioned. The great harm was to yourself."

"Thank you," whispered Halina. "You are a very kind young man. If I had met you—someone like you—in Warsaw before the war, I know my life would have been different. I would have gone on trying to keep alive from day to day because I would have had something to look forward to. But I met Adam Feder instead."

"What about Feder?" I asked. "Was he all right?"

Halina shrugged. "I took care of the him until the last. No harm came to him that I know of."

"Halina, you were a young girl with few experiences with men, suddenly under the thumb of a monster, while at the same time trying to get revenge on an egotistical bastard. You must be about my mother's age. Do you know what she was doing in the forties? Going to college dances and football games!"

Halina patted my hand. "Wait, wait. I'm not through yet. It's true that, with the exception of my father, I had known only bad men intimately, but I did finally discover other kinds of men. This was in 1945 and the war had ended.

"I don't need to describe the condition of our camp. You've seen the photographs, although they don't begin to tell the story. For one thing, they can't convey the stench that hung in the air like a poisonous gas, the smell of death. You couldn't escape it for a second. That dreadful odor terrified me more than anything. I had a horror of dying and becoming nothing more than a nauseating piece of putrefaction. The smell made me lose my appetite; I had to force myself to eat. Food was scarce, even for a relatively pampered creature like myself. I grew very thin but I looked positively radiant with health compared to the living skeletons that wandered about the camp. I tried not to look at them, and to hide myself from *their* sight. But they were everywhere—my fellow Jews—dying wherever they happened to fall down. Nobody picked them up. The SS tried to make the other prisoners put the bodies into piles so they wouldn't be underfoot. But since there was nobody left who had the strength for this kind of work, even this attempt at orderliness was abandoned.

"Everyone around me was perishing of disease and starvation with the exception of the Germans and their foreign guards, the Ukrainians, Czechs and whatnot. For my part, I was already dead, only I didn't know it. It took me many years to come back to life, even though I can't say I have ever really enjoyed it since. Are you familiar with Moussorgsky's musical work *Pictures at an Exhibition*? That is what I have in my head—all these pictures from the most horrifying exhibition the world has ever seen—and I must look at them until the day I die once and for all.

"When we heard the British were only some kilometers away, the camp personnel immediately fled, including Lentz, who dragged me with him. There was no question of leaving me behind. He would have forced me, if necessary, but there was no need. I was sick of Lentz, but I was more sick of the camp and wanted desperately to get out. The *kommandant* was not going back to his family, but I hoped that, once out in the world, I could get rid of him. And so we all scurried off. Some of the SS and their helpers got away, but most were caught before long and tried by the British for their crimes. Nor did Lentz make good his escape. He and I were on foot with nothing but the clothes on our backs. Lentz, naturally, was not wearing a uniform or carrying a weapon in case we were searched. All he took was some money. He was convinced we could blend into the population and eventually receive some help from a Nazi organization.

"On the road we saw a detachment of British soldiers coming toward us. Lentz pulled me into some bushes. We might have gone unnoticed but something inside me snapped. I had had enough of Lentz's company, God knows, and when I saw those Tommies pass me by, it was more than I could bear. I let out a scream and ran toward the soldiers. I tried to cling to a lorry, but it knocked me to the ground. Everything halted. Still lying in the dust, I began to shout in English, 'There he is over there! Catch him! Don't let him go!'

"Are you surprised? Yes, I denounced my protector, the man who had saved my life. I knew English even then. In school I won a prize for learning this language, but I had never had the occasion to use it until that day. While I was studying English I had the idea I might someday make a trip to London. Later on, from the way the Germans were boasting, I was sure London had been totally destroyed.

"Lentz was captured and we were taken back to the camp together. Lentz refused to look at me, but I noticed tears in his eyes. Yes, even the lowest beast has feelings. There was no doubt in my mind that I had broken the German's heart. Perhaps, in his madness, he had assumed that I had grown to love him. Love thine enemy.

"When we entered the camp most of us—Lentz, the British and I—all wept. Lentz had his disappointment, the Englishmen their shock and grief and I . . . well, the tears that had been collecting inside me for years burst forth in a hysterical fit that lasted for hours. I was shut away in a room, sobbing and shrieking like a madwoman, but after a while I calmed down. Our liberators told me I was free to join the camp population, but I was cautioned against running away. After all, they had no idea who I was or what my function in the camp had been. I was more or less under arrest until my innocence could be established. With my normal-looking physique, clean hair and a dress instead of rags, I was a suspicious character. Many of the women there didn't even have rags and walked about naked, if they walked at all, which I could tell deeply unsettled the proper English. But soon they had so much to attend to that they took no further notice of me. I hid in that room for as long as I was able to delude myself that I might be safe there. When nobody came to see me or bring me any food, I knew that I would have to emerge and face whatever was waiting outside.

"Gathering all the courage that was left in me, I walked out into the yard and stood waiting. I did not have to wait long. Within minutes a group of women, indescribably miserable in their condition and appearance, descended on me, pushing and shrieking curses and obscenities. I was called a Polish whore and worse. I knew the women wanted to kill me and I remember wondering if they had the strength to do it. Handfuls of hair were torn from my scalp and I was beaten all over, but I didn't resist at all. I somehow felt the wretched women had the right to do with me whatever they pleased.

"Lying in the mud and filth, I closed my eyes and prepared to die, but suddenly I heard a man's voice ordering the frenzied cadavers to stop. The voice spoke in German, yet I knew there were no more Germans left to issue commands. Perhaps out of habit, the women obeyed.

"I opened my eyes to see a man in pajamas, a rather elderly Jew, peering at me through spectacles with only one lens left intact. I didn't know him, but I later learned he was a German, a professor or a famous rabbi—perhaps both. He looked horribly emaciated, but what inner strength that man, at his age, must have possessed in order to survive this hell on earth. Everybody seemed familiar with him, except me. I had made a point of avoiding the inmates as much as possible. He had been a very well known personage in his country before the war and continued on to even greater renown in Jewish circles in America afterward.

"This rabbi had a brief discussion with the women. They argued with him in German and Yiddish, but respectfully.

"I heard him raise his voice in an effort to drown them out.

"'No! No excuses! Are we Jews or animals? We must not become like they were, to sink to their level, no matter what. If we do, we have not truly survived at all!'

"This gave the women pause. 'Now,' demanded the rabbi, 'let me hear which of you this woman has harmed, and I will report it to the proper authority.'

"Nobody could say anything, as I had certainly never done anything to hurt any of them. A few of the other inmates who had come over to see what was happening even began to volunteer that I had given them food at times, which was true. If someone had come near the Kommandant's quarters for some reason or had a job to do there, I did as much as I could for that person, which was little enough in any case. Sometimes I had fairly ached to confide to someone that I was a Jew and just as much a prisoner as anyone, but of course, I knew better than to be so stupid. But that didn't mean I thought enough of myself to feel my life ought to be spared because of my Jewishness. Yet, a miracle had happened once again. With a few words, a kindly and honorable man had restored order, and for the second time my, skin, worthless as it seemed even to me, was saved. This time it was different, however; the German rabbi wanted nothing from me. The idea that this learned Jew, having undergone what amounted to a process of dehumanization, still clung to the precepts of justice and mercy showed us that people *need not* be changed or corrupted by extreme adversity.

"All of a sudden I remembered Adam Feder. Surely he must have heard the commotion and had come to find out what was going on. Now there was nothing to prevent him from getting even with me by revealing my true identity, but Feder was nowhere in sight. In fact, I couldn't recall seeing him since I'd returned to the camp. Perhaps he'd run off or died. Despite the best efforts of the British, a great many survivors were beyond help and continued to die every day.

"The good rabbi helped me to my feet, saying that he wanted to place me in the protection of the British. On our way to search for someone in charge, I thanked the man for his concern. He made light of it as a person with very fine manners might and caught my arm when I tripped over something in the appalling mess that was our prison grounds. I remember the rabbi looking at the numbers on my arm in the same surprised way that you did when we first met. He searched my face, looking for some answer there, while something rose in my throat, preventing me from saying another word. But the rabbi had no questions for me. Through an interpreter he explained my predicament to an officer, who seemed to accept his word that I needed looking after. I said good-bye to the rabbi, who only replied sadly, 'God help you, my poor child.' I felt that somehow he had guessed everything about me. I never saw him again in person after that, although, as I said, I found out who he was much later in the States. As it turned out, the rabbi was one of two decent men who came to my aid in the camp.

"I was now a prisoner of the British, who kept me confined at the advice of the rabbi until they could determine just what category I fell under and what was to be done with me. I was made to under-stand that nothing could happen along these lines until the Military Investigation Team arrived to interview the inmates, who were now being cared for by English doctors and nurses, before they could scatter into the four winds. Their affidavits and testimonies were to play a crucial role in bringing those who had run the camp to justice. The latter had all been taken away to some prison, but for some reason, I remained where I was.

"Some of the Tommies took pity on me once they made sure I wasn't German, even tried to flirt with me in a good-natured way, as I was the only woman around who still looked presentable. A few of the British nurses were attractive, but most were formidable types who tolerated no nonsense. The soldiers gave me things like a comb, pocket mirror and candies. All of them behaved like gentle-men and I had no qualms about accepting gifts from them. My own things had been confiscated by the prisoners almost immediately. As far as I was concerned, they were welcome to everything.

"I was completely without self-esteem and felt sure that I would be punished and humiliated for the way I had lived with Lentz. I hated the very thought of my past and grew physically ill recalling it.

I was constantly retching and could eat nothing but the hard bon-bons the men gave me.

"But whenever I did chance to speak from then on, it was always in English. That is how readily human beings can adapt themselves. First I talked only in Polish, and then German out of necessity. Now I think in English and can't even remember certain words in my native language.

"One day a young soldier poked his head into my little makeshift cell and said, 'Hey, Greta Garbo,'—that's what they jokingly called me—'polish yourself up a bit. The big guns are coming.'

"Then I knew my day of judgment had arrived. I decided to take the Tommie's advice and at least comb my hair. When I looked into my little mirror, I was once again astonished to see how stubbornly my looks had refused to change. I felt old and ill at twenty-four, but somehow the mirror reflected a face that was still young and pretty. Strangely, this gave me no comfort at all. I would have preferred to have grown haggard in payment for my sins. It seemed monstrous in those terrible surroundings to be left with a face that looked as though it had never known a day of suffering. As you can see, something finally did catch up with me and left its mark. One can't age gracefully under certain conditions, but I won't go into that now. It's too long a story even for me to tell. I'll stick to my experiences during the war, with which I'm nearly done, except that I can't omit the part about the Englishman. I can still see his face. He represented civilization, something I was no longer a part of in my own mind.

"The 'big guns' proved to be some high-ranking officers, most of them lawyers in civilian life. They were expected to investigate what had transpired in the camp and to prosecute those responsible for the atrocities. One of the arrivals, whom I watched through a crack in my boarded-up window, immediately struck me with his appearance. Oh, he was very handsome to be sure, the most remark-able-looking man I had ever seen, even more handsome than Adam Feder had been in the old days. But what interested me about this man more than anything else was that he looked Jewish. How can I explain it? He didn't have what some call a Jewish nose and his face wasn't exactly 'a map of Israel,' as they say, but certain things about him reminded me of Jewish men I had known back home—his hair, the way his eyes dominated his face. He didn't seem like the other English I saw every day, men whose collective good looks impressed me from the start. They were tall and lanky with narrow faces. This officer was rather short and compact, but his dark beauty made the rest look bland. When one of my soldier acquaintances stopped to check on me later that day, I asked who the black-haired man was.

"'That's Colonel Canning,' I was told. 'He's in charge of the investigation team.'

"The colonel's name didn't sound like a Jewish one to me, but a name didn't mean much. English surnames were alien things to me, anyway. Who knew what their Jews called themselves?

"'Please, Eddie,' I impulsively begged the soldier. 'Please ask him to talk to me.'

"'Oh, I couldn't do that, Miss,' Eddie replied. 'He's got his plate full right now as it is. Don't worry. Your case'll come up in due course.'

"Well, that was that. Days went by and I waited. Eddie dropped by again with some rations.

"'Come on, Ducks,' he coaxed in his funny accent, so different from the one I had been taught in school. 'You've got to eat something besides sweeties. You're looking right peckish now. No need to go starving yourself, is there?'

"'I hope I die,' I said to him, 'before I ever go to trial. I can't stand this place any longer. I've got to get away from here!'

"Eddie seemed perplexed. 'Trial? You ain't been charged with anything. What you done, then?'

"When I told him, Eddie simply shrugged. 'Cor, ain't nobody never been hung for that. If they was, Piccadilly Circus would be fair empty tonight.'

"I had no idea what he meant, of course, and felt no better when he left. I felt certain the investigators would find something to charge me with and I dreaded the notion of having to describe my actions of the last couple of years in detail. I regarded the English as an idealistic people who had suffered a great deal and who were highly intolerant of those less valiant than themselves. Yet perhaps among them were some better disposed to be understanding.

"I was watching through the crack the next morning when the officers passed right under my window, Colonel Canning among them. Well, I thought, here goes. Although in Poland I never spoke Yiddish, my parents sometimes did and most of our neighbors spoke it as a rule, so I knew something of the language. In Warsaw, when a Jew greeted another he would say, 'Vos macht a Yid?' or 'How goes it with a Jew?' So that is what I said, or rather yelled at the top of my lungs. The party halted in surprise, but my eyes were on Colonel Canning, who made a funny sort of face.

"Somebody said, 'Good Lord, what was that?'

"'It's the one they call Greta Garbo,' said a Tommie who knew me.

"'Why is that?' asked Colonel Canning. 'Is she an actress?'

"'Not likely,' answered the soldier, laughing. 'Just a little blonde smasher.'

"The Colonel raised an eyebrow and the soldier drew himself up. 'Polish prisoner, Sir! Collaborator!'

"'Well, bring her out here. Let's have a look at this Garbo person.'

"When I was brought to the officers, my eyes were wet and stinging because I had grown unaccustomed to bright sunlight. Or perhaps I had begun to cry. Far from appearing a glamorous film star, I knew I looked the worse for my confinement and was now so skinny that my dress hung on me like a shapeless sack. I hoped I didn't smell too fearfully.

"I said to the dark-haired officer, in English this time, 'Sir, I must speak with you, please. Only for a few minutes, I beg you.'

"This got a bit of amusement out of the others. One man, a captain or major or something, said, 'It seems she fancies you, old man.'

"'I shouldn't wonder,' said Colonel Canning with a smile, but his eyes were serious. I'd never seen such beautiful eyes in my life. I couldn't stop staring at them, they fascinated me so.

"'Please,' I repeated.

"The colonel told the private to take me to his office, the same one Kommandant Lentz had occupied so recently. I waited for him there. At last he came, alone as I had hoped, and sat down at his desk. He wasn't a young man, about forty or so. He looked terribly weary in the half-light of the room. What he had witnessed since arriving at the camp was enough to wear down even the most stoic emotional makeup, including the legendary stiff upper lip. He lit his pipe and shook out the match. His fine eyes were even blacker than I had previously thought, and when he removed his hat, I saw that his hair was curly at the ends in the same way my poor father's had been. This was a Jew; I was sure of it.

"'Well,' he said, 'do you have something to say to me?'

"'Yes,' I replied. 'My name is Halina Zylberberg and I am a Jewess from Warsaw.'

"The Colonel seemed to digest this for a moment. Then he said, 'Recite the Jewish Prayer for the Dead.'

"I had never had much occasion to say the Kaddish in my time, but I began to say the prayer as well as I could, stumbling through to the end. I managed to remember all of it.

"'You're the girl who turned in the commanding officer of this hellhole, I'm told,' Colonel Canning went on. 'What was he to you?'

"'Nothing,' I said, and that was as much the truth as I had ever spoken. 'I was his housemaid, his slave. I obeyed him like a dog. What he wanted he got. That is all.'

"'Did he mistreat you?'

"'Never. He told me he loved me.'

"The silence in that office was so heavy I began to have difficulty breathing. I was perspiring, too. If only those black eyes would regard me with the tiniest bit of benevolence.

"'Did Lentz know you were a Jewess? You're very fair in your coloring. He might have been deceived about you.'

"'He knew,' I said, 'because he was present in Warsaw when I was transported. He spoke to me then and I had a Jewish star on my jacket.'

"'Evidently it didn't trouble him,' Canning said. 'How extraordinary!'

"'It was mad—everything. He was mad, I was mad and we lived here in a madhouse. I don't know any other way to explain it to you.'

"'Then allow me to explain something to you,' began Canning. 'Before the war, in London, I was a barrister. I was often called upon to defend people in court who pleaded they had done certain crimes because they were hopelessly insane or had simply gone mad for a time. Sometimes this proved an effective defense, and the accused were dealt with leniently. Should this be my defense of you now?'

"'If it pleases you,' I told him, not quite understanding what he was driving at. 'If I need a defense. Have I committed a crime, in your opinion?'

"'You want me to be the judge and jury all at once, don't you?' Canning said. 'Yet I'm only an attorney, after all. I can inform you of your rights, but I don't think that's what you want from me.'

"He was right, you know. I wanted him to absolve me, to tell me that the fact that I was still alive was all that mattered. I looked into those devastating eyes and could only say feebly, 'I want to go home. Please let me go home.'

"'My dear young lady,' said the colonel, 'you have no home. Don't you know that?' What a beautiful voice he had, like an actor. How is it that some Englishmen are able to say any sort of ordinary, even unpleasant, thing and still make it sound like a poem?

"'To me, home is anywhere but here!' I blurted out. 'I wanted to live; can't you understand that? I've done nothing to anyone here. Ask the people, if you don't believe me. I was very young and I didn't want to die so soon. Can you honestly say you would not have done the same in my place—done anything to stay alive?' I remember clutching at my head like I had a headache. 'No, no! I wouldn't have done anything, not just anything. I wouldn't have taken so much as a piece of bread from anyone else.'

"Canning puffed on his pipe. 'I can't answer you. I could never be in your place, nor even imagine what it was like to be you on the day the Nazi decided you were his cup of tea.'

"He was beginning to make me angry. 'It was *my* body,' I nearly shouted. 'If I chose to have it violated in order to survive, then that was my business. Others let themselves be beaten, didn't they, and the guards took pleasure from doing that, let me tell you!'

"The eyes had seemed to soften. 'Well, well, it seems you don't need me to defend you after all.'

"I was sullen now. 'Defend! You're here to accuse, remember?'

"'Um-hum,' said Canning. 'I do. When I was assigned this duty, I thought, oh no, this is bound to drag on a good long time. Here the war was over and I still had no prospect of going home. I longed to sit

in my own library, feet toward the fire, with a good brandy. Yet
when I saw all this, all of you people, I changed my mind. Now I
don't care if it takes forever, if I have to examine and prosecute a line
of devils that reaches all the way to China. Now let me ask you something. What would you do now in my place with a young woman
named Halina . . .'

"'Zylberberg,' I finished. I didn't have to think at all. It came to
me in a rush just what I should say. 'If I were you,' I told the colonel,
'I would just for two minutes be a Jew and nothing else.'

"For a moment I thought the man would smile, but he managed
to compose his wonderful face and pointed a finger at me.

"'Stand up,' he said, and his finger beckoned me to come closer. I,
who had for so long lived in fear of anyone wearing a uniform, found
I had no dread of this officer whatsoever.

"He took hold of the little twig of an arm I had then, this one with
the tattoo, handling it like a fragile relic that might crumble in his
hand.

"'I'm not sure if I have the authority to release you,' Canning said.
'In fact, I'm even fairly certain I don't. But you may go. You've
served your time; we both agree on that. I'll have you driven to a
refugee camp where no one will know you. Is that what you would
have done in my place? I certainly hope so.' He did actually smile
then. He looked so marvelous I had an urge to kiss him, but of
course, I did no such thing.

"'You mean I can just go?' I wondered. 'Without any punishment?'

"The colonel grew serious at once. 'Oh, you can go, all right. As
for the punishment, I know I can leave that to you. I have the idea
that this punishment will be long and harsh.'

"And, oh, how very astute he was, this Canning.

"The colonel was as good as his word.

"I was transferred, fattened up and began working for the Red
Cross. Pardon my saying so, but I became beautiful once again,
more beautiful than ever because I was older now. People told me
every day what a lovely girl I was. And, would you believe it, a tremendous thing happened. Colonel Canning came to visit me. He
took me to lunch and told me he had a bit of a holiday before the war

crimes trial in which he was participating was to begin. I believe Canning only meant to find out what had become of the odd girl who had called to him from a window—you know, just out of curiosity. But he wound up spending every day of his holiday with me. He even had me excused from my work. He entertained me and fell in love with me. I swear it's true. Colonel Canning asked me to come to England with him when his duties were finished and become his wife. How do you like that, eh?"

I loved it. "Well, did you?" I cried. But Halina was not in London. She was sitting with me in a dingy eatery in the good old U.S. of A. "Oh, God, you didn't . . . you couldn't have."

"Of course I didn't," Halina said, almost sneering. "That would have been too lucky, too wonderful. The colonel had said I was to be punished, but he afterward changed his mind. But I had not changed mine. No, I still thought I needed to pay for my cowardice, my compliancy. Besides, I had already promised to marry someone else, someone I met while working with the Red Cross."

"What do you mean?" I scoffed. "I could tell you fell for that Englishman from the moment you set eyes on him!"

Halina shook her head. "You don't understand. Yes, the English officer attracted me very much, but I had forgotten how to love. You see, young man, I had come to realize why I could feel no more revulsion for Kommandant Lentz than I did. I didn't even have a crumb of hate to spare for that one. I told you I protected Adam Feder, but not out of compassion. I hated him, only him. Believe me, I would have been glad to spend the rest of my life persecuting him. He was a murderer, too, in his way."

"But what did that have to do with a nice guy like Canning? He could have helped you, changed you."

"Or maybe I would have changed Canning," said Halina. "He was all right the way he was, wouldn't you say? He didn't need me. On the outside, I was a nice-looking young woman. I did my job, nursed sick people, smiled at them, even kissed them if they happened to be children. I dated Canning—a man who obviously cared for me—and even kissed him. But it was no use. All the while, my insides kept churning with hatred. I wanted it to stop. I wanted to see myself as Canning had come to view me, but secretly I thought he was a fool. I hated myself even more than I had loathed Adam Feder, the man who began it all. You see, Bob Samuels, I was then really quite insane."

"I'll say," I told her. "Not marrying the colonel was the dumbest thing you could have done. I suppose you went ahead and married that other guy."

Halina nodded. "Yes. This person was a concentration camp survivor like myself. He understood what I was all about."

"Oh, yeah?" I said. "You weren't happy with your choice, were you? I know that without asking."

"Happy?" Halina grinned, showing her yellow teeth. "Do you think it was ever my goal to be happy? Young man, use your good Jewish head. Or have I been talking to you all day for nothing."

I shook my head, no longer knowing what to say. I felt tired and confused. The cafeteria now seemed as gloomy as a cave and Halina appeared haggard, witchlike. Her thin hands looked to me like claws. I had a fleeting image of them tearing the flesh of Adam Feder, venting her hatred on him one last time as the Allies approached. I had been prepared, even eager, to feel sympathy for this woman, for the horrors that had constituted her young life, but now I saw that she had never solicited my pity. She had told her story matter-of-factly, and had I pronounced her a monster, I don't believe she would have been upset. I envisioned her recounting the same tale to everyone who would listen, smiling inwardly as she waited for the listener to pass judgment on her, laughing silently at his inept attempt to explain her behavior, the lack of feeling that enabled her to endure the caresses of a slaughterer of her own kind. Heroine or betrayer of her people, Halina waited for the answer, always waited. Perhaps it was like a game. At least she spared Colonel Canning a lifetime of this sort of mental exercise. Later blinded by Halina's beauty, he had correctly guessed in that first meeting the role she really wanted him to play. Judge and jury all at once; he said it himself.

I gazed at the people walking by the window and was momentarily unsettled by how sinister they appeared, how singularly incapable of doing good.

Perhaps Halina had read my thoughts. "Why are you so sad? All of it happened long ago. It was a bad dream, but it passed."

"I'm not upset," I lied. "I'm just thinking."

"I know what you're thinking—how can this old lady go around telling such things about herself so calmly? Doesn't she care what people think? Well, I don't care. I only know what I think, how I feel about myself. Do you want to know what that is?"

"What is it?" I said, rather nastily.

"I was wrong," said Halina. "I thought because I was young and pretty and a victim that I had the right to preserve my life. But that was false. Many persons younger and prettier and certainly more gifted were reduced to ashes. What I had was a great opportunity and I refused to make use of it. I had fallen into Lentz's hands, certainly, but in a way, he had also fallen into mine. Every night I could have taken his pistol and put a bullet into his head. I could have killed him more easily than Yael did Sisera in the tents of ancient Israel. That is what I *should* have done."

"What good would that have been? You would have been killed yourself and somebody just as bad would have come to take Lentz's place."

"That's true. There's a never-ending supply of evil in this world, but so what? It's up to every decent person to strike a blow where he can, not simply survive and let the others do the striking. Canning knew that very well, but he was too fine a gentleman to tell it to my face." Halina gave a little moan. "Well, I received my punishment, just as he had predicted. That part I didn't leave to others."

"I don't get it," I told her. "You mean that, out of guilt, you did something to hurt yourself?"

Halina smiled wanly. "I guarantee it. You'd better go now, Bob Samuels. I've exhausted myself and probably have gotten you into trouble. Go, nice young man. You've been as patient as a saint."

I left Halina and I never went back to the cafeteria again. I didn't have the courage. For a long time I felt burdened with the thought of what I would have done had I been Halina in her awful circumstances. Ultimately, I had to give up wondering. Like Canning the barrister, I realized the futility of trying to put oneself in the place of another.

That same day I went back to work just as the office was about to close. I made up a story for my boss about having been detained by the police after witnessing a car accident. He looked at me rather quizzically but only said, "You look like you've been in an accident yourself."

On the way to the bus stop while going home, a funny notion came to me. On a hunch, I slowed down in front of a little store that had a display of hats in the window—flamboyant hats like those black men are given to wearing. Also on display were ties—wide crazy ones with palm trees and setting suns. Through the dirty glass I caught sight of Halina, hunched over the counter, conversing with an old man. At first I thought he was a customer, but then I realized he was wearing a classy, well-cut suit and that his accessories would never come from this shop. I knew he wasn't a customer when Halina spoke sharply to him and gave him a dirty look before she went into the back room.

But the old fellow didn't leave. He got behind the counter, and turned a mirror stand around so that it faced him. Carefully adjusting his own tie, he looked at his reflection with one eyebrow cocked, as if he were a sharp-looking thirty-year-old getting ready to impress a date. The old man was so busy preening, he never noticed me at all.

There was no question in my mind that I was observing none other than Adam Feder, Halina's husband, a survivor in every sense of the word.

Professor Mondshane

L UDWIG MONDSHANE, Professor Mondshane, as he called himself, perspired quietly on a Sunday afternoon. It was a Volksfest
Association gathering on the grounds of the Volksfest Haus, and
most of the company present were wearing appropriate summer
clothing. Some of the women had donned what passed for traditional Bavarian costume and a few of the men sported lederhosen.
An accordionist played and, despite the June heat, amateur dancers
slapped their soles to the rhythm of the *Schuhplattler.*

Professor Mondshane watched their efforts, thinking quite
rightly that two minutes of this folk dance would give him a massive
coronary. The temperature was at least eighty-five degrees. Nevertheless, he was the only spectator wearing a jacket and tie. Mondshane never went anywhere in shirtsleeves, nor did he have a suit
that wasn't black. In winter he wore a coat with a big fur collar that
made him look like an old-world impresario. The coat, made of
cloth-of-iron, he had bought in 1945 in Vienna. The only hat Mondshane owned was a homburg. When he first came to America, the
professor had used a walking stick, but he had discarded that long
ago, his only concession to modern fashion.

Some members of the Volksfest Association were second-gen-
eration Americans, but most were, like Ludwig Mondshane, im-
migrants from Germany and Austria. The professor listened to bits

of the surrounding conversation, for the main in German dialects and heavily accented English. Mondshane, of course, spoke English with an accent, but his German was high-class. Yet he spoke to nobody and none thought to address him. Nor was he particularly bothered by the stares his appearance elicited. The heavy, ruddy faces about him gazed with benign amusement at his overly formal attire, his sallow complexion and Mediterranean features, for Mondshane was as conspicuous in this assembly as a raven in a poultry yard. Professor Mondshane was, to the Volksfest crowd, as unmistakably a Jew as when he had worn a yellow star on his coat so many years ago.

Unlike then, however, no one begrudged him his Jewishness this Sunday afternoon. At length, someone even decided to sound him out. A man in a baseball cap said, "Hot, isn't it?" Mondshane replied that it certainly was.

"You look like you could use a beer," observed the man, taking a swallow of his own from a plastic cup. "You from Germany?"

"Austria," Mondshane told him. "Vienna."

"My granddaddy came from over there," the man volunteered. "I don't speak the lingo but I wish I did. I think it's great how these people here keep the traditions going and everything. You sure look like you need a beer."

Professor Mondshane conceded that the man in the baseball cap and shirt with the little green reptile was right. A beer was entirely in order, even though Mondshane ordinarily never touched the stuff. He made his way to the refreshment stand and paid his fifty cents for a cup of brew. Announcements were being made from the wooden platform, where the entertainment took place, but Mondshane only half listened. None of the information had anything to do with him. He was not a member of the association and had nothing to contribute to the perpetuation of German ethnicity in America. The professor was fond of saying that he had attended the best German finishing school, only they hadn't finished him—not altogether. Yet Mondshane held no grudges. At least not here. The leather shorts and other assorted German memorabilia on display brought back no associations, good or bad. His life in Vienna had, after all, not consisted of beer-hall tunes and apple strudel. Even the beer he sipped from the plastic container tasted totally different from any he had ever been served in his native land.

The truth was that Ludwig Mondshane had never meant to attend this Teutonic garden party. He lived only a few blocks from the Volksfest Haus, had been taking a stroll and was attracted by the music. Listening to music, even this kind, under the shade of an elm was, to the professor, a welcome diversion on a dull Sunday, for Mondshane was a profoundly lonely man.

As Mondshane walked back to his tree, something happened that finally commanded his full attention. The tone of the music suddenly changed, and the professor's ear picked up the opening bars to a song that was as familiar to him as his own name. Then he heard the words sung in German: "There once was a Vilia, a maid of the woods . . ." Even the second-rate sound system couldn't distort the crystalline soprano interpreting the lovely Lehar melody. Mondshane, as was his custom, not only listened but swiftly analyzed. The voice was young but had strength, shimmered in the middle and upper registers but lacked absolute control in the lower. Still, it was a gorgeous sound. Mondshane had heard far worse on the stages of Vienna from those who were called prima donnas. Certainly, he had heard less deserving professional voices in the midwestern city in which he now lived.

Mondshane abandoned all politeness and elbowed his way nearer the plywood dais. It was then that an even greater excitement gripped him for he saw that the singer was not a woman, really, but only a girl of not more than sixteen or seventeen. The young soprano finished her "Vilia Song" on a B-flat that was like a shower of stars. When a singer was able to float a high B like that, it was said in operatic circles that she had the $100,000 note. It was a feat that normally required years of practice to bring off, yet this child had secured it already! Mondshane wanted to applaud wildly, but he had the accursed cup in his hand. He finished the beer in one gulp and discarded the container. Drawing out his handkerchief, he wiped his face for he had broken out in a cold sweat. Mondshane's moment had arrived. Fate, for once, had steered him in the right direction. The rest was up to him.

The girl stepped down to considerable applause and walked

across the lawn toward the refreshments. Professor Mondshane pursued her at once.

The woman selling the cold drinks seemed to understand just why Mondshane would offer to buy the singer a cola, but the girl, not yet accustomed to having her talent saluted in this manner, looked bewildered.

"Well, I guess," she said, looking at Mondshane uncertainly. She was a rather pretty creature, though a bit on the plump side. Her shiny hair, which was long and rippling, reminded him of a Titian painting. An adolescent blemish or two did not detract much from the pleasing effect.

As a music teacher, Professor Mondshane was accustomed to young people. For years they had tramped up the stairs to his studio, their sheet music mixed in with their schoolbooks. He told them what to do, and they did it—if they were able. Since they regarded Mondshane as a sort of oracle, he was probably the only adult in their lives for whom they made no trouble. Some of his pupils were quite gifted. These he much preferred over his older pupils who doggedly strove for something they would never attain. Mondshane accepted the latter's fees in retribution for his frayed nerves and assaulted ears.

"Tell me," he said, "where did you learn to sing like that?"

"You liked the song, huh?"

"The song I have always liked. What I want to know is who taught you to sing it with such authority."

"Elisabeth Schwarzkopf," replied the girl, her gaze darting about as though searching for an escape route. Mondshane knew that she sensed herself in immediate danger of being bored to death.

"You studied with Elisabeth Schwarzkopf?"

The girl smirked at him. "Sort of. I listen to her records."

"Are you telling me that you learned to sing from recordings?" Mondshane demanded.

"Sure," she said, licking the cola from her upper lip.

The professor's eyes narrowed. It occurred to him that the girl might be pulling his leg, even though her answer was the only one he had really wanted to hear.

"What is your name, young lady?"

"Lanie Twardowski."

"Miss Twardowski, I must speak with you. Do you mind coming into the shade for a moment?"

Lanie Twardowski indicated a point past Mondshane's ear. "I really gotta go. My parents are over—"

"No, no, no," said Mondshane. "Wait, wait." He delved into his coat, retrieving a dampish wallet. "My card, if you please."

"Professor Ludwig Mondshane," the girl read, mispronouncing his name in the usual American way. "Voice." She regarded Mondshane with a new interest. "Does that mean you teach people how to sing?"

Mondshane decided she wasn't putting him on. The girl knew nothing about the art of singing—except how to do it beautifully.

"To sing better," he told her. "Would you be interested in studying with me?"

"Don't I sing good now?" asked Lanie Twardowski, somewhat fearfully. "People seem to think—"

"What people?" said Mondshane irritably. "These people here whose idea of great music is 'The Beer Barrel Polka'? Your choir director in school? Your silly friends who know nothing but Elvis Presley, eh? You have a very fine voice, but that is only the beginning. And listening to phonograph records is very nice but it is not the way to proceed in training. There is much, much more involved . . . Well, what is so funny?"

"You are," laughed the girl. "Nobody listens to Elvis anymore."

Professor Mondshane pulled a face. "No? Maybe that is because he did not have me for a teacher."

Lanie Twardowski leaned toward him, rocking lightly on one foot. Evidently she no longer thought Mondshane such a fatal bore.

"You talk like someone from the old country," said Lanie. "Like my mom and dad. But you're different somehow. I can't put my finger on it, but you're definitely different. How old are you?"

Professor Mondshane was surprised at the question, but he replied, "Fifty-five. A Stone Age man."

"That's not so old," said Lanie Twardowski, and Mondshane was surprised again. "You like to dance?" she asked, nodding toward the pavilion on the opposite side of the grounds, where couples were moving to the sounds of "You Can't Be True Dear."

"Well, I . . ." Mondshane began.

"I mean with me."

Ludwig Mondshane looked up at the blazing sky, at Lanie Twardowski and then back at the pavilion. He sighed inwardly but removed his black jacket and laid it on the grass. The professor even went so far as to roll up his sleeves. For this girl, no, for the opportunity of shaping this girl's voice, Mondshane was willing to take a few turns around a dance floor, even though he couldn't recall the last time he'd actually done any dancing.

And so Mondshane loosened his tie and gingerly put his arm around Lanie Twardowski. Fortunately, it was only a waltz, and after a moment's hesitation, he fell easily into step.

Lanie looked up at him. "I know what's so different about you. It's your eyes. I've never seen eyes like yours before. I mean, they're totally fascinating."

"What year is it?" asked Mondshane.

"1975," said the girl, smiling. "June . . . ."

"Very good," said Mondshane. "Now you're talking sense. Keep it up."

Mondshane could have sworn the girl cuddled up to him. She was really very appealing, more than marginally pretty, but the professor felt ill at ease. He made it a rule never to touch any of his female students. Clearly, with this one he was beginning on the wrong foot.

"How old are you?" It was Mondshane's turn to ask.

"Seventeen going on eighteen."

"Just the right age."

"For what?"

"Beginning vocal studies."

"Are you married, Professor?"

Mondshane explained that he was a widower and had been for ten years.

"Gee, that's too bad," commented Lanie, but something in her blue eyes told Mondshane she found it no great tragedy.

The waltz set finally ended, and Ludwig Mondshane firmly steered his protégé away from the pavilion lest she take it upon herself to dance on.

"I would like to speak with your parents," he told Lanie.

"They don't like music," she said, looking at the ground.

"Oh, come now! Surely they must want you to develop your talent."

"They want me to be a stenographer."

Mondshane raised a knowing eyebrow. "I see. You are teasing me again. The biggest philistine on earth wouldn't want to turn you into a typist, not with that voice, and you do have Schwarzkopf records at home."

Lanie tossed back her hair, her full mouth twisted in a wry smile. "They're from the public library! When I play them, my folks yell at me to turn down the noise."

"Lanie" said Mondshane, "do you want to sing or not?"

"You mean like a career?"

"Of course that is what I mean!"

"And you'll help me?"

"I want to, if you'll allow me."

Lanie Twardowski picked thoughtfully at a blemish on her chin. "Okay," she said abruptly. "Let's go."

Mr. and Mrs. Twardowski sat on lawn chairs they had brought from home. Although they were European-born and accustomed to shaking hands on introduction, neither extended a hand to Mondshane. They regarded him sourly, as though he were a flea-ridden dog their daughter wanted to adopt. As it turned out, Mrs. Twardowski, a heavier, coarser version of Lanie, originated from Hamburg. Her husband was a Pole she had met and married in Germany, a common arrangement due to the shortage of eligible German men following the war. The little man, with his suspicious, close-set eyes and sharp features, seemed shriveled next to the robust form of his wife, whose vast shelf of a bosom alone was enough to intimidate anyone.

Mondshane thought fleetingly of Maestro Toscanini, who once allegedly grasped a soprano's prodigious endowments, exclaiming, "If only these were brains!"

Mrs. Twardowski addressed Mondshane in a German that was as far removed from his own as a cockney's English is from that of the Queen.

"How do you come to be here then?"

Professor Mondshane assumed she meant what was he doing in that very place at the given moment, although the question held many implications.

"I am a music lover, after all," Mondshane replied indicating the accordion player, who was at it again. "In fact, I am a teacher of music, vocal music. I would be honored if it could be arranged that Lanie would study with me."

"My daughter sings just beautiful already," protested the mother. "Don't *you* think so?"

"Well, yes," said the professor, "but she needs training."

"Ah, crazy singing," scoffed Mr. Twardowski in English. "Better study secretary."

"We're only poor working people," said Mrs. Twardowski. "We can't afford expensive lessons. How much do you charge, anyway?"

"Eight dollars per half-hour." This was actually the going rate for local voice teachers, but the Twardowskis looked at one another as though Mondshane had said something outrageous.

"I come this country work ninety cents hour," growled Lanie's father. He evidently understood German very well but didn't deign to speak it.

"That was years ago, Papa," said Lanie.

"We're only poor working people," repeated the mother, eyeing Ludwig Mondshane like he was an enemy of working people everywhere.

I know your type, thought Mondshane. These people had elevated the idea of manual labor to Work with a capital W until it became a sort of blue-collar snobbery. To slave away at some backbreaking job meant you sweated for your wages, perhaps gave more than you got. Artists, even lowly music teachers like himself, were suspect. They probably enjoyed their livelihood. To the Twardowskis of this world, this somehow didn't seem right. Mondshane had also known Jews who felt the same way. When he first saw the legend "Arbeit Macht Frei" (Work Makes You Free) on the gates of the concentration camp, he hadn't been a bit surprised.

"All right," said the teacher, "I understand these things. Perhaps we can come to terms. It is very important that Lanie begins her studies as soon as possible. She cannot keep on singing with a technique that might ruin her voice." Mondshane wiped his face. "So make me an offer."

Mr. Twardowski laughed. "A quarter!" he bellowed.

Mondshane bitterly reflected that the Pole had probably been waiting for Mondshane to reveal himself as the haggling Jew.

He drew himself up. "Actually, I have so much faith in your daughter's ability that I would be willing to teach her for nothing."

"Is that so," said Mrs. Twardowski, squinting. "For free? Very unusual, it seems to me."

"Free!" chortled her husband. "Free! Best joke I hear all day!"

"Besides," added the woman from Hamburg, "how do we know what kind of a teacher you are? Do you teach in a school, a conservatory? No? In your home! It's impossible. We have to be careful. What kind of parents would send a young girl to a strange man's house?"

"She need not come alone," said Mondshane, highly offended. "Surely you don't think—"

"It's impossible," Mrs. Twardowski declared anew. "I work days and my husband works nights. We barely have time to sleep, much less act as chaperones. Lanie is still in high school and has plenty of homework every evening. It was kind of you to offer, but we are not interested."

"In that case, good day," said Mondshane, bowing curtly. "It was enchanting to meet you, I'm sure."

"I warned you," muttered Lanie Twardowski as Mondshane walked away.

Much later Professor Mondshane trudged up the stairs leading to his apartment, the upper story of an old, Tudor-style house. He had not gone directly home from the Volksfest Haus, taking a long walk instead to rid himself of the turmoil his encounter with the Twardowskis had aroused. Now, however, he was completely exhausted, too tired even to fix himself supper. He switched on the air conditioner in the spacious room that served as both his parlor and the studio where he gave lessons. Mondshane's late wife had had good taste in furnishings, and so the flat was an attractive one, maintained by Mondshane, himself, and a woman who came in once a week.

Yet this particular evening, the familiar surroundings struck him as being oppressively gloomy, filled with fading museum pieces.

The professor sank into his favorite chair and gazed at the corner where his old Steinway stood. On the wall behind the piano hung numerous photographs, all of singers and musicians he had once known, some of them famous, most of them dead. Lotte Lehmann's portrait was there, and so was Maria Jeritza's. These two divas had personally autographed their pictures, although Mondshane had really not known them well. He had been a very young man in those pre-war days, only an obscure rehearsal accompanist at the *Staatsoper*, the great opera house of Vienna. Still, his position there had afforded him meetings with many celebrities, if only in passing. The wonderful Richard Tauber even sang with him on occasion. It was the famed tenor himself, who had first warned Ludwig Mondshane to leave Austria; the Jewish Tauber soon fled, seeking refuge for himself and his unique voice in England. Upon learning this, Mondshane finally made up his mind to go. But by then it was too late.

At any rate, while he accompanied, Mondshane had observed the great singers and had tried to figure out their techniques, what they did to produce such beautiful sounds. Sometimes he had even asked them about certain things, and all were only too happy to explain— if they could. Singers never tire of talking about singing, their own or anybody else's. Still, in those days, he had never considered becoming a voice teacher. Mondshane's great love had been composing, although he now realized how limited his ability in that direction had been. In any case, after the war and Mondshane's struggle for survival were over, whatever flair Mondshane had had for composition completely dried up. Inexplicably, he found himself unable to string together the notes for even the simplest tune.

When Mondshane came to the States, to this town where he had some distant relatives, he had to make a living. So he hit upon the idea of passing himself off as a voice teacher. To give himself prestige, he added the title of "professor." Who would know the difference? After a while, through the actual process of teaching or attempting to teach, Mondshane did learn a thing or two about vocal pedagogy. At least he believed he hadn't ruined anybody's voice.

How much good he did his pupils was up to them to determine.

Of course, none of the students ever had what amounted to a real career, much less achieved renown. Mondshane consoled himself that this was not entirely his fault. The truly gifted ones did not seek out the likes of Ludwig Mondshane but took themselves off to New York, to Juilliard. And so, on days when a would-be singer made a little progress or overcame a vocal stumbling block, the professor rejoiced in his having a hand in it. But late in the evenings, when he found himself alone staring at the television, Ludwig Mondshane called himself a charlatan and a fake. Yet teaching voice was all that was left to him. In Mondshane's heart there was always the hope that somehow someone with a great talent, a marvelous potential, would find his or her way to Mondshane's studio. Painstakingly, lovingly, the professor would mold this individual's voice into a glorious instrument, a ticket to stardom. But this opportunity had never presented itself in all the years—until today. In Lanie Twardowski, Mondshane felt he had found his vindication, his right to exist. Yet his chance had been snatched from him by the work-callused fingers of her anti-Semitic parents. The darker side of Ludwig Mondshane's mind wondered briefly whether even they, the ignorant Twardowskis, had somehow perceived that he was not everything he claimed to be. At last, Mondshane's chin dropped to his breast and he fell into a troubled sleep, dreaming, as he invariably did, of the days when he was a man transformed into a beast, beaten and driven by others who refused to be convinced of his authenticity.

As the week wore on, the teacher had begun to settle himself into his routine of lessons, solitary meals and early bedtimes. On Thursday evening the telephone rang. Mondshane hoped one of his acquaintances was inviting him for a Sabbath meal the next day, but instead he heard the speaking voice of the little soprano.

"Professor Munching, this is Lanie Twardowski—you know, from the German picnic."

"Yes," breathed Mondshane, willing her to tell him that her parents had had a change of heart. "How are you?"

"Great. Listen, Professor, can I come to see you? I kept your card."

"Good. Have your parents consented to let you study with me?"

Lanie Twardowski sighed into the receiver at the other end. "Nah, they're really out of it. I mean, couldn't you tell? Are you busy now? If you're not, I wish you'd let me talk to you in person. I'm not far from where you live."

"What are you doing in this neighborhood at this time of night?" asked Mondshane. "You told me you live way across town!"

"I took the bus," replied the girl cheerfully. "Besides, it's not late. I came because I knew you'd want me to."

Mondshane was at a loss. Common sense told him he should tell Lanie he was too busy to see her and that, without her parents' approval, there was nothing for them to talk about, but he heard himself saying, "Are you sure you can find the address? It's growing dark already."

"I'll find you," said the girl and hung up.

Ten minutes later, Lanie Twardowski was ringing Mondshane's buzzer. Had the child called him from a shop down the street? Was she that certain of his desire to talk with her?

He let her in, and she gave him a bright grin, her singer's lungs apparently not protesting at the climb that always left Mondshane breathless.

"Wow!" Lanie exclaimed. "What a groovy apartment! I just knew you'd live in a place like this."

"Make yourself comfortable," said Mondshane, showing her to the parlor. "Sit down."

But Lanie Twardowski wasn't ready to sit. She wandered slowly about the room inspecting his wife's treasures, stopping at the piano.

"Man, look at those pictures! Are these your friends?"

"Yes," said Mondshane, making a simple job of it.

"Great-looking people."

"They used to be. They're mostly all dead now."

"Wow," said Lanie, making perhaps the ultimate comment on the human condition.

Mondshane seated himself on the piano bench.

"Now then, what is it you wish to speak to me about?"

"You know—about taking lessons."

"But I recall your mother informing me that it is impossible."

Lanie made a face. "Aw, she's full of it! You know, I hated like hell to have you meet my folks, but I guess you had to see them for yourself." She put her head inside the open Steinway, studying its works. "They told me you're a Jew."

"How astute of them to figure it out," said Mondshane.

"Yeah, well, I guess they don't trust Jews."

"What about you? Are you the trusting kind?"

Lanie raised her head. "Me? Sure I am. I always trust people until they do something to hurt me. Besides, I don't know any Jews—except you. Anyway, I guess Jews are human beings, no different from anybody else."

"Don't you believe it!" Mondshane told her.

"Okay, then, how are they different?"

"That is a complicated matter, I assure you."

"A secret, huh? Well, you're different all right, and I like you. Then I guess I must like Jews."

"A woman of logic," said Mondshane, not unhappily. He played a chord and then another. "As long as you are here, let's see what you can do tonight. What can you sing for me?"

Lanie thought about it. "Do you know Brahms' 'Lullaby'?"

"I think I have heard it," murmured the professor, and he played the introduction.

Lanie Twardowski sang the simple cradle song with as much feeling and beauty of tone as she had the operetta piece a few days ago. Only now, being closer to her voice, Mondshane was even more deeply affected by it. And her German diction was flawless. How did it all come to be? In Jewish lore there were spirits called dybbuks who entered humans, causing them to do unaccountable things. Could such a phenomenon have invaded the person of Lanie, making a sensitive classical singer out of a teenager in blue jeans whose vocabulary and demeanor otherwise marked her as being downright common? But who was he, Ludwig Mondshane, to question such miracles?

"Come here," said Mondshane, and when Lanie approached him, he took both her hands and kissed them. "You are an angel from God, totally sublime."

"Does that mean I can study with you?" Lanie wanted to know.

"How?" shrugged the professor.

"You weren't kidding, were you, when you said I could take lessons free?"

"Of course not. I always mean what I say."

"So do I," said the girl. "Listen, just because my mom and dad
weren't impressed with you, doesn't mean I was going to forget
everything we discussed. I'm not a kid; I've got a mind of my own,
haven't I? I hardly slept these last few days thinking of a way to get
around my folks."

Lanie told Mondshane her plan. The elder Twardowskis, predictably enough, were bugging her to get a part-time job now that
school was out. Lanie would find one. She knew of several places
that wanted to hire high school students, but she would make sure
that she would have one or two evenings off for lessons with
Mondshane. The Twardowskis would never notice the difference.
How did that grab him, the girl wanted to know.

The professor felt himself "grabbed" by great misgivings. Never
in his entire career had he been a party to such intrigues. The necessity, of course, had never arisen. But then, no one with the potential
of Lanie Twardowski had ever come his way. Even Mondshane,
who had so often closed his eyes to professional ethics, was overwhelmed by the girl's eagerness to deceive her parents. Surely no
teacher could be excused for aiding a youngster in making fools of...

"Professor Munching," he heard Lanie cry out, "aren't you going
to say something?"

The professor looked at the candid young face before him. The
blue eyes pleaded with him. The Twardowskis were at fault here,
Mondshane felt sure. Were they not already such fools, no one
would need to deceive them. They clearly did not deserve such a
wunderkind. Yes, Lanie Twardowski was a genius, a budding artist.
The elder Twardowskis were nothing.

"Are you sure you can manage all this?" Mondshane asked the
girl. "And how will you practice what I teach you?"

Lanie smiled in a Mona Lisa way, full of the confidence of youth.

"I'm always practicing," she said. "Can't you tell? When I'm not
singing out loud, I'm singing in my mind. You'll see. I can swing it."

Within a few days, Ludwig Mondshane heard from Lanie again.

She had obtained a position as a waitress and made arrangements with her boss to have every Monday and Thursday night off. Was that okay with Mondshane? The professor, already working out the problem of rescheduling his later students on those days, muttered his assent.

"Can you come between seven and eight?" he asked.

"No problem," was the reply. "You're a doll," Lanie added and before Mondshane could say any more, the line was dead.

The difficulties connected with teaching Lanie Twardowski were greater than Mondshane had anticipated. For one thing, the girl didn't read music, but when the professor tried to explain to her the values of notes, she grew impatient with such technicalities. Although she did her vocal exercises with precision, Mondshane was aware they also made her restive, that she failed to find a connection between them and "real singing," as she called it. However, Mondshane had discovered this to be true of many beginning pupils. Because of her background, Lanie was proficient in German, but the professor had to teach her how to pronounce Italian and French. First, however, he had to teach her how to pronounce his own name. Fortunately, Lanie was able to mimic the Romance languages as surely as she had the good German of Schwarzkopf. She was also one of those lucky creatures who knew how to breathe from the diaphragm by instinct, and the placement of her voice was already generally good. Mondshane saw his task as being one of helping her to control her air flow in order to sustain her phrases better and to strengthen the wobbly lower register. Lanie complained the breathing exercises made her dizzy. She bewailed her chances of ever becoming a musician and sometimes Mondshane was inclined to think she was right. If only he could get her some piano lessons! But when? How? Whenever the girl felt things were not going well, she would attempt to lure Mondshane into conversations that had no bearing on the work in progress. She seemed extraordinarily curious about Mondshane's life, past and present. Most of the time he was able to divert her back to singing, but often he let himself be lured. Every so often Lanie would call him at very short notice to tell him that her employer needed her and that she was unable to come. At other times she would be on the telephone wanting to know if she could come over right away. Yet Mondshane was always glad to see her, no matter how great the irritation. The fascination her voice held for him was endless. He was also intrigued by the unexpected things that popped out of her mouth, odd statements and questions that very often shocked the correct teacher with their frankness. Thus, the lessons continued throughout the summer and into the early fall.

"What did I do wrong now?" Lanie groaned one evening, pulling her shirt out of her jeans. "Ugh, it's hot in here. Can't you open the window?"

The teacher complied. "Is that better? Can we go on?"

"No. Open it all the way."

"Cold air is bad for the voice. Now then, back to the passage. You can't take a breath at that point. It chops up the phrase."

"Either I breathe or I turn blue."

"The ribs, Lanie, remember. The ribs must be held firm. Otherwise you can't get proper support."

"I'll never get it right," sighed the girl. "All these things you want me to do—I can't remember them all at once."

"They must become second nature," said Mondshane, "so that you won't need to remember. Here, let me show you."

Completely forgetting his rule about not touching female students, he got up and placed his palms on Lanie's rib cage.

"Breathe," he ordered, "and hold it in here. Never let the ribs cave in. It must be like an iron bar is in here holding them up and out. The chest must stay up, also. Yes, just like that. Always good posture. Understand now?"

"I hope so," said Lanie. "How come you never showed me this before?"

"I can't teach you everything at once," murmured the teacher.

"Yeah, I guess not," said the girl. "Listen, what time is it? It must be after eight."

Mondshane consulted his watch. "It's 8:32. Do you want to stop?"

"I'm kind of tired."

Mondshane raised an eyebrow. "A young girl like you? Oh, yes, I forgot. Your parents may be worried."

"Who knows," shrugged Lanie. "Who cares."

"You don't have to run off, you know. I've been thinking, Lanie. I've got a lot of wonderful recordings here. It would be a very good thing for you to listen to some great singers perform the pieces you are learning. It would teach you a good deal about style and phrasing."

What he did not say was that it often saddened and worried Mondshane to send Lanie off, week after week, without anything to sustain her, into an environment devoid of culture or love of beauty, much less encouragement of the girl's endeavors. He had considered offering to buy her tickets to operas and concerts, even taking her himself. After all, who else would? But he rejected the idea for reasons that were not altogether clear to him. Very likely the girl would find the idea of being seen in public with him ludicrous, anyway. It's not your responsibility, Mondshane told himself, but somehow he felt it was.

Lanie chewed on her bottom lip in uncharacteristic confusion.

"Thanks, but not tonight," she said. "I've really got to go. There's a lot going on right now."

"Ah, yes," said Mondshane with a resigned smile. "Well, then off you go, my dear. Remember the ribs. Practice holding them the way I showed you."

"I will," promised the girl, "and next time we'll listen to records. I'd really love to, honestly."

"We'll see."

"Well, good night, then."

"Good night, Lanie." Mondshane, in his gentlemanly fashion, got up to show his pupil to the door. He held it open for her.

Suddenly she said, "Professor Mondshane, I don't really want to leave. You think I do, but I don't."

"Then stay. Don't be silly."

"I can't. I have a date."

"Why didn't you say so? Why shouldn't a pretty young girl have a date?"

"Well, it's not a very important date, really. No great shakes, if you know what I mean."

"I'm not sure," chuckled the professor.

"If I'd known you were going to ask me to stay, I wouldn't have made the date."

"Don't apologize, Lanie. It's all right. Go on. I'll see you next time."

"It's just that I never thought—"

"Good night, Lanie," said Mondshane firmly.

"Yeah. Good night."

As he heard Lanie running down the stairs, Mondshane couldn't resist the urge to go to the window. To his embarrassment, the girl stood on the darkened sidewalk gazing up at him. She smiled and then pressed her fingers to her mouth in a kissing gesture. Juliet to an unlikely Romeo, Mondshane thought and waved at her lamely. Then she was gone.

He stood there awkwardly for a few minutes but felt somehow strangely pleased. At once it came to him why he so enjoyed teaching Lanie, outside of the delight he took in her voice. When she looked at him, Mondshane had the idea she was seeing not a creaking mentor with a tiresome devotion to detail, but a man, a man whose touch was still worth a couple of extra heartbeats. Hadn't he felt them, himself, just a while ago? Idiot, Mondshane castigated himself, you probably make the girl nervous, that's all. She probably tells her girlfriends, not to mention her dates, what an old *yente* you are, always nattering at her about this and that. Mondshane wondered what the English equivalent of *yente* was. Some time ago he had heard someone referred to as a real "square." Perhaps that would be Lanie's word for him. What awful language the child used. Of course, it was really not her fault that her manners were so bad. In America everybody seemed to swear in public, even the President. But a lyric soprano?

Mondshane resolved to speak to her on this subject next time. He lit up one of the eight daily cigarettes he allowed himself and began to pace around. What was the matter with him? Why was he so agitated tonight? He really ought to be getting out more, instead of hanging about the house all the time. There were plenty of things he could be doing—if only he could summon the will to pick up his coat and go out the door. Why did everything appear so stale and redundant to him lately? Nothing seemed worth the effort. With one exception.

Mondshane stopped himself sharply. You're putting all your energy into that girl, you fool, he told himself. Who do you think you are—Pygmalion, Dr. Frankenstein? Is this girl's life your business once she leaves your studio? You have a life, too, or at least you used to. Don't be such an *alte kocker;* it's still early. Get going!

The teacher wondered if he should phone one of the women he used to go out with but decided he didn't want to start up again with any of them. Instead, he called Glicenstein, another refugee he had known for years. They made plans to meet downtown at a cafeteria where aging Jewish men like themselves dropped in for coffee and a good argument.

Glicenstein had saved a table. He was a stocky individual with mere wisps of hair left on his head. The smoke from his cigar permeated the all-night cafeteria. Glicenstein, older than Mondshane by more than a decade, was a retired tradesman. The music teacher did not have a great deal in common with him, yet Glicenstein radiated geniality and good sense and could converse intelligently on almost any subject except the arts. In short, Glicenstein was a real *mensch*, a decent human being.

"So where have you been, Mondshane?" Glicenstein demanded by way of a greeting. "Some of the boys are worried you died."

The professor put down his cup of coffee. "Weren't you worried?"

"Naw," said Glicenstein. "I told 'em Mondshane's too elegant to die. So what have you been up to?"

Mondshane shrugged. "The same."

"Still teaching the singers, eh? How come you ain't been down lately?"

"Too busy and too tired."

"A young guy like you tired! Get outta town!"

Mondshane smiled. Moishe Glicenstein spoke with a strong Yiddish accent, but he always seemed to be up on the latest slang expressions.

"Listen, Mondshane, you still got your hair and most of your own teeth, as far as I can tell, so why don't you give some nice lady a break and get married? They say you're loaded. So don't be a cheapskate *yekke* [a German Jew] and find somebody who'll spend it for you. Whatta you say, huh? Some broad told me the other day she thought you made Gregory Peck look like the Hunchback of Notre Dame."

"Forget it," laughed Mondshane.

"On second thought, you're right. Who could stand to be married to a guy what's got people screaming their heads off in his house all day long? Deaf as a doorpost is what you need!"

"It's not so bad," Mondshane told him. "I have an exceptional young soprano coming to me right now."

"Sopranos are fat," said Glicenstein.

"How would you know? Anyway, I have high hopes for this one, even though she's a very low-class type." Mondshane sighed. "Such a mouth on this girl. Her parents don't even know I'm teaching her."

Mondshane told Glicenstein the whole story, glad to be getting it off his chest.

His friend wagged his head slowly. "I don't believe it. You're really going out on a limb here. What's in it for you?"

"If you have to ask," said the teacher, "then it's no use my explaining it to you."

"Rosenfeld's in the hospital," said Glicenstein abruptly. "Heart attack."

"No!" Mondshane recalled Rosenfeld as being a man not much older than himself, one who had been introduced to him as an avid piano player. Or was it pinochle player?

"Over a week ago. I just visited him and he don't look so hot."

"Too bad. Tell him hello for me next time."

"You'll probably wind up in the bed right beside him," predicted Glicenstein. "I sense danger."

"Why do you say that?" asked the teacher.

"If you have to ask, it's no use explaining."

The two men drank their coffee and made companionable use of the time. All of a sudden, Mondshane happened to glance up at the window facing the street. It was fogged up from the cold and someone seemed to be trying to clear a space in order to peer inside. The door opened and in rushed none other than Lanie Twardowski.

"Professor Mondshane!" she cried out. "I thought it was you."

"Who's that?" said Glicenstein. "Another student?"

"That's the one," whispered Mondshane.

The girl straightaway grabbed Mondshane's napkin and blew her nose none too quietly.

"Lanie, what are you doing here so late?"

"The movie just let out. I'm on my way home."

"I should hope so! You look frozen." The professor seized Lanie's hands. "Like an icicle. Sit down and drink some chocolate."

"I'll miss my bus."

"You're not taking the bus anymore. It's nearly midnight. Sit down!"

Lanie was seated and Mondshane introduced her to Glicenstein. To his surprise, she extended her hand to his friend and said, "Very nice to meet you," in an entirely ladylike way.

"I'll get the hot chocolate," offered Glicenstein.

When he was gone, the teacher took hold of Lanie's arm and gave her a shake. "Are you crazy? Look at you—nothing on your head or around your throat. And no gloves. Do you want to catch pneumonia?"

"Come on, lighten up a little. Isn't this a one-in-a-million chance, us meeting like this?"

"A wonderful coincidence," said Mondshane dryly. "Where is your young man?"

"He takes a different bus. I guess you're not too glad to see me."

"Not at this hour. Here," Mondshane got out his wallet, "take this and call a taxi." He pushed ten dollars into the girl's hand.

"Okay, but can't I even have my drink?"

"Yes, while you're waiting for the cab."

Glicenstein came back and looked around. "Where's the little girl?"

"Making a phone call. Can you believe it—running around by herself in the middle of the night?"

"This is your great discovery—a runny-nose kid?"

"You should hear her," said Mondshane. "Besides, even Caruso was young once."

"The cab'll be here in a minute," announced Lanie, resuming her seat. "Thank you very much," she said to Glicenstein. "It's just what I need." But she was only able to take a few sips before there was a loud honking outside.

"There you are," said Mondshane. "Hurry up now. Wipe your mouth first."

A rather crestfallen Lanie picked up her purse. "Well, good night,

I guess." She threw her arms around Mondshane and gave him a hug. "He's the greatest," she told Glicenstein. "One hell of a teacher." The horn sounded again and she was gone.

"You were kind of short with her, weren't you?" Glicenstein remarked.

"Short! I sent her home where she belongs."

"The kid's crazy about you."

"Don't talk goofy," Mondshane scoffed. "I get along fine with all my pupils."

"Nice girl," said Glicenstein. "Polite."

"How would you know," muttered the teacher, although he was overcome by the feeling that he had behaved badly toward Lanie, that he had treated her totally opposite the deference he usually bestowed on women of all ages. He had no idea what made him do it.

"I smell danger," Glicenstein said. "I'm just warning you."

"Who are you—the prophet from the mountain?"

"You poor schmuck," was his friend's response.

One day Mondshane managed to shock Lanie. When she asked him to demonstrate something she was unable to grasp, he had to tell her it was impossible. He was not a singer, himself; in fact, he had a terrible voice.

"You mean you can't do any of this yourself? Not at all?"

"No. I wasn't blessed with whatever it takes to make a voice. Anyway, it wouldn't help you if I could sing. You have to do it all yourself ultimately."

Lanie digested this information with visible suspicion.

"What did you do when you were my age?" she said suddenly.

"Practiced the piano six hours each day," Mondshane answered. He pointed to the wall. "There I am following one of my recitals. I never became a concert pianist, either."

A much younger Ludwig Mondshane, dressed up in a double-breasted tuxedo, standing before a grand piano, beamed down at them. His wavy, then-black hair glistened only less brilliantly than his teeth. He was bowing slightly.

"That's you!" screamed the girl. "My God, you're gorgeous!"

She glanced back and forth between Mondshane and his earlier self as if trying to reconcile the two images. From her expression Mondshane perceived she had just pardoned him for not being able to sing. "Christ, I mean, you must have had a lot of girlfriends back then!"

Mondshane protested that he had found little time for girls in his youth. He told Lanie about his job with the *Staatsoper* and of his associations with the personages whose photographs he displayed.

"See that blonde lady up there," said Lanie, indicating Maria Jeritza. "She looks a lot like the lady in my dreams."

"Dreams?" echoed Mondshane.

"Well, not exactly dreams, more like a fantasy I used to have before I went to sleep. When I was younger, I mean. I used to pretend that my parents weren't my real folks, but that they'd found me in an orphanage when I was a baby. I knew that I didn't actually belong to them, even though they beat me whenever I brought it up. In this fantasy I grow up to be a famous opera singer—you know, diamonds, furs, singing at the Met and everything. And then one day, a beautiful blonde lady comes back stage after my performance and says to me, 'I'm your real mother. I've been searching for you all these years.' After that we both cry and hug each other. Then she stays with me and takes care of me."

"You mean like a maid?" asked Mondshane.

"No! Like a mother, of course. Then my real mom and dad—I mean the ones who adopted me—find out and make a big stink. But they can't do a thing, see, because I'm outta their class now, too much of a celebrity and all. Nutty, isn't it?"

Mondshane laughed softly. "So the Twardowskis—your false parents—simply fade away, eh?"

"Naw," said Lanie, laughing also. "I guess they sue me or something."

"Don't you like your parents, Lanie?" said the teacher.

"Oh, they're okay. I guess they haven't had much of a life. Not like you. You know that guy Franz Lehar, the one whose songs I like so much? Well, I used to imagine, before I met you even, that he looked like you, sort of distinguished and kind. You are nice, you know. About the most beautiful person I've ever met. I never feel good now unless I'm here with you. Anyway, this Lehar, was he Jewish, too?"

"I don't think so," said Mondshane. Although her words had touched him deeply, he did not dare thank her for the compliments. Mondshane was aware that he rarely knew how to reply to the things Lanie told him.

"Oh well. I know he lived in Vienna—what a great place that must have been. Why did you ever leave?"

"I had to."

"Why?"

"It had to do with being Jewish, Lanie. Don't you know what happened to the Jews? Don't they teach you that in school?"

"Oh, my God," breathed Lanie Twardowski as though something vague and formless had revealed itself clearly to her for the first time in its glaring ugliness. "Oh, gross!"

"Yes," said Ludwig Mondshane.

The next time Lanie arrived for her lesson, Professor Mondshane was compelled to tell her how lovely she looked. Her hair was combed in a different style and she had on—wonder of wonders—a dress. He couldn't recall her having previously worn so much as lipstick, but today she had painted her face with all sorts of makeup. The effect was disconcertingly attractive, as if Mondshane were ushering in an alluring stranger.

When they walked over to the piano to begin, Mondshane noticed Lanie looking at his recital photograph. He cleared his throat to get her attention, and for the rest of the hour, she obeyed him without hesitation or question, her new mature appearance finally matching the womanly quality of her voice.

Afterward he said, "That was very good, Lanie. You are doing very well these days. The voice sounds better than ever. But I wonder . . . do you think your parents believe you are going to work in such a beautiful dress?"

"Oh, that's nothing. I change into my uniform at work, anyhow."

"Then they suspect nothing?"

"No," said the girl, "not a thing. They don't notice much, believe me."

"Hmmm," was Mondshane's comment. He wondered how anyone could fail to notice Lanie as she looked tonight.

"Professor Mondshane, what do you do after I leave here?"

Mondshane shrugged. "What do I do? I relax, or try to. I read, watch television, perhaps listen to music. Sometimes I go out or have a visitor."

"Really? Do you mean like a girlfriend?"

"I do have one or two acquaintances, you know. My whole life is not just my pupils."

"What kind of friends do you have? I mean, they're not all just men."

"I see. You will not be satisfied until you have determined whether or not I have what you call a girlfriend. The answer is no."

"You kidding? You're a good-looking guy for your age, I mean it. Haven't you ever had a girlfriend since your wife died?"

Mondshane said that he had had one or two, but nothing had come of the relationships.

"Why not?" Lanie persisted.

"Well, I don't know. Then, perhaps I wasn't ready. Now, perhaps I am too old."

"No!" the girl fairly shouted. "I don't believe that for a second. I'll be your girlfriend, if you want."

Mondshane was startled. This he had not expected. His face apparently reflected his alarm because the girl said, "Hey, don't pass out. It's no big deal. As long as I'm here every Monday and Thursday, we might as well have some fun."

"Fun!" gasped Mondshane.

"Sure. I like you and I think you like me. So what's to stop us?"

Mondshane rose from his seat. "Lanie, you are an intelligent girl, more than you want people to realize, I think. If you don't know what is to stop us, then I—"

"You don't go for me," said the singer darkly.

"My dear, that is not the point at all."

"With a guy that's always the point."

"Oh? You're an expert on men now?"

"I'm not a virgin, if that's what you mean."

Mondshane slammed the cover down over the keys. "I don't want to hear about it! Here is your music. Go home and study it when you can. I want you to know the piece by heart next time." He shoved the book of soprano arias at her.

She ignored it. "I have to know if you like me, Professor Mond-shane," she said, "because I love you."

"I like you very much, Lanie. Don't you know this without ask-ing?"

Lanie sighed. "Yes, I guess I know it, but I need more from you."

"More!" said Mondshane raising his voice. "What more? I am giving you everything that is in me, all the knowledge, all the pa-tience I possess. Even when you are not trying very hard, even when you are completely bored, it is a joy for me to teach you because your future as a singer means everything to me. Now you ask for more? Well, more is what you are not getting! Do you want to ruin every-thing, you silly girl?"

"You don't care anything about me," said Lanie angrily. "All you care about is my fucking voice. Well, screw you, Mondshane!" Lanie pushed the anthology into Mondshane's chest and ran to the door, slamming it on her way out.

Ludwig Mondshane was devastated. Not knowing what else to do, he shut off all the lights and put on a recording of Erich Korn-gold's glorious tragic opera *Die Tote Stadt*, translated, "The Dead City." The music, in all its mournful splendor, washed over him, the singers pouring forth their tales of sadness and longing while Mond-shane felt he would momentarily choke on his own. What made him sad, he surely knew, but exactly what he was longing for es-caped him. Perhaps if he, too, had a voice, it would all gush out of him. That's what opera singers were good for, after all; they ex-pressed for us, in loud soaring tones, all the emotions normally so difficult to utter. If only some singers were a little better at suppress-ing their own feelings.

Where had he failed with this strange girl, Lanie? Had he inadver-tently done something to make her think he desired intimacy with her? Mondshane shuddered. Sexual relations with a pupil! As rep-rehensible as a psychiatrist having intercourse with a patient, in his opinion. Then Mondshane remembered the girl had said she loved him. Could such a thing really be true? Surely it was an unprece-dented occurrence in his case. If any other female student had ever developed a crush on him, he had never noticed. Mondshane con-sidered himself to be as vain as the next man, but he could honestly think of no reason why a young girl would have such feelings for him.

On an impulse he ran into the bedroom and stared into the mirror over the dresser. He saw nothing there to enlighten him, nothing but gray hair and grayish features. Heavy-lidded dark eyes stared at him in wonder. Mondshane felt the tip of what his wife used to call his "surprise" nose because while perfectly straight and Aryan-looking from a frontal view, it was definitely Semitic in profile. His wife had adored his nose, saying it was the sort all men should have. She had often playfully bitten it. But Mondshane's wife had been a woman of culture and educated tastes. The hairy pop idols of young girls these days certainly bore no resemblance to his saturnine appearance.

Mondshane gave up on his morose reflection and went back into the parlor, where he had a bottle or two hidden away in case a guest might want a cognac or a glass of schnapps. Mondshane himself rarely drank. Nevertheless, he felt in need of something alcoholic now. He filled a glass and sat down just in time to hear the soprano sing the beautiful "Lute Song" from the opera. As he listened, all he could think was how much better Lanie Twardowski could have sung it. But Lanie, like the tenor's dead wife in *Die Tote Stadt*, would never return.

But Mondshane, to his amazement, was proved wrong. On the next appointed evening, Lanie Twardowski arrived punctually at seven. Not expecting anyone, Mondshane was in his old slippers and had not bothered to do anything about his five o'clock shadow. Lanie, for her part, wore another pretty dress and makeup as on the last terrible occasion. The professor took this as an ill omen. She walked past him into the apartment, seeming not the least contrite, yet her face looked weary and as shadowed as his own. Mondshane concluded that the long hours in school and at the restaurant were wearing her down. She appeared to have aged years since he had last seen her.

"How you doing, Mondshane?" she said lightly, glancing down at his frayed red velvet house shoes.

The teacher was so delighted to see her, he would have kissed her had he dared, but he said stiffly, "Excuse me, please. I must change my clothes."

"What for? Hang loose for once. You look okay."

Mondshane didn't insist. "Very well, take me as I am, then. Shall we begin?"

Lanie did her warm-up vocalizing in a hollow, listless tone. Normally, she watched Mondshane's face for his reaction to her efforts, but this time she looked off into the distance. After a half-hour, Mondshane could bear it no longer.

"Come here to me, Lanie," he urged gently. "Let us have a little talk."

"I can't come closer," said the girl. "If I do, I'll start crying."

"If you don't, I will cry," Mondshane threatened quite truthfully. "Oh, come on now!"

Lanie complied. "Professor Mondshane, I'm sorry I swore at you. I can't believe I talked to you that way."

"Believe it or not, I've heard bad language before. Forget it. It is all my fault, I think. I should have explained it better to you. Let me try now. You see, the relationship between student and teacher is a very special one. Each must like the other; that is important. But this relationship is also a very delicate one. The pupil and the teacher must feel close, especially in that the student must trust the teacher. But there must also remain a little distance. Nothing must happen to interfere with the work being done. Do you understand that, Lanie?"

"Sure, I get it," said Lanie. "I understood even last week. I could tell you were tempted to take me up on my offer, but you're a decent guy, so you said no. I was the one who behaved like a slut."

Mondshane blinked at her. Was the girl a witch with the ability to fathom his soul? Or had he become as transparent as glass, his face no longer the mask of his thoughts? The professor groaned. How was he to continue with this creature? He felt the delicate balance of which he had just spoken was already irreparably upset. He wanted to say, Yes, for the tiniest moment I desired you, but surely I can be forgiven this moment. A man does not lust after his own saviour. But instead he said, dully, "Don't talk nonsense. We are great friends, you and I. No amount of foolishness can change that."

Lanie put her hand on his shoulder. "I still love you, Mondshane. What does that do to our student-teacher relationship?"

Mondshane looked at the girl's face and then at her arm. It was then that he noticed both were bruised, the one cleverly concealed by cosmetics and the other almost hidden by a sleeve.

"What's this?" he said, pushing up the material. "And what has happened to your face?"

"I've got bad news, Mondshane. My parents found out I lied to them. They decided to have a bite at the restaurant last Thursday, thinking I'd be there. But I was here instead, wasn't I? My dad blew his top at me when I got home."

"Lieber Gott!" said Mondshane, forgetting to speak English. "Your father did this to you? And what will happen when you get home tonight?"

"Who cares?" said Lanie, shrugging. "I don't give a damn."

"But I do!" shouted Mondshane. "Do you think I would allow you to come here and be beaten for it afterward?"

"I never told them I was here."

"No? Where do they think you were?"

"With my boyfriend," said Lanie Twardowski.

The boyfriend's name was Terry. He was several years her senior, a high school dropout who worked as a garage mechanic. The Twardowskis didn't like Terry, even though he was a hard worker who earned a decent salary. The Twardowskis didn't mind dirtying their own hands, but they wanted a husband for their only daughter who didn't have grease under his nails. Besides that, Terry wasn't a Catholic and he ran around with a motorcycle gang who sometimes drank too much and got into trouble. Terry had even been arrested; his name had been in the newspaper. All these things made him highly undesirable in the eyes of the Twardowskis. Mondshane didn't blame them. He would have felt the same in their position. At any rate, after Terry's arrest, Lani was forbidden to see him again.

"Did you obey your parents?" Mondshane heard himself asking. "Or is that too much to expect?"

"I thought I loved Terry. And I know he loves me."

"So," said the professor heatedly, "this young man whom you thought you loved—was he waiting for you at eight o'clock after your lessons with me?"

"Yes," said Lanie.

"How convenient," hissed Mondshane. "Two birds with one stone. What a clever girl you are. Several times I asked you if you wanted to stay longer. I would have given you all the time on earth—you knew that, I'm sure. But you were always too tired. No wonder you are tired—schoolwork, waiting on tables, music lessons and making love with a motorcycle hoodlum! Too much for even an iron constitution, I would say. Even someone as hard as nails as you are."

Outside it had begun to rain. Water beat against the window panes as if trying to penetrate them by force. Thunder rumbled and Mondshane felt the house shake. Or was it he who was trembling? He began to pace, horrified by the idea that he, himself, was tempted to slap the girl's face.

Lanie walked over and laid her head on Mondshane's chest.

"Don't yell at me," she said, beginning to sob. "I can't stand it from you. Put your arms around me, for God's sake! It won't kill you. I know you love me, at least part of me. The best part, I guess. That's better than nothing."

Mondshane pulled her closer and stroked her hair. His legs grew weak under him, so great was his desire for her. I am lost, he said to himself. This is the end. This terrible child has bewitched me out of my senses. What kind of a teacher am I now? The Twardowskis were right not to trust me with their daughter, he admitted bitterly. They knew I needed her more than she needed me.

This realization, sobering as it was, did little to diminish Mondshane's lust. He sucked the tears from Lanie's face like a man perishing of thirst. Just when Mondshane felt that nothing in the world could have prevented him from pushing her onto the sofa, something actually did. The phone rang. Mondshane and Lanie both stared at it as if it were an alien object never before seen in a human dwelling. After the eighth ring, Lanie said, "You'd better get it before it gets you."

A deflated Mondshane made for the phone. But when he said hello, the caller abruptly hung up.

"Who was it?" asked Lanie.

"Probably God," said the professor, lowering himself onto the couch. He was sweating so hard that the perspiration stung his eyes.

Lanie bent over him. "Are you okay? You look kind of sick."

"I am," said Mondshane.

"Here, lay down," the girl said, pushing his head to the cushions. She began to laugh. "You poor thing. I've heard of people's consciences pricking them, but yours looks like it's drowning you!"

"It's not right," said Mondshane. "I know it's not right, but I do love you. I love you, my darling girl."

"I'm a woman," said Lanie.

"I know," murmured the professor. "A strong-willed, beautiful young woman. Go home, Lanie, please. I'm too tired even to think. Come back tomorrow if you can, and we'll talk things over."

"It's raining, for Christ's sake!" protested Lanie, but her eyes were shining. "Can't I stay here? I'll be good; I swear! Hell, can't you adopt me or something so I'll never have to leave?"

"Adopt! You are not a stray cat or dog in the street. You have a family. Your parents know better than you think. Go home."

"They don't know shit! If I were older, would you marry me?"

"Yes. Go home and get older. Maybe by that time I shall have done you the favor of dying."

"God, you're a mess," said Lanie. "Wait a sec."

Lanie went to get her purse. She pulled out tissues and began to blot the moisture from Mondshane's face.

"Have mercy," he pleaded.

"I never have mercy," Lanie replied, kissing him on the mouth.

As if by design, the telephone shrilled again. This is the craziest night of my life, thought Mondshane. He felt so weary he began to wonder if he hadn't had a heart episode or a stroke. This is what came of trying to fulfill one's dream when one never had any right to dream in the first place.

"Aren't you going to answer it?"

Mondshane shook his head. "I'm not moving. You answer it. I have a feeling it's for you, anyway."

Lanie made a face, but she got up, angrily snatching the receiver from its cradle. "Professor Mondshane's residence!" she snapped. She seemed to listen briefly and then slammed down the receiver.

"Damn! That was Terry."

Mondshane was not at all surprised. "What did he want?"

"He's down the street. He says when I leave here he's going to kill me."

"Why? Have you quarreled?"

"Quarreled, hell! He's jealous of you. He knows I love you and not him. The guy's gone bananas. I'm telling you, Mondshane, I can't leave here."

Mondshane pulled himself up. His head reeled. "Yes, you can. You are leaving right now. I am going to take you home." Mondshane went to get his coat.

"But you don't even have a car!" wailed Lanie.

"I'll call a taxi."

"Terry'll be out there waiting. I don't know what he'll do. Mondshane, get serious! Do you want to wind up in the hospital?"

"Better there than in jail," said Ludwig Mondshane.

Lanie put herself between Mondshane and the closet.

"Okay," she said, "call a cab. I'll go by myself. You don't look all that great. Maybe you'd better go to bed. I don't want to cause you any trouble."

At that even Mondshane had to laugh. "Trouble! Think nothing of it. I'm going with you. I'm not afraid of this boy, this Terry of yours. Trouble has become my middle name."

"I told you he's no Terry of mine. We're all done. Finito! Besides, he's full of hot air. He says he'll kill me, but that's a lot of crap. He doesn't want to go to jail again, either."

"Are you sure?"

"Positive."

"And your father—what about him?"

"He'll be at work. Don't worry about it, Sweetie. I'll call you tomorrow." She gave him a quick kiss. "Bye now. I love you like hell."

Mondshane seized her arm. "Listen to me. I think you must tell your father the truth. Do you hear me, Lanie? No more secrets from the parents. From now on, you are with me, not this Terry. We must find a way to stay together. Perhaps your parents won't mind so much your studying now. Certainly they will think me more harmless than this motorcycle fellow."

Lanie shook her head. "Poor Mondshane, you don't know a thing, do you?"

"I only want what's best for you. That's all I ever wanted. Now you have forced me to admit to you, and to myself, that my feelings for you are more complicated than I thought. But my intentions have not changed."

"I'd bet anything on that," said Lanie. "*Ich liebe Dich!*" She opened the door and ran down the stairs.

"Lanie, the taxi!" Mondshane called after her. "Wait!"

But Lanie couldn't wait.

Nor did he hear from her the following day. He did his work half-heartedly, listening not to his pupils but for the telephone, which remained obstinately silent. By afternoon, his insides were knotted with worry. Why didn't the girl call? Something must have happened. What a stupid fool he had been to let her go out in the night like that. Mondshane tried to calm himself, reasoning that she would probably ring him when she got to work. But evening came and still nothing. Mondshane found the number of the restaurant, but when he asked for Lanie, he was informed that she had quit her job.

The next afternoon, an ashen, unkempt Mondshane waited for the girl outside her school. There were several girls who looked and dressed like Lanie. But Lanie herself did not appear. Some of the young people passing by looked at the professor like they thought he ought to be arrested. Others giggled behind their hands. But Mondshane was now beyond feeling foolish. A panic had taken hold of him that made him nauseous and light-headed. He had not known such fear since his time in the concentration camps.

The professor, in desperation, called the Twardowski home several times, but on each occasion Lanie's mother answered. He would have spoken to the woman except that she seemed to be as agitated as himself. No doubt the Twardowskis had learned everything by now and had decided on some severe course of punishment, even locking the girl in her room. If Mondshane asked to speak to her, it would surely make things worse. Lanie would have to reach him on her own. If she didn't soon, it could only mean that her parents forbade it and there would be no more lessons. The professor began to wish with all his being that he was a young man of twenty who could go to the Twardowskis and argue a case for himself, Jew or no Jew. To do this at the age of fifty-five would be to invite certain scorn and ridicule. Yes, in this instance fifty-five was the same as ninety. No one was going to believe in the purity of his motives. In fact, he was beginning to doubt them, himself.

By the end of the week, the teacher had resigned himself to the fact that Lanie Twardowski was no longer a part of his life. He told himself that it was all for the best. One simply could not have a pupil under such conditions. It was bad enough that the parents disapproved—but to become entangled in a romance! Not that Mondshane would ever have allowed *that* to go any further. But still, the girl was very bold and he—well, he did love her in a sense. How in the devil had he come to love her at all? Yes, it was a very good thing that it was all over. Yet telling himself these things did not help. Mondshane had turned his face to the wall—he was now a mourner. Sniffling into his handkerchief several times a day, the teacher realized that it was not for the loss of his one great opportunity that he grieved but for the loss of Lanie herself. Over and over he asked himself how she could be so cruel as not even to call him one last time. Ludwig Mondshane, who had lost so many things in his lifetime, feared he was losing his mind.

One night, two months later, the teacher was awakened by his buzzer. At first he thought he was dreaming, but when he finally sat up, and saw by the clock that it was 2:00 A.M., he realized that someone wanted to be let in. The people downstairs probably needed Mondshane's assistance. He put on his robe and turned on the hall light, muttering "Ja, ja!" In the foyer, he opened the door against the chain and the party outside seemed to fall forward. It was Lanie.

When she came inside, she needed to lean against the wall for support. Mondshane was shocked by her wild appearance. Her hair hung in greasy strings over a face that looked as battered as a prizefighter's. A strong odor of alcohol emanated from her person. Mondshane was aghast, but he was also angry. He had only recently begun to feel better, to have found some measure of peace in his work and regulated existence. Doubtless, the girl had returned to unsettle him as only she knew how. The professor was determined not to allow it to happen.

"What do you want?" he demanded sharply. "Do you know the time?"

"Hell no. The bar's closed—that's all I know."

"And so you come here? Now? What has happened to you? Why did I not hear from you before this?"

"Mondshane, help me," the girl whispered.

"I have always tried to help you," answered Mondshane, assuming his most Germanic bearing.

"Well, hell, then help me to the bathroom."

Mondshane saw that he had no choice but to oblige unless he wanted his Oriental carpet ruined. Pushing her into the bathroom, he held Lanie over the toilet bowl while she vomited repeatedly.

"I'm dying, Mondshane," she sobbed between retching.

"Go ahead," he told her. "Find out what it's like to die."

At last she stopped and Mondshane let her sink to the floor. The teacher cleaned up the mess and filled the bathtub with water. He removed the girl's smelly garments and lifted her into the tub. Mondshane saw that Lanie had grown thin and that her whole body was full of bruises. So much abuse to the tender, white skin, as vulnerable in appearance as that of a child, caused Mondshane's anger to begin to dissipate. He felt a little sick himself. He sponged her gently, fearful of hurting her more, while she continued to sob and whimper.

"*Shah, Liebchen,*" he murmured. "Don't carry on so. You'll be all right."

Well, he thought, now I have become a nursemaid to this wretched girl. Little thanks I will receive for it and probably a good deal more trouble.

"Try to stand up."

"I can't do it," Lanie whined. Mondshane struggled to get her out of the tub, soaking himself in the process. He took off his damp robe and put it on Lanie.

After he had deposited the girl on the sofa, Mondshane went to make her some tea. His spirits began to lift; he felt almost happy. He also felt in control. The girl was in no condition to bedevil him now. It was obvious she had paid dearly for all her transgressions.

Lanie was able to keep the hot tea down. Afterward, she even asked Mondshane for a cigarette. Mondshane, his ire rising in him again, swore at her in German. She had the right to ruin her insignificant self if she chose, but not her superb voice, which only had the misfortune of belonging to such an unworthy creature.

"Okay, okay," she said. "Forget it. I guess you hate me now."

"I am not in the hating business. Do you feel better now? If so, please get dressed and go home. There is nothing more I can do for you."

"I haven't got a home," Lanie told Mondshane. "Not anymore."

Lanie had not lived with her parents for quite some time. She had run off with her boyfriend, the one who had threatened to kill her. A few days ago, they had gotten into an argument, the result being the battered shape Lanie was in. She had left Terry and wandered around on her own. This evening, she had spent the last of her money in a bar.

"Why did you run away with this crazy boy?"

"Because you didn't want me," the girl said simply.

"You are a seventeen-year-old girl!" bellowed Mondshane. "What should I have done?"

"Terry didn't mind the risk. I guess he loved me more than you did."

"A wonderful love," spat the teacher. "Always you are talking of love and you have not the least idea what love is. But I never thought you were so stupid. First a father who beat you and now this Terry!"

"My dad never touched me," said Lanie. "I lied to you. It was Terry the whole time."

"Did it ever occur to you that if you truly loved me you could never have disappeared with this awful young man? That maybe just having a peaceful friendship with me was better than being mauled to death by that idiot? Well, answer!"

"For me it would have been worse."

Mondshane's fingers raked his hair. "I see. Well, what do you want now? Is it money? I will give you some money—this time. But there will not be a next time!"

"No!" Lanie held out her hand beseechingly. "Mondshane, my head hurts. Can't you just sit down with me for a second and talk to me nice like you used to? Come on. I won't bite."

"Let me at least put my trousers on," mumbled the teacher.

"Put on a suit of armor if you want," laughed the girl. "Get all the protection you can!"

Mondshane got dressed and sat down at Lanie's feet. She nudged him with her toes.

"Professor, you devil, you saw me naked! You gave me a bath. You've got more guts than I thought. Anyway, listen. I came here because I had a dream about you."

Mondshane covered his ears. "Don't tell me. Any dream you would have is not the kind I want to hear."

"No, no, don't get worried. Remember I told you I used to have this fantasy when I was a kid about finding my real mother? Well, last night I had a real dream. God! You know where I slept? In a car parked on the street that somebody forgot to lock."

"No," said Mondshane. "Oh, Lanie!"

"Wild, huh? So I dreamed about being a famous soprano in the back of this old green Chevy. But this time, no blonde lady showed up to claim me. The one who came was you, Mondshane. That's when I knew how much you missed me and that I had to see you. But I didn't have the nerve, I guess, so I got drunk. I know I disappointed you, Mondshane. I'm sorry, but I knew the whole thing was no good. If I'd come back for my lessons, all we'd be thinking about was going to bed."

Mondshane glowered at her. "Is that so? Do you think I have no self-control? That I am some kind of beast like this Terry of yours?"

"Oh, hell, Mondshane, where are you from—the planet Zaronga? Why don't you wake up in the real world? I know we'd have wound up being lovers sooner or later. But you would have hated it. You would have hated yourself and me too."

"You are only seventeen and you know all this," Mondshane wondered.

"I'm eighteen," Lanie corrected him. "I can do whatever I want."

"Except," said the professor, "you'd better learn that we can't always do what we want—at least not without hurting other people."

"Did I hurt you, Mondshane?"

"Yes. I am ashamed to tell you how I was after you left me. I thought you'd killed me."

"Really?" inquired the girl. "That bad? I never thought you'd take it so hard. I figured—well—that we were sort of on the same wavelength. I thought you'd know I was doing it for your own good!"

Mondshane stared at the girl. Could she be telling the truth? Had she actually run off with another man in order to be able to stay away from him? In her crazy little mind, had that been the only possible course of action?

The teacher slapped the girl's foot. "Lanie, you stupid girl! Why didn't you trust me? Why didn't you just leave everything to me? I am older than you, God knows. You should have at least given me some credit. I would have known how to handle this situation."

Lanie got up, shaking her head. "You're the dumb one, Sweetheart. You couldn't have handled me in a million years. I was crazy about you. You're the only person I ever really loved. It would have been better to keep a safe distance, but I'm not the type. That I have to leave to you." She leaned on the piano. "Why couldn't you have stayed that guy in the picture?" she sighed.

"It is him you love, not me."

"Maybe. Do you think he would have gone for me?"

"No," admitted the teacher. "That smiling young man is not as carefree as he looks. He is a good Jewish boy, hard-working and earnest, full of yearning to succeed at something but not quite sure of what. A girl like you, even though lovely and talented, would have struck him as too wild, too much of a drain on his own lesser spirit. He needed a proper Jewish girl who lived only for him, wanted only to please him. And that is what he ultimately got. No, Lanie, you would not have liked that young man, although he was, as you say, rather handsome. He was what people call nowadays a stick-in-the-mud."

"Really?" said Lanie with a little wail. "Gee, I wish you hadn't told me. Well, to hell with him then. What about you? What do you want? Mondshane, this is the deal, now or never. Either I stay or I get dressed and leave for good. I can make it without you, but I'd rather not. And don't tell me to go away and grow up because, Mondshane, there is no way I could ever get any older."

Mondshane, arms folded, pondered the "deal" that had been tossed in his lap. A greater folly than keeping this girl was hard to imagine. Moishe Glicenstein's face loomed before him, puffing his cigar and saying, "I smell danger, you poor schmuck." Yes, prophets still flourished in the midst of the Jewish people; that was clear.

And what would his other pupils think of a nubile young woman ensconced in their teacher's home? It wouldn't do, of course. If he took Lanie in, he would have to give up the others and concentrate on her alone. That would be expensive, although Mondshane had no financial worries. Even so, he couldn't count on Lanie becoming a serious student. What if she was right; what if the possibility of a student–teacher relationship no longer existed between them? The girl obviously loved to play games with him. Mondshane wondered what would become of him if he lost his resistance and got too deeply caught up in those games. The teacher envisioned a titanic struggle between art and frivolity.

But he also imagined a disappointed Lanie, dismissed from his life and left to her own devices. Doubtless, she would find a new boyfriend, another Terry, or at best a steady but unimaginative young man who would require her full attention, domesticate her, impregnate her and ruin her chances forever. Ludwig Mondshane, the man who had always longed to be the catapult that launched a brilliant career, now felt perversely resentful that Lanie Twardowski's future had become his responsibility.

"Mondshane!" he heard the girl cry out. "Say something! You're slipping into a coma!"

"Lanie," said Mondshane at last, "this is my home, not a reform school, a house of detention for wayward juveniles. You may stay here, but only on my terms. Believe it or not, I had a life before I met you. Boring perhaps, but my life had order, Lanie, and I will not let you throw it into chaos. From now on, if you stay, you will have no ideas except those I put into your head. You will do exactly as I tell you from the moment you get up until you go to sleep. When you go to bed, you will be very tired, I assure you. You are going to work with me all day long and finish your schooling at night. You will have time for nothing else, especially romances. Do you hear me, little girl? You think Mondshane will make a nice playmate for you, eh? Well, Mondshane never had time for games, and he was a failure. Just imagine what you are going to endure to become a success!"

"You really mean it, don't you?" said Lanie. "What are you, a train that nobody can flag down? I haven't got a one-track mind like you. Sure, I want a career, but that isn't everything to me."

"Then you'll never amount to anything."

"You mean, that's how it's got to be?"

"Unfortunately, yes. At least for now."

"Then there's going to be nothing between us?"

"I didn't say that," the teacher told her. "There is already something between us; more than you understand, I think. But, for the moment, I am not prepared to put myself into your careless little hands. If the day comes when I see that you are able to take yourself and your talent seriously, then I might be persuaded that you could take me seriously as well."

Lanie regarded Mondshane in bewilderment. The teacher saw, with some relish, that his words had, for once, unsettled her in the way that she had always been able to shake him. For a moment, he was sure she had no reply, but he should have known better.

"God damn!" she exclaimed, laughing. "Can I pick 'em or what!"

"Don't make fun, Lanie. I'm very serious."

"You're always serious," said the girl. "Why the hell do you think I took to you in the first place? There you were, this funny man sweating bullets from the heat, looking at me like I was the eighth wonder of the world. At first I thought you were nuts, but all of a sudden it hit me: This guy is serious! He always has been and he always will be. That's when I realized you were the guy for me, I guess, but I couldn't believe it. I was always expecting somebody different."

"I shouldn't wonder," said Mondshane. "Lanie, it's nearly morning. Put your head down and get some sleep."

"Oh, Christ, I've done everything wrong! If only I hadn't come on to you the way I did. Why didn't I have the sense to keep quiet and let you get to know me? I mean, the real me. Oh, shit, I don't even know who the hell I am!"

"That's enough now," said Mondshane, putting his arm around Lanie. "You're very tired."

"Tired! I feel like I could sleep for the next thousand years. Thanks for not throwing me out, Mondshane. I'm telling you, it's a cold world out there."

"Is that so?" remarked Mondshane with a little smile.

"Hell, yes," sighed the girl. "I know you think I had it all coming to me. Well, maybe, if being a dope is a crime. What do you think,

Mondshane? If I hadn't turned you off by being such a little shit, do you think you might have wanted to get to know me better?"

"I don't know," said the teacher humbly, pulling the girl nearer. "I am ashamed to tell you that I really don't know."

When nine o'clock came, Lanie Twardowski was still on Mondshane's couch, sleeping with no apparent intention of seeing any part of the morning. The buzzer summoned and Mondshane, coffee cup in hand, opened the door for his cleaning lady, Mrs. Coonan.

The old lady put down her things, her gaze stopping at the sofa. She squinted at the teacher as if seeing him for the first time.

"Ah, Mr. Munching," she said in her Irish brogue, "what's taken hold of you, then? I see you've been a naughty lad for a change."

"Mrs. Coonan," said Mondshane, "allow me to present Lanie, a singer who will be living here depending upon whether or not she behaves herself. However, she is in no condition for any vacuuming, I'm afraid."

"A little bit of a thing, isn't she? Well, the saints be praised, Munching, you've had a real donnybrook here, by the looks of it. Didn't break anything, did you? Your nice china knickknacks and all."

Mondshane couldn't help laughing at the idea of Mrs. Coonan thinking he had beaten up Lanie. He helped the woman with her coat.

"No, no, it's all right. She came that way."

"Well, thank heaven. I never really picked you for that sort. What shall we do with the little darling, then? Cart her off into the bedroom?"

Mondshane shook his head. "Just clean around her."

Of course, the day would have to come when Ludwig Mondshane would have another interview with the Twardowskis. Fortunately, this meeting was postponed for quite some time.

They burst upon him on another Sunday afternoon when Mondshane was by himself. The Twardowskis, even in their indignation, seemed surprised that the teacher would admit them so readily, even asking them to take a seat.

"Stow your nice manners!" Mrs. Twardowski told him in German. "What have you done with our daughter, Lanie?"

"Lanie isn't here," answered Mondshane.

"You lie!" Twardowski accused menacingly.

"No, I don't lie. Look around for yourselves, if you don't believe me."

The pair looked at one another for support, but each had run out of ammunition.

Mondshane took charge. "What made you think your daughter would be here?" he asked.

Mrs. Twardowski showed Mondshane his own crumpled card. "This. I found it in Lanie's room along with some music that had your name stamped on it. Also, she is no longer with that no-good Terry."

"In jail again," said Lanie's father. "No-good motorcycles."

"Very well, sit down," said Mondshane. "You are entitled to know the truth. Sit!"

The Twardowskis obeyed, cowed by Mondshane's direct manner, something he felt they hadn't expected.

"Lanie ran away with Terry because neither you nor I had the wisdom to prevent it. Yes, Lanie had been studying with me against your wishes. After she left Terry, she came to me again. That was several months ago."

"She lived with you?" exclaimed Lanie's mother.

"Yes, with me. I love the girl with all my heart."

Mrs. Twardowski was stunned. "Lanie? A man like you is in love with our Lanie?"

Mondshane nodded. "However, she is not here now. Lanie is in New York."

"New York!" cried the mother. "Why New York?"

"That's where she is going to school."

"Lanie is in school?" wondered her father. "She hate school!" Then something else dawned on him. "And you give the money?"

"I give the money," said Mondshane.

The Pole whistled. "Holy Mary!"

"A good school?" asked Mrs. Twardowski.

"The best for her. Juilliard School of Music."

Mrs. Twardowski fanned herself with Mondshane's card. "But why are you doing this? Why are you going to so much expense for our daughter? I hate to say this, but she is not a very good girl. Very ungrateful."

"Because that is what is best for her."

"*Ach*," the woman from Hamburg sighed. "For a moment I thought you might have gone so far as to marry her. Not that she deserves it, mind!"

"I've thought about it," Mondshane informed her. "But don't worry. By the time Lanie comes back, if ever she does, she will most certainly have forgotten me."

"Marry! No be crazy," Twardowski advised albeit mildly. "My girl too much trouble. You be sorry."

"Casimir is right," said his wife. "Before the war he wanted to be a psychologist."

Mondshane's eyebrows flew up. "Really?"

The little man shrugged. "I go into army, get taken prisoner. No study for me, just slave for Germans. They make me factory work. I still factory work and I still slave for Germans."

The two Twardowskis laughed heartily at this witticism. Now that he had warmed up verbally, Casimir was not about to quit.

"What you do in war?" he asked of Mondshane.

"Same as you," the teacher replied. "I was a slave, but not in a factory. I don't even want to describe to you the different kinds of work I did."

Twardowski took a turn around the room, inspecting everything in the same way Lanie had once done. He too stopped at the piano, peering closely at Mondshane's photographs. All of a sudden he appeared to take a leap backward.

"You piano player!" he cried, gesturing at the teacher's glitzy recital picture.

"So I thought," Mondshane told him.

"You in camp, right? Which one?"

"Several," answered Mondshane. "Buna and Auschwitz—"

"Buna!" yelled Lanie's father. He slapped his forehead. "Stinky Buna where they make the rubber. Phew! I am there for few weeks, believe or not." The Pole pointed a finger at Mondshane. "And I know you! I think all the time I know you. You Jew what use to play piano for kommandant, the big shot! Holy mother!" Twardowski ran over and shook his wife in great excitement. "The Nazi crazy for this boy. All the time he play. We all hear him—Chopin's *Grand Polonaise*—very hard piece, but he play it like lightning. Beautiful, beautiful! I cry; everybody cry. All people in camp feel better for little while. Now I here and you here, too. So many die, but the good God watch out for Jew with golden hands. I am so happy!" Twardowski pulled out his handkerchief and blew into it with gusto.

Mondshane, naturally, was too stunned by this unexpected development to say a word.

Mrs. Twardowski shrugged helplessly. "I was only a teenager in those days. What did I know?"

"You have a wonderful memory," Mondshane finally said to Twardowski. "I did play—until the kommandant grew tired of me. I wasn't all that good, you see."

"No say that," Twardowski chided him. "You maybe save you life."

"He should have been a psychologist," said Lanie's mother. "Listen to him."

"Too bad he didn't recognize me at the German picnic," retorted Mondshane. "It would have saved a great deal of trouble. He might have analyzed that I only meant well, after all."

"Of course you meant well," the woman surprised him by saying. "We all meant well. But where Lanie is concerned, there could only be trouble. I was only trying to warn you, but you didn't take the hint. Casimir acted the fool; I told him so after we got home."

"My English so-so," said Twardowski, squirming a little. "Same for German. Too bad you don't know Polish. Then I could tell you some story—yes, plenty bad one. You listen my wife. She talking machine." Twardowski guffawed, winking at the professor as though they had suddenly become conspirators.

"Please, Casimir," his spouse importuned. "You are not on TV."

"Tv!" Casimir's mirth redoubled. "Polish channel 4 and ½!"

The woman directed a long-suffering look at Mondshane.

"So what could we do? We were ashamed to tell a total stranger that our daughter is a big pain in the—"

"Tochas," Mondshane finished for her. He laughed. He was really not having that bad a time. Life, after all, was only a joke whose punchline continually changed. Of all the people in this city, it turned out the only one who knew him from the old days was Casimir Twardowski, Lanie's own father. Or perhaps the Pole had merely gotten him mixed up with another wavy-haired Jewish musician, one of thousands who played while the Angel of Death capered.

"I'm glad you have kept your sense of humor," remarked Mrs. Twardowski, whose first name he later learned was Emma. ("Call me Emmy," she was to tell him. "After all, we have been through so much together.") But now she said, "When it comes to Lanie, mine flew out the window years ago. Look at us. We did everything for Lanie, our only child. Worked night and day but what good did it do? She did badly in school, except in choir, of course. Singing is all she was ever good for. Who knows where she got such a beautiful voice! When Lanie wasn't singing, she was running around with motorcycle gangsters. For this we did not come to America, let me tell you. The girl never listened to us one day since she was twelve, and then, on her eighteenth birthday, she vanishes without even a good-bye. Professor, prepare yourself. You will never see her again."

"Actually," said Mondshane, "I hope to visit Lanie next week." He did not tell the Twardowskis that he still received tearful phone calls from the girl saying she missed him terribly and threatening to leave school if he did not come to visit her every few months. It all cost the dear earth, but Mondshane wasn't worried. He wasn't a rich man, but he had made some shrewd investments over the years, and since his wife passed away, there wasn't much else to spend his money on.

"Go to New York more money waste," was Twardowski's comment. "Jew should be more smart."

"Well, he certainly has a lovely home," said Mrs. Twardowski, looking around appreciatively. "You must make a nice living with your music lessons, Professor. Frankly, that is the reason why I was so worried that Lanie might marry that boy, Terry. I always wanted her to find a professional man, someone with a little culture. You know what I mean, I'm sure. You are much older than Lanie, but you seem very well established here. There is no question in my mind, at least, that you must be a very smart person, even though you fell in love with our daughter. And they always said when I was a girl that Jewish men make very good husbands."

"They did?" said an astonished Mondshane.

"I bet he own whole house," said Twardowski.

"I'm sure he does," said the mother smugly. "So what do you think, Herr Professor? Do you think you can make Lanie come back?"

Mondshane sighed. "So far, she always has."

And Casimir Twardowski, apparently now at peace where the fate of his wayward child was concerned, seated himself at the Steinway and with much rolling of eyes and tossing of head began to pound out his own choppy version of Chopin's *Grand Polonaise*.

The Jew of Bath

SOMETIMES THE SUN shines in England in July. The writer, who now never left her small bedroom, felt that each brilliant day viewed through the bow window was a mockery to her own waning forces. Her body had become her enemy. It was willing itself to die, Mr. Lyford, her physician, had told her. Even he could give no name to her mysterious malady. During the day the writer often felt too tired even to breathe, and at night, her flesh crawled with fever.

For a time, the writer had been able to take up her pen and work on her novel for an hour or two each day. Eventually, she had lost the heart for this activity and had not written a fictional word since March. "Pretend," Mr. Lyford—a famous doctor, after all—had said, "that each time you dip into your inkwell, you dip into a font of life, life flows from your pen. I believe your brain has gone awry and is sending false messages to your body. You must fight back by sending positive ones."

The writer had moved from the village of Chawton to Winchester to be near Mr. Lyford, and so she had tried to do as he suggested. Nevertheless, she wished he would bring her something in a bottle to drink, but he told her there was nothing he knew of that would do any good.

There was never any pain. Some died in great anguish, she reminded herself. The writer tried to take comfort from the notion that she would not be one of those.

In due course the wellspring that nourished the novel in progress, *Sanditon,* dried up and the authoress's writing started to consist only of letters. That is to say, The Letter, the completion of which the writer began to despair as it grew longer and longer.

The writer's world had dwindled to the various sounds that rose from the street—birds, twittering or raucous, annoying dogs, a dray clattering on the cobblestones, the tinkle of a shopbell, snatches of people talking. How her heart ached each time she heard a child's bleating voice. She wept then like a forsaken little girl, herself.

On the fourteenth of July, the writer awoke feeling rather stronger than usual, but she knew that as on other occasions, this would only be followed by more illness. The writer kept a little hand mirror on her nightstand. She amused herself by gazing into it at times, even though only a strange woman's face looked back at her. She had the feeling that soon this unknown woman would reveal something about herself that the writer longed to know.

Her brother, Henry, came. Henry was a man in the service of God, but he refrained from any undue mention of God's name to the writer. For this the writer was grateful, although, when alone, she would sometimes cry out to the Lord in a little moan, both reproachful and pleading. But she, a vicar's daughter, never seriously prayed for renewed health. The writer, modest person at heart, did not presume to expect any favors from a higher power. Something told her that she had once been given a gift so singular and satisfying that it would be sheer greed to ask for anything more. In the words of her father, every good fairy in the kingdom had gathered round her cradle and bestowed their blessings upon her. But Papa had always dearly loved his Jane, his little brown hazelnut, the one among his many children whose quick spirit made the sparks fly. How pained he would have been had he lived to see her reduced to a creature of the shadows whose wit failed her when she could no longer attend to her own bodily functions.

"Sitting up today, Jane," said Henry, who, it seemed to the writer, was grown so like their father that it startled her each time she saw him. "Very good, indeed."

"My face is always dirty, Henry," the writer observed. "Don't you agree that my skin appears very dirty now?"

Her brother tugged the mirror gently from her grasp.

"The illness has made you a bit sallow; that is all. You don't get into the sun these days, so what can you expect?"

"I expect nothing yet I still want. I want to bloom like a rose."

To this, Henry—who was later to write of his beloved sister, "her eloquent blood spoke through her modest cheek"—said, "I still pray you shall, my dearest girl."

"If a rose blooms not in summer, Henry, then surely it will never at all. Well, you are an excellent brother, and a good brother makes a good husband. Why do you not remarry?"

"Ah," replied Henry, "it is not so simple a matter. My poor Eliza taught me that I am a man partial to a great flirt. Yet now I am become a clergyman, all the ladies become instantly grave and circumspect in my presence."

"How vexing it must be for you. Although it seems to me that a man once wed to a matchless coquette would be content never to meet another."

Henry pulled a comic face. "Oh well, I will own that her French-ified ways did appeal more in the beginning, but—bless me— Eliza was as silly as God ever made woman, but she was my destiny, I suppose, and only a very light cross to bear."

The writer smiled. "I'm glad your courage in the face of Mama's opposition wasn't in vain—her own darling boy and the much older widow of a guillotined French count! Mama said it would never do, but you thought it would and I admired you for it, Henry. Only I forgot to say so."

"What brings you to this, Jane? Since you never bore fools gladly, I cannot imagine my Eliza appealed to you overmuch."

"It appealed to me that you loved whom you pleased and the rest be damned!"

Henry Austen felt his sister's arm to see if she had fever.

"What is it, Jane?" he asked quietly. "Why are you so vehement?"

"Henry, have you ever known a Jew?"

"A Jew? Why, yes, in London, but only to buy things from oc-casionally."

"But has a Jew never said to you a civil word, passed the time of day with you for even a moment under circumstances having nothing to do with commerce?"

"Certainly not that I can recall," said Henry. "Besides, Jews don't particularly seek out Anglican vicars for the purpose of amiable chatter. Now why do you ask me such a thing? Surely you can never even have seen a Jew or known one if you had. —Ah, I nearly forgot. Cassandra wants to know if you'll have tea."

"Yes, I will," answered the writer with a little sigh. "And I would like my writing things as well, if you please."

Her brother brought a little portable desk to her, placing it on her lap.

"I shall return with your tea."

"Our Lord was a Jew, Henry."

"Yes, I know, Jane," said Henry, peering at her with a worried frown. "Don't overtax yourself, whatever you do. If the writing gets too difficult, you must promise to stop."

"The writing's always hard," remarked Jane Austen in a tone of voice that her brother was glad to note sounded much more like her old self. "It's overcoming the difficulty that gives us our greatest satisfaction."

Each time she worked on The Letter, the authoress read it over from the beginning, as her concentration was not what it was and she feared she would repeat herself otherwise. Thus it went:

College Street, Winchester
July, 1817
Fanny Knight
Godmersham, Kent

My Dearest Fanny,

What a good sort of girl you are to write such kind and concerned words to your aunt. I am still very much the same as when I wrote you last, confined to bed and often without strength to place as much as a foot upon the floor. I judge by the look of my good physician that I shall never make old bones, although I am ashamed to admit that when I was somewhat younger than you, I was not shocked by the death of a person of forty. Indeed, it seemed to me then that one managed to live to such a great age as fifty only through an excess of obstinacy.

I know you will be amazed to receive so many pages from me. I shall, of course, be gone by the time you read them, so let them, in part, be my way of comforting you. I feel I am talking with you as I used to do, and I hope that you will feel it, too. It should be no surprise to you that some of the happiest hours I have ever spent were in your company. Yes, we were very giddy together and the whole world suffered not a little from our viewing it in tandem, but what does that signify? People who understand one another perfectly always fall to gossiping, but I think there was too much mirth in our conversations to allow for any real malice.

You know, dearest creature, how jealously I have always guarded my solitude and how vexed the others would become with me for shutting myself away so much. I once fancied myself happiest when putting words to paper, losing myself in the adventures of my heroines. Now it appears I have plenty of time to write; in fact, it is the only activity I can manage in my present state. Perversely, I am no longer content with my scribbling but find myself staring out the window, longing to have my old vigour back if only for a day. How gladly I would lay down my pen and fly out into the street, under the old gate and into the heart of the town, greeting everyone I met there. I would throw myself into the vortex of activity like a person perishing of thirst into a stream. Too often I am burdened with the woeful notion that I was never truly a participant in my own life but a mere spectator to a theatrical. It seems to me I noticed everything except that time was racing forward and that nothing had actually ever happened to Jane yet.

Yet I did dream, Fanny. I dreamt of renown, immortality, financial security and even love—oh, yes, that too. My longings are all contained in pages, frail leaves that are doomed to crumble, just as have all my hopes of attaining those things of which I dreamt.

I have instructed Henry, that dearest and most valued of brothers, to make an effort to publish *Northanger Abbey* after I am dead—under my own name this time. You see, I haven't yet left off dreaming. How I wish I had not published the others anonymously! Such paths lead to oblivion and ought never to be taken, especially for the sake of womanly modesty. A man would never even consider it. Oh Fanny, my novels are my only children, and to think I did not have

the fortitude to give them my name (it was not their fault they had no
father) and simply left them on England's doorstep like foundlings!

Sometimes lately I amuse myself with speculating what people
will say of me after I am gone. There are, to be sure, certain immut-
able facts of birth and circumstance, yet an unsettling worry has
crept into my consciousness. I have come to think people will con-
clude that Jane Austen, spinster, wrote of love, courtship and romance despite never having been privy to those experiences. Oh
yes, one or two misguided members of the male sex did try to win
her affection but were greeted with the same enthusiasm as were
Penelope's thwarted suitors in the Greek *Odyssey*.

Fanny, I never feared men, but I believe they may have sometimes feared me. I am prone to think men prefer softness and tender-
ness to sharpness. Mama often said I had wit but not the wit to con-
ceal it. Nevertheless, I never set out to wear the spinster's cap, nor
put it on gladly when at last it seemed the proper thing to do.

At twenty I flirted with Tom Lefroy and expected he would propose, but he did not, and married a lady of fortune in Ireland. A
Cambridge don named Samuel Blackall wooed me but did not
commit himself. As there was too much sense in him and not
enough love, I was satisfied with the outcome. Harris Bigg-Wither
of Manydown Park did beg for the honour, but he was younger than
myself, and I was an old twenty-seven at that. Besides, he was not
Mr. Darcy, although he had plenty to recommend him as young
gentlemen of leisure go.

Did you think I had invented Mr. Darcy, Fanny? How could I
have, when there was no one in my acquaintances at Steventon or
Chawton or even London who was anything like him. Yet Mr.
Darcy was as real and as dear to me as he was to Elizabeth Bennet
because I met him in Bath, already created by a greater power than
my own. I loved him, Fanny dearest, but I could not have him and so
I gave him to Elizabeth, instead.

Did you ever doubt that someone like myself could have had a
secret passion? You laugh, I know, and I rouse myself to laugh a little
with you. Yet passion is the theme here, the motive behind this very
long—and soon to be much longer—letter. I want you to know and
to let it be known when I am no more, that Jane Austen did not spend

all her feelings on her writing and stint her fellow man. Had she had her way, she would have been engaged, wed and brought to child-bed like any other English woman—but not without love. Yet in the town of Bath in the year 1799, love flourished but availed noth-ing. You are wondering, no doubt, why I did not mention it before. Well you may wonder! Now you shall know all. I will set it down in the form of a memoir, a story. I could entitle the story *Pride and Prejudice,* for there was a good deal of both in evidence. Or perhaps *Sense and Sensibility* would be more appropriate. However, wishing to be original, I will call my tale *Jane Austen in Bath.* Does that not evoke a fanciful picture? Read on.

One day, while trying to interest myself in the fortunes of my her-oine, Susan, my sister burst into the room with the strangest of dec-larations.

"Whatever do you think, Jane? Aunt Perrot has gone to gaol!"

As I said, I was engaged in writing and only thought Cassandra meant to amuse herself at my expense. I am rather loathe to admit that my first reaction to this bit of information was to wish I could devise a means to put my Susan into prison, as the novel was pro-gressing very dully, I'm afraid. Later on, this Susan became Cath-arine Morland and went to Northanger Abbey. But I digress.

"Jane, do listen," said my sister. "The letter has just arrived. Mama is in a faint, of course. Lord, it promises to be the most awful scandal. Imagine Aunt Perrot doing anything so sly! Come and help me re-vive Mama. Oh, where can those smelling salts be?"

We found Mama just as Cassandra had left her, sprawled across a chaise lounge, groaning and weakly fanning herself with a sheet of paper. The smelling salts were found at last in Mama's mending bag. As I held the vial beneath her nose, she gasped and bolted upright. I perceived, from her unquiet eye, that we had only tindered a fresh spark to her smouldering sensibilities.

"Ruined!" declared Mama in a voice uncommonly strong for a swooning lady. "Absolutely done for! When news of this gets out, we won't be received in any decent home in Hampshire. And what will become of the two of you now? Oh, my poor maligned girls!"

My sister and I exchanged a look, fearing our mother was about to embark on her favourite theme: the Misses Austen and their standing in relation to men, matrimony and society in general. Mama's view of this panorama had grown considerably dimmer as Cassandra and I attained twenty-six and twenty-four, respectively.

"Maligned, Mama?" wondered Cassandra. "Surely no one could possibly connect Jane and myself to any sort of crime."

"What Mama means," I clarified, "is that where before there was scant hope, now there is likely none at all."

Mama held up a finger. "People have a way of connecting others to any sort of thing they choose. Think of it, your poor Aunt Perrot confined in Ilchester gaol and my brother gone with her. It isn't possible, I tell you!"

But I understood, from reading my uncle's letter, that it was all too true. James Leigh-Perrot and his wife, another Jane, residents of the city of Bath, had always been the most respectable among our more prosperous relatives. Somehow it was ordained that we Austens at Steventon Rectory should supply the poor relations to more well-to-do parties than is usual for one family in England. But we shouldered this surprisingly unrewarding burden with equanimity, even pride, in the case of Mama.

Aunt Perrot, who surely could afford to purchase any amount of lace she desired, had been accused of stealing a small quantity of same from a shop. Somehow, unthinkably, this great lady was now confined at Ilchester for her alleged wrong where she awaited trial. Her husband had chosen, out of devotion, to accompany her. Uncle wrote that they were there if for no other reason than *on principle*, for he suspected the shopkeeper could easily have been *persuaded* not to press the matter. Uncle said the motive was blackmail from the outset.

I had to admit that this was a scandal of the first water, whose odour was likely to cling to the whole family whether Aunt Perrot was found guilty or not.

"What else does Uncle James say?" asked Cassandra while fanning Mama. "Does he mention how Aunt Perrot is bearing up?"

"Aunt Perrot's stoicism in the face of her ordeal," I replied, "is a fact that must go without saying."

"True," answered Cassandra. "But Aunt Perrot in irons! Too grim!"

"I doubt that irons are involved, though if there were any *principle* on test, I feel sure Uncle James would not think Aunt Perrot in irons too great a sacrifice."

I made a moue at my sister, who hid a smile behind her hand. Being blessed with dimples, I frequently made faces that brought them into play.

Cassandra peered at the letter. "Why, Uncle James writes of us, Jane! He wants us to come to Bath!"

When George Austen, rector of Steventon, arrived home, he was at once assaulted with the dreadful report. The poor man was at a loss. The scholarly Mr. Austen usually left matters of gossip and the occasionally unsavoury affairs of the neighborhood to his wife and those two of his children who remained with them (all of whom dealt much too handily with that sort of thing, in his opinion) but this was clearly a family matter. The Reverend Mr. Austen longed to retreat to the quiet of his library, but there was no help for it. Some comment had to be made.

"Too puzzling, really. I can't think why Jane had such an urgent need for a bit of lace."

"Father!" exploded Cassandra. "You don't understand. Aunt Perrot is innocent!"

"Nevertheless," opined Mrs. Austen, "I cannot imagine what James is thinking of in asking the girls to come to Bath to live in the house while they are away. How can they go there now in view of everything that's occurred? And who would chaperone them with the Perrots indisposed?"

"Why do you not go, my dear?" Mr. Austen asked his spouse.

"I?" gasped that worthy woman. "Upon my life, never! Go to Bath and look a proper laughingstock! What a bold suggestion, indeed, Mr. Austen."

"Mama may never again so much as leave the house," said I with a wink at my father.

Mr. Austen, known in his youth as "the handsome proctor," dreaded this possibility as much as any placid man with a highly excitable wife might, but the devilish expression in his younger daughter's eyes made him smile. He had those same hazel eyes, but his shone with a far milder light.

"On the contrary, Madam," said Mr. Austen. "I only presumed upon your eagerness to help your brother in his hour of need. If you do not go to Bath, it will appear a very ill thing on your part, I'm sure."

Mrs. Austen frowned. "George, if it were in your power to take notice of anything in this house outside of your books, you would have seen that I already appear as ill as I possibly can. Just this past year I have suspected asthma, dropsy, water on my chest, a troublesome liver—"

"Heavens, Mama," I cut in before my mother could progress in her litany to her unsettled bowels, "you have been giving us such a masterful account of your ailments that even father cannot be ignorant of them."

"True," said my father to Mama, "and it is also clear to me that no one could benefit from the waters of Bath more than yourself."

"Mama take the water cure!" exclaimed Cassandra. "What a capital idea!"

"Fiddlesticks," said Mrs. Austen, springing to her feet. She pushed her disordered hair into her cap. "I'll drink tea and nothing else! Come, girls, we'll serve it up in the garden."

Thus went the conversation over the Event, a scene played not unlike many others at the rectory, each actor taking his accustomed role. As it turned out, the possibility of curing all her ailments wholesale at the famous spa quickly overcame Mama's dread of scandal, and she readily convinced herself that she was too righteous a figure for anyone to attach anything to *her,* try though he might. And so it was arranged that the three of us journey to Bath, but at the very last moment, Cassandra caught a bad cold and could not go. As a result, it was left to Mama and myself to brave whatever storm was brewing there.

"Oh! who can ever be tired of Bath!" I once wrote. I did weary of it much later when we removed there after father retired, but my first sight of Bath made me exclaim in wonder. With all its fine yellow stone houses, the city appears to have been touched by some Midas. How beautiful is Bath, indeed! But best of all, there is never a lack of activity, people to encounter, fashions from London, balls every other day. Mama thought Bath very noisome, but what is a bit of hubbub to the young? I missed the company of my sister very sorely, for the diversions of such a place as Bath are only half of what they might be were they shared by another of one's own age and inclinations.

Mama and I settled at the Leigh-Perrot's and were well tended there by the servants. At first Mama was hesitant to enter into society, to venture near the Pump Room, the centre of life in Bath, due to her fear of being pointed out as a connection of Aunt Perrot, but her gregarious nature surmounted that hurdle. Soon Mrs. Austen and her daughter became regulars at the Assembly Rooms and baths if not downright denizens.

Far from being ostracized when it was discovered she was the sister of the husband of an accused thief, Mama at once became a popular cause, and people took great pains to show their sympathy and indignation at the outrage against Aunt Jane, who still languished with Uncle in gaol.

I wonder today how I could have found Bath so gay in those days when, were one to own it, a great many of the people one saw were either mildly disgusting or positively pitiful in their unsightliness. The more handsome persons of both sexes came not for their health but to secure their futures. Some of these made the journey, one regrets to say, to enrich themselves at the expense of others. Fortunes were lost at cards every day. Many men—nay, even women, their wattled faces cracked and caked with powder and riddled with out-of-date beauty patches—already teetering on the edge of the grave found themselves engaged to be married to those who already envisioned themselves richly widowed. Yes, one saw every sort of deformity and illness, and the accompanying odours were most distracting at times. But if folly had a smell, Bath should certainly have reeked beyond endurance.

I never cared for the baths overmuch. Indeed, what reasonably fastidious person could fail to cringe at the notion of what unwashed flesh, what manner of open sores had preceded one into those hot, murky waters, bubbling and dubious as the contents of a witch's cauldron. Mama, however, maintained that the springs feeding the baths purified them continuously, and so, if only to be companionable, I wallowed and perspired with the rest.

How ludicrous we must have appeared in our ugly, ill-fitting bathing shifts, our caps with their silly ribbons and those little floating trays suspended round our necks on which we kept our smelling salts, handkerchiefs, nosegays and other indispensables. I describe only the women. The opposite sex looked frightful beyond telling, the old men who still wore wigs sweating beneath them, the powder running in white rivulets down their faces, which were red unto apoplexy. The waters made them lecherous too, if the truth be known, and as more wine was imbibed than mineral water, they lost all inhibition. Indeed, men and women bathed together, united in the effort of courting renewed health and even, in some instances, salvation, but I have heard things went on in the baths that are not for us to consider.

One day Mama directed my attention to a truly heart-wrenching sight. A young girl of sixteen or thereabouts was being lowered into the "stew pot" by her attendants. Her limbs, what could be seen of them, were well formed but abnormally thin, and she was yellow all over. In her face shone a pair of marvelously dark eyes, larger and more grieving than any I had ever chanced upon in a human creature. I perceived that the unfortunate invalid anticipated her immersion with even less relish than myself, but she was either too weak or resigned to make a murmur.

Turning her back, Mama whispered, "That is a Spanish girl, I am told. Of all things, having to come to England for her health!"

"How cold she must be," I said, "having come from a land where the sun always shines."

"She'll thaw out here right enough," observed Mrs. Heywood, a new acquaintance of Mama's from London, whose manners and speech were rather quaint, to be charitable. The wife of a wealthy brewer, she had enough jewelry to outdazzle any duchess. However, I quite liked the woman. Her set of ailments matched those of Mama to perfection, and a bond sprang up between them on this account that, I believe, will stand while empires fall. They still write one another to this day, letters fit to rival a physician's journal.

"Dear, dear, how poorly she is," said Mama with what may have been, for all I know, a touch of envy. "They say she is called Miss Terragon or Terrapin or God-knows-what foreign-sounding name."

"What lovely clothes she has," Mrs. Heywood's daughter, Livinia, informed us. This was a young woman much better spoken than her mother but, somehow, twice as common. "They are far too grand to be wasted upon such an ugly little monkey of a Portugee."

This amazed me, for despite her all-too-obvious infirmity, the Spanish girl had struck me as being not in the least ugly but as being possessed of a definite, if tortured, prettiness.

"I believe I must introduce myself," I suddenly said.

"But Jane, dear, what if she has no English?" Mama fretted. "How will you get on?"

"We shall splash one another once or twice and go about our business," said I and excused myself.

Perhaps Mama was right. I was making myself civil to the foreign bather only to spite Miss Heywood, whom I found odious from the start of our acquaintance. I began to rack my brain for some word of Spanish I might have come across in my reading.

"How do you do, Señorita?" I asked of her. "My name is Jane Austen. May I know yours?"

Even I was startled by the poor girl's response, which was a beatific smile that gave even further charm to her remarkable eyes.

"I am done to a turn," she replied, extending a thin hand, "and my name is Olivia D'Aragon. How delightful to meet you."

The young Spanish lady's accent was precisely the same as mine and not a whit otherwise.

"I thought you were from Spain," I told her. "What a fool I am!"

"Not at all," she said kindly. "My name is very Spanish. It means 'from Aragon,' a city I wish I could see but fear I never shall. Indeed, what would I not give to be back in London this very moment. How dreary it is here!"

I was about to protest but suddenly realised that Bath, to a young person who could neither dance nor promenade, much less feel inclined to flirt or gad about in general, was nothing more than a watering hole frequented by a cantankerous old herd who could hardly offer her any amusement.

"If it suits you, Miss D'Aragon," I ventured, "there is to be a ball in the Grand Assembly Room tomorrow evening. I know no one here myself and do not expect to be dancing, but I should be glad of someone to talk to. Believe me, sitting in a room filled with music and gay people is vastly better than sitting in a chair at home."

Miss Olivia D'Aragon seemed perplexed. It occurred to me that she was unaccustomed to invitations of any sort, that people did not as a rule include her in anything so lively as a party or a ball.

"Yes, all right," she nearly stammered. "I should be very glad of your company. If only I—"

"If your health does not permit, I shall understand completely. But I shall be very sorry not to see you."

Miss D'Aragon's attendants announced it was time she left the water, which the poor girl seemed glad enough to do. In point of fact, she appeared rather the worse for her brief immersion.

The Grand Assembly Room has several great chandeliers, brightly waxed floorboards, a bevy of Roman goddesses looking down from their niches in the walls and more French gilding than an enlightened civilization ought rightfully to tolerate.

I suppose I was a bit surprised to see Olivia D'Aragon already seated and waiting for me. From Miss Heywood's remark, however, I was quite prepared for her beautiful embroidered gown. Diamonds glittered on her bony neck and wrists.

"Miss D'Aragon! How pretty you look!"

This was absolutely true and no flattery of mine. Granted the boon of health, Olivia D'Aragon would surely have been the most beautiful woman in the hall.

"How kind you are, Miss Austen," replied the invalid, taking my hands in her own. "And it is you who ought to be admired. If some gentleman does not ask you to dance tonight, then we are in the company of blind fools and ought to go home at once."

I replied sincerely that it was quite sufficient to my happiness to have her present. Truly, I did not expect to dance, having as yet been introduced to no suitable young men. Yet I could not help wonder aloud why Miss D'Aragon had been left unattended.

"Oh, I have been left alone for only a little while," she informed me. "Don't concern yourself on that account."

"Forgive me, Miss D'Aragon, but I must tell you that your diamonds are too wonderful. I have never seen anything to compare with them in my life."

"Do you know, Miss Austen, that I have never before had the occasion to wear my late mama's jewelry. I'm glad of the chance, for I know she would have wanted me to put them on if only once. I don't remember my mother really. She died when I was a very little girl, but they tell me she was a beauty. Now a poor stick like myself is nothing to hang gems upon. I look ridiculous in them, no doubt, but I don't care at all tonight."

I squeezed Miss D'Aragon's hand. The girl's cheeks had a bit of color to them, but I was sure it was not a healthy sort of rosiness—not that I suspected that someone like my sad new friend would resort to artifice. Miss D'Aragon's face bore the deadly flush of consumption.

Miss D'Aragon bade me call her Olivia and promised to call me Jane in spite of the difference in our ages. She did not demure. Being but seventeen did not deter a girl in her woeful condition from numbering herself among us spinsters.

This was all we were able to have in the way of a private chat before we were joined by Mama, Mrs. Heywood and Livinia. The spirited and rather aggressive conversation of the two matrons cowed Olivia into silence and rather had the same numbing effect on Miss Heywood and myself. When the music began and the hall had filled up, I had nearly settled myself to watch the dancing when a florid young man wearing a shocking waistcoat burst upon us without any warning at all.

"Heigh ho, Mama! I have put on my dancing shoes for nothing. There is no one here worth the trouble."

"Percy!" cried Miss Heywood. "For heaven's sake go away!"

"May I present my son," said Mrs. Heywood without the least enthusiasm. "Percy, have you been drinking?"

"Not a drop, I swear, Mama!" chortled Percy Heywood.

"He has too," said Livinia.

"Well," said Mrs. Heywood firmly, "while you're still on your feet, Percy, kindly pay your respects to Mrs. Austen, Miss Jane Austen and Miss Olivia D' . . . Miss Olivia."

"Howdye do, ladies," said the young man, actually having the effrontery to peer at us through some silly sort of glass hanging from a chain on his coat. "I say, I spoke hastily, didn't I?"

"You always do, Percy," his mother reminded him.

"Damme, but you're right, Mama! Miss Austen, is it? May I have the pleasure of this dance?"

You have by now guessed how much pleasure *I* thought I should derive from standing up with Mr. Heywood, but seeing the look on poor Mrs. Heywood's face, I did not have the heart to refuse.

I have never in all my days seen a young man so startling in his address as Mr. Percy Heywood, newly arrived from London the day before. I cannot imagine how someone so sensible and well meaning as old Mrs. Heywood could have produced two such offsprings as Percy and Livinia, but there they were! To his credit, I will own that Mr. Heywood was of a somewhat kinder disposition than his sister. Unfortunately, he was also an energetic but awkward dancer who, it appeared, found in me a partner very much to his taste. His remarks to me that evening were very much the same as the following speech and probably a good deal worse:

"I say, Miss Austen, you are a cracking good dancer—unlike my sister who might be a clubfoot for all she's worth as a partner. Heigh ho, doesn't she look ugly wearing that peeved expression because I won't play the victim and ask her to stand up with me! Won't I just let her fret! By and by I'll dance with her or Mama will pull a fit, don't you know. Who's that odd creature sitting with you? I don't mean your mater but that shrivelled little body with the jewels. A pretty penny they'd fetch at a pawnshop, what? By Jove, call me a Turk if that gel lives through the evening. My mater can be depended upon to bore her to death if all else fails. Doesn't that gel over there dancing with that officer look a perfect witch in that gown? Egad! Oh, look, there is Brownlow, a friend of mine. We shall quiz him presently over a glass of punch. Damme, what a killing ball this is, as good as any I've ever been to or I'll be cut for bait!"

I was about to remind Mr. Heywood that he had only just moments before pronounced the ball a failure due to a dearth of pretty girls, but he was not to be interrupted for an instant. After the third dance, I made up my mind to cool Percy Heywood's interest and mentally rehearsed various excuses. As it turned out, none was necessary, for just as Mr. Heywood began to entreat me to join him in yet another foray, a voice behind me spoke.

"Heywood, how can you be so selfish? Allow someone else the pleasure of standing up with Miss Austen."

I turned round in surprise to see a very fine-looking man standing behind Miss D'Aragon, his hands on her shoulders. I perceived at once that he was very like her in the darkness of their hair and the liquid beauty of their eyes, but where one read only mute suffering and fatigue in the face of one, the other was vibrant with every sort of energy and charming attribute permitted to Man.

"Allow me to present my brother, Benjamin D'Aragon," said Olivia with obvious pride.

"Good gracious!" proclaimed Mama, looking rather stunned by the sudden appearance of such a splendid gentleman.

Mr. D'Aragon bowed to the ladies while Mr. Heywood astonished us by exclaiming, "Why, damme if it isn't old Dragon! How the devil do you do?" For the edification of the rest of us, he added, "We were at school together until I got sent down. Egad! Let me shake your hand, you croaking fellow. You look prosperous enough, I must say, although I suppose that is only to be expected, what? Dance with Miss Austen, if you must, but remember, I saw her first!"

"Do sit down and rest, Percy," advised his mother. "You're dripping sweat on my gown. Take this chair here next to Miss Olivia and try to make yourself agreeable, if you can."

"Don't mind if I do," replied Mr. Heywood, viewing Miss D'Aragon's necklace with much the same expression as a jeweller with a loupe screwed into his eye.

"I very much admire your dancing, Mr. Heywood," said the gentle Olivia. "I was just saying to your sister that you are quite the most fun to watch."

"Percy is a great show-off," I heard Miss Heywood scoff. "Pray don't encourage him."

As Mr. Benjamin D'Aragon led me away, I cast back a regretful glance at his sister.

"Don't worry," said my new partner, the skin about his great eyes crinkling in a merry way. "Olivia doesn't dislike Mr. Heywood as much as you do."

"And how do you know that I dislike Mr. Heywood, Sir?"

"Everyone who saw you knew it, except poor Heywood himself."

"Mr. Heywood is a perfectly dreadful man."

"Not perfectly dreadful. Only by half, perhaps."

"Why do you defend him?" I wondered. "Did you not hear what he called you?"

Mr. D'Aragon actually laughed. "You refer to the title of 'old Dragon.' Heywood meant no harm by it. It is as near as his English tongue can come to pronouncing my outlandish surname. If he had real intent, he could call me much worse."

"Are you quizzing me, Mr. D'Aragon?"

"Quizzing? What does that mean?"

"Ask Mr. Heywood. He will tell you at once."

"Oh, yes, I see," said Mr. D'Aragon, laughing again. How easily amused he was! "Heywood was rather decent to me at school. Perhaps he felt a kinship because his people and mine were both in trade. So you see, Miss Austen, I am no more a gentleman than Percy Heywood."

This notion so outraged me that, I am afraid, I uttered a vulgar sound. "Pah! You come to Mr. Heywood's defence out of gratitude? Why should he not have been decent to you?"

"Oh, I don't know," my partner replied casually. "He might have found some reason had he wished to be unpleasant."

I scarcely knew how to reply to this and, so, concentrated on keeping time with the music. When at last the dance ended, I was not a little relieved. My cheeks burnt uncomfortably. For some reason, even though Mr. D'Aragon had behaved beyond reproach and had even come to my rescue, I felt he was mocking me. Chiefly to blame for my discomfort, I think, were his black eyes, which gazed at me so unwaveringly yet inscrutably.

Livinia Heywood, I learnt, had been taken away to dance by that same Mr. Brownlow who was a friend of her brother. The latter was still, somewhat to my surprise, seated beside Miss D'Aragon and appeared to be entertaining her with a choice sampling of his very odd remarks. Far from seeming annoyed, Olivia laughed gaily, as though Percy Heywood were a rare wit instead of merely a rattle.

"Oh, do leave off, Mr. Heywood!" I heard her beg between peals of merriment. "You are making me cough. I cannot catch my breath!"

"What a pity you are bound to that chair, Miss Dragon," said Percy Heywood, "for I am certain, did you dance, you would dance very well, indeed, and be just the sort of partner I like best."

"Are you feeling well, my dear?" Mr. D'Aragon inquired of his sister.

"Oh," she replied, "I am rather tired now. Mr. Heywood has quite worn me out."

"Upon my word," said Mr. Heywood, "I never meant to. Dragon, old fellow, why did you never tell me you had such a charmer of a sister? Damme, but chatting with women is such a chore. They never want to talk about anything worthwhile, do they? But Miss Dragon converses so well I can scarcely credit her with being a female."

"Nevertheless," said Mama, "Miss D'Aragon must go to bed or she will pay for it tomorrow. I myself was delicate at her age and never stayed up past ten o'clock."

Although I did not presume to contradict, I had certainly heard otherwise where Mama was concerned.

"You are very wise, Madam," Mr. D'Aragon told my mother. "Olivia is past her bedtime and we should make our way home now."

"Oh, bother!" was Olivia's comment.

"Dash it all," said Mr. Heywood. "Just when I was enjoying myself too. Well, drag the poor gel away if you must, old boy, but come back afterward for a game of cards. Bring all your ducats with you, ha, ha!"

I fully expected Mr. D'Aragon to make some polite refusal, but he said, "Very well, I shall look for you later, Heywood. Shall I see you as well, Miss Austen?"

"I fear not," was my answer. "We are leaving this very moment ourselves."

"Well," said Mama, looking a bit vexed, "I suppose we must be off if Jane insists. Though I myself am not in the least tired."

"Well, I am," declared Mrs. Heywood. "Music invariably gives me the headache. I will go with you."

"Leaving Livinia on my hands, naturally," said Mr. Heywood, his eyes rolling in his head. "What a deuce of a mother you are, Lord love you!"

No sooner had he said this than the subject of his discontent came into view along with Mr. Brownlow. This gentleman was introduced to me in an offhand manner by Livinia, who then turned to Mr. D'Aragon, saying, "And this gentleman is Mr. Benjamin D'Aragon, whom Percy knew at school." An innocent enough statement, one would think, but Livinia Heywood managed to sound as though she found it incredible that her brother and a man like Mr. D'Aragon could inhabit the same universe, much less be old schoolfellows. In fact, judging by the gleam in her eye and the rather frightening, tooth-baring smile she directed at him, it was obvious that Miss Heywood admired no man present more than the handsome "Portugee" standing before her.

Miss D'Aragon was helped to her feet by her brother.

"Good night, Jane," she said to me. "Were it not for you, I should never have come. I liked the ball immensely!"

Her eyes were shining, I saw, as I arranged her shawl, and doing so, I glanced surreptitiously at Mr. D'Aragon, who seemed to be gazing at me in such a way that pains me now because I find that I am powerless to even begin to describe it. Dear Fanny, it is a proven fact that some men grow more likeable on further acquaintance while others become exposed, but there are a few who blaze like the sun, lighting up our hearts, no making of them veritable torches, so that though we grow old, their fateful glances forever haunt us.

"I hope to see you again soon, Miss Austen," said Mr. D'Aragon. Mr. Heywood, not to be outdone, came forward with "Yes, damn soon, I hope."

And I, having become so distracted by that sudden burning in my breast, went so far as to tell Percy Heywood that I wished to see him quite soon as well, although in reality, I dreaded nothing so much as a reunion with Mr. Heywood, whether in this life or the next.

Upon the following morning, I rose early, a certain restlessness drawing me into the street, where I began to walk as with a purpose, if not a destination in mind. It was thus I hurried toward the solitary figure of Mr. Benjamin D'Aragon coming from the opposite direction, although I had no way of knowing he would be there.

But what a different Mr. D'Aragon I beheld that morning! Elegance and proud bearing had vanished with the night, leaving a bowed man who walked with stooped shoulders and weary expression. As he drew nearer, I saw that his beard had grown out in stubble, and I knew that Benjamin D'Aragon had never been to bed and had doubtless spent the entire night gambling with Mr. Heywood and his cronies.

So lost in thought was this gentleman that he failed to see me until I was right under his nose.

"Miss Austen!" he exclaimed. "Up so early?"

"We seem to keep the same hours, Sir," I told him.

"Not quite," was his answer. "You look very pretty indeed, if I may say so."

"Very kind of you," I murmured.

"Not at all. It is you who are kind. Last evening you made my sister very happy and this morning—well, you are no doubt thinking I am profligate and unkempt, but out of kindness, shake my hand as though you were glad to see me."

"We are not shaking hands, Mr. D'Aragon," I said.

He held out his hand and, oh, I had no choice in the world but to place my own in it. It moved quite of its own accord, knowing better than I where it belonged.

"Did you lose a great deal, Mr. D'Aragon?"

At this he gave his quick little laugh. "Just enough. Believe me, Miss Austen, sometimes it is better to lose."

Those were the circumstances under which I became acquainted with Mr. D'Aragon and Olivia, his sweet sister, both of whom I was to see on many more happy occasions while waiting out the tragedy of Aunt Perrot's confinement—which, as it turned out, was never in a cell at all, but in the gaoler's house with all its comforts.

I should very much like to describe some of these meetings in detail, especially my talks with Mr. D'Aragon, who for an East India merchant, knew a great deal of those subjects usually expected of a scholar's conversation. What he gave up of his knowledge he exposed with just the right amount of wit and good humour, and I made no secret of the fact I liked nothing better than to walk or sit or dance or ride with Benjamin D'Aragon. Indeed, I quickly grew to feel that Bath would be unbearable without him. Although I knew very well that this man might easily attract a great beauty or an heiress, I felt that he had remained unmarried due to the responsibility of caring for Olivia, as their parents were dead. Nevertheless, he must have realised that I should certainly never have considered his sister a burden. Because of this and because he so frequently sought my society, I hoped against hope that Mr. D'Aragon might yet propose.

Dear Fanny, my supply of paper is running low, so I must rush to put an end to this narrative. Even so, I must go on a little further, although the following is very painful for me to relate.

Mama and I were giving a little supper—the Heywoods, Mr. Brownlow and, of course, Mr. D'Aragon and Olivia were all to attend. To my great surprise, Percy Heywood was announced early with the excuse that he wished to speak to me in private.

"I know you think I'm a bit of a dolt and all," Mr. Heywood began, "but, as I am to go into the brewery, in any case, it would be a waste of time for me to try to become anything more than what God made me. I shall be able to keep a wife very well, Miss Austen, and Miss Olivia is the gel for me, by Jove!"

"Miss D'Aragon!" I cried out. "You wish to marry Miss D'Aragon!"

"You're mighty quick! Damme if I haven't gone and fallen in love with the little minx with her pretty eyes and all. Egad! Cast a proper spell on me, she has, and I aim to mend my ways, if you get my meaning. Only there's old Dragon—got to get past him, don't you know. There's where you come into it, Miss Jane. Dragon likes you. You're the apple of his eye, make no mistake. That's why I implore you to speak to Dragon on my behalf."

"But Miss Dragon—Miss D'Aragon—is an invalid," I protested. "She may not live—"

"Don't say that, Miss Jane," Mr. Heywood entreated and I knew, by the fear in his eyes, that this young man, known as a whip and a wag and a rattle by his equally frivolous friends in London, truly felt himself to be in love with poor Olivia. Even though Olivia was an heiress to no small fortune, Mr. Heywood had no need of it, standing to inherit a brewery himself. And perhaps Miss D'Aragon, in her inexperience of men, had found something in Mr. Heywood that made it possible for her to return his affection.

"Well," I told him with a sigh, "Mr. D'Aragon seems to like you well enough. You need have no fear of approaching him, I am certain."

"He never liked me much at that," admitted Percy Heywood. "He only allows me to visit Olivia because she falls to laughing whenever I'm about. You see, Miss Jane, Olivia needs a witty fellow about her to lift her spirits, not a gloomy old body like Dragon who's always got his nose in a book. He was like that at school as well—always swotting the books, no fun in him. He did my lessons for me, though, because I once knocked down a fellow who called him a filthy Jew."

"Is Mr. D'Aragon a Jew?" I asked. I must admit the possibility had never occurred to me. I thought the D'Aragons to be of Spanish descent. Mr. D'Aragon had told me that his ancestor had journeyed to England in the service of an infanta who married King Henry VIII, Catherine of Aragon.

"Lord love you, girl, what else could he be? Smart as a whip and rich as Croesus, there's a Jew for you. Of course, you being from the country wouldn't know that. You wouldn't know a Jew if he fell on you. Now me, I'm a great favourite with the Jews. I've borrowed from them on my expectations and owe them a king's ransom. They're always glad to see me in London, and I've gotten to know their ways, don't you see. That's how I know that Jews only like to marry other Jews, which rather leaves me dangling, doesn't it? It might be Dragon will make an exception in Miss Olivia's case, what with her being a bit sickly and all." Mr. Heywood looked at me pointedly. "And perhaps, just perhaps, old Dragon will make an exception in his *own* case, what?"

In spite of my confusion about what he had revealed to me, I duly scolded Percy Heywood for presuming to anticipate Mr. D'Aragon's intentions and went on to disabuse him of his mistaken notion that Miss D'Aragon was "a bit sickly" when, in truth, she was very ill indeed. I rejected, of course, his plea to help him present his suit to Mr. D'Aragon and only agreed to be his second when he broke the news of his intent to his mother and sister upon their arrival.

When this happened, old Mrs. Heywood began to weep, but

declared through her tears that Percy, while showing as little common sense as ever, had finally said something his mother could like him for.

Livinia, for her part, saw no more merit in Mr. Heywood than she had previously and took great pains to tell him so.

"Besides," she added with a sniff, "when I get a sister-in-law, if ever I do, I hope that she will at least be an English woman like myself!"

"I fear, Miss Heywood," I could not help but say, "that any woman resembling yourself would be of no benefit to your brother whatsoever."

"Amen to that, I say!" crowed Mr. Heywood. "I'd sooner be hung at Newgate."

Luckily, a note was sent round from the D'Aragons. They would not be coming after all, due to Olivia being indisposed. What an uncomfortable, edgy supper it should have been had they arrived just then! In fact, it was none too pleasant as matters stood. With the exception of the mother, I fervently hoped never to be in the company of any member of the Heywood family again.

Within two days, Miss D'Aragon came to call on me without her brother. I perceived that her spirits were very low and her little face paler and more pinched than I had ever seen it. It came to me at once that Mr. Heywood had, indeed, made the offer for her hand, had been refused, and now Olivia was full of grief over it.

"How sad it makes me, dearest Jane," she said, taking my hand, "to have to tell you that Ben and I are leaving Bath immediately."

"Well," I said in a trembling voice, "you were never so fond of Bath."

"Not at first, perhaps, but now I am loathe to go because I have found someone very dear to me in this place."

"Mr. Heywood?"

"Not Mr. Heywood!" cried the girl with a little sob of a laugh. "Although I shall be rather sorry to part from such an amusing companion. It is you I mean, Jane. I shall miss you terribly!"

"Are you going, Olivia, because Mr. Heywood wants to marry you and your brother won't have it?"

"No, that's not why," said Olivia gravely. "It is true that Ben has

refused Mr. Heywood permission to marry me, but I don't wish to
marry Mr. Heywood, in any event. It is not Mr. Heywood we are
running away from. It is you, Jane."

"I?" I gasped. "What have I done?"

"Nothing and everything. You are you and that is wonder
enough. I had to come and speak to you, to explain to you why I
cannot invite you to visit me in London as I should want to do. It is
because of the way Ben feels about you, Jane."

"I rather thought your brother liked me," I said, dully. "Or perhaps my great liking for him made me want to believe that he did."

Miss D'Aragon tightened her grip on my hand.

"Ben loves you, Jane! He finds himself very much in love, even
against his will, and he doesn't know what to do about it." Olivia
lowered her head. "I was determined to make you understand why
he feels he must leave you, but suddenly, I doubt that I am equal to
such a task. I fear I might make a muddle of it and offend you in some
way, and this I should never want to do."

"I believe I understand," I told her. "You need say no more, my
dear Olivia. I understand very well."

That is what I said, my dear Fanny, and I believed my own words,
but deep within me, there was no reconciliation. Benjamin D'Aragon, the one man whom I might have loved until the breath left my
body, departed from me without so much as an adieu. He did write
a note, a polite and even kindly message, but he knew better than any
living soul that it was not sufficient. Dear God, how he must have
known it! If he is still living, I wonder what he has done with that
knowledge. Where has he hidden it so that it cannot trouble him—
or does it trouble him a little sometimes? I don't think there has been
a day since that it has not troubled me.

I know Mr. D'Aragon left Bath because he was a Jew. What is a
Jew, then? Immediately upon returning to Steventon, I asked father
this question and was given a long, sad speech about the history and
suffering of a people, of how, even in our own land, in our time, a
Jew has none of the rights and privileges of other Englishmen. How
amazed and dismayed I was to learn that a Jew cannot own property,
that he might go to school if he has sufficient means but, nevertheless, cannot earn a degree. All professions are barred to him save

brokerage and usury, and of course, he is reviled for that, although kings and nations have been known to be saved by the generous loan of a Jew. All these impediments, father related rather gleefully, could not stand in the way of a man called "Mendoza the Jew," who was boxing champion of all England from 1792 to 1795!

Papa said that the difficulty with the Jews is that they do not accept Our Saviour, although they are a civilized people in every sense. That is, of course, most curious, but even stranger was my father's reply when I ventured the opinion that, would the Jews only embrace Our Lord, their troubles would certainly come to an end.

"I should like to affirm that as the truth," said Papa, "but I daresay, were it all so simple, each Jew would have become a Christian long ago. What I mean to say is, perhaps there is a benefit in the Hebrew remaining as he is that is more apparent to himself than to those who do not comprehend his ways."

These words of my dear papa struck me quite dumb and ended my inquiries into the matter. How wise he was, my father, and how kindly in his speech and manner, but even so, I had not the heart to confess to him that I had come to love a man who was an unbeliever, the fact of which had failed to diminish him in my eyes in any way.

Mr. D'Aragon, however, was not to know that. I should have been glad of the chance to tell him so, but this he never afforded me. Nor did he consider it fitting to say the words I longed to hear from him: "In vain have I struggled. It will not do. My feelings will not be repressed. You must allow me to tell you how ardently I admire and love you." This I gave Mr. Darcy to say to Elizabeth Bennet, and although she rejected his declaration on account of his excess of pride, any reader must know that poor Eliza was already quite lost. Oh, had Mr. D'Aragon only been able to pronounce what I had already glimpsed in his eyes, I might have forgiven him his sudden departure!

On the contrary, Mr. D'Aragon, that man with whom I had spent so many felicitous hours in perfect harmony of temperament, spirit and contemplation of the world that was Bath, left me with the feeling that he thought me as different from himself as had he been a dog and I a cat.

Now I ask you, what dreadful forces have conspired in order for this to be possible! Injustices exist aplenty, but Mr. D'Aragon and myself were neither the cause nor the remedy of any of them. He certainly was not poor and, far from being reviled, was admired wherever he went for the beauty of his person. The only misfortune Mr. D'Aragon ever complained of was his sister's illness. Therefore, I continue to wonder, as I always will, what made Benjamin D'Aragon, the only Jew in Bath in 1799 that I knew of and surely the handsomest Jew in Christendom, so positive that to break my heart and very possibly his own by silent withdrawal was the only course open to him . . .

At this point the writer broke off, never to take up her pen again. On July 18,1817, she died of her illness before the sun rose, not yet having seen her forty-second year. In due course, the authoress was buried in Winchester Cathedral. Meanwhile, her grief-stricken family inserted this notice in the *Courier* on July 22nd, the first published admission of her authorship of the four novels then published:

"On the 18th inst. at Winchester, Miss Jane Austen, youngest daughter of the late Rev. George Austen, Rector of Steventon, in Hampshire, and the authoress of *Emma, Mansfield Park, Pride and Prejudice,* and *Sense and Sensibility.* Her manners were most gentle; her affections ardent; her candor was not to be surpassed, and she lived and died as became a humble Christian."

Some time later, the authoress's sister, Miss Cassandra Austen, set herself about the task of sorting out Jane Austen's papers, which consisted mainly of the unfinished novel and letters the writer had received in her lifetime. Added to this was an unusually long letter intended for Fanny Knight.

Cassandra read through this letter and was so shocked by its content that she immediately consigned it to the fire, along with several other letters written to her sister that contained references to matters of which she did not approve.

The Samaritan Treasure

THE FATE OF THE HILL is desolation, darkness and decay. For thousands of years there has not been so much as a small light to wink back at the stars on the summit at night. In the morning, the mist rises amid crumbling masonry and fluted columns that have teetered for ages and have finally crashed, unheeded, to the ground. Living creatures inhabit the hill: bats, owls, lizards, every kind of rodent, sometimes jackals. These emit a strange cacophony by night, but in the occasional stillness a much eerier sound can be heard—stones talking. The baking heat of day and the subsequent sharp drop in temperature cause them to split audibly. If the stones do not actually speak, they are surely groaning, for a lonelier place than the Hill can scarcely be imagined. That the Hill is accursed is apparent. By moonlight, the enduring power of the curse pervades all, but there is in it only a tangible, throat-constricting, unbearable melancholy.

The name of the hill is Samaria, and it was bought by an Israelite king for twenty talents of silver. Samaria, how many were your masters and how varied! Much of their bric-a-brac still lies on the summit, slowly becoming dust, except that which the British unearthed and took away. The English, the most powerful, kindest and oddest of all the masters of Samaria, instead of building anything new, delighted in digging up everything old. But perhaps not everything.

The masters of the Hill have vanished. Of those who did battle for this poor place, few came to a peaceful end. Even the last of the black-eyed sovereigns, the unhappy Hussein of Jordan had it wrenched from him in war. And now, Samaria belongs to the Israelites once again—a far from tranquil proprietorship, for the dreary hill is in the middle of a fierce seemingly never-ending strife.

There certainly seems to be a curse, but to whom it extends and what must be done to lift it, not even the wisest in Israel know. Yet the lore of Samaria is well documented by a people who love to remember.

In the days of its full glory, the hill, rising gradually above the surrounding plain, resembled a great altar festooned with vineyards and olive groves. On the summit, encircled by walls and garden, stood a house of huge, square stones. This was the home of the King, the seventh ruler of Israel, the madman.

For a long time the king's madness was accepted as a characteristic of royalty and was more than compensated for by his mastery over the Arameans whenever they threatened. In fact, the Samaritans suspected their ruler's lunacy to be an asset to his military duties, as a saner man might perhaps resent the vulnerability associated with being king. After all, at least 7,000 from Aram-Damascus coveted his head on a spike. Useful, too, was the King's fearful reputation among children— mothers having difficulty getting their little ones to bed, warned that he would come to devour them unless they obeyed. His name was Ahab, the son of Omri.

Many of the king's servants had relatives in towns throughout the province, and to these kinfolk they would carry tales of their lord, even though none were on speaking terms with him. Ben-Omri, it seemed, was a taciturn eccentric, as elusive as a shade in his own palace. Some contended that his jaw was so glumly set that words could barely hiss through his teeth. When handed clothing, food or documents, he would either nod absently or appear momentarily startled, as though he found it odd that others continually waited upon him. All his orders were conveyed to his steward, Obadiah, who saw to it that they were carried out. This was agreeable with the servants, who tried to keep out of the king's way as much as possible, lest he happen to look at them as he passed. His eyes, dark and glossy as pitch, were reputed to be able to cast spells.

Sometimes the king had a few words to say to his heir, Ahaziah, but mainly in angry tones that echoed through the halls. It was said that the king had managed to produce seventy sons, but somehow it happened that only this one remained in favor with him. Many thought it was due to the memory of Ahaziah's long-mourned mother as, more often than not, the king cursed his son in a voice that rumbled in his chest.

So no one blamed the prince, being the son of such a father, for his need to travel from one city in the province to another, drinking and wagering away his monthly allotment. The king's displeasure with Ahaziah began when the boy did not bother to learn the poem that dealt with the seasons for planting and reaping, something no true Samaritan failed to memorize.

The king, Ahab, was possessed of a fierce and restless vigor. He paced endlessly within the confines of his courtyard, shoulders forward, hands clasped behind his back, eyes to the ground or squinting at the sky. And when bothered by an old wound in his leg, using a cane, he walked even more briskly, as if to escape the pain. He was a disquieting sight on those days, the fringes of his robe whirling as he hobbled about, his face dark as murder, cursing and flaying at any hapless fowl that strayed across his path. When the king went inside, his hoary dog, whom he had never been known to mistreat, lay in wait in the doorway and, growling, nipped toothlessly at his heels.

Every so often the king was stricken with bouts of wheezing and gasping for breath. It seemed then that he would surely die. When, on his birthday, a soothsayer told the king that his fate was written in blood, he came to greatly fear the "wasting sickness" and was sometimes observed inspecting his sputum for signs of color. After a particularly awesome coughing fit, he was heard to say quietly but distinctly "God help me," a plea the six previous kings of Israel had never been known to utter. Yet the 7,000 from Aram-Damascus or the increasingly hostile Assyrians caused him no more anxiety than did the flies that buzzed about his earlocks and teetered on the rim of his wine cup when he took his evening libation.

The actual truth was that the king's mind was as sound as any man's. It was only that his nervous system, hopelessly inadequate due to the pride of his ancestors, gave him these odd quirks and mannerisms. For although royal only as far back as a single generation, when Ahab's father had overthrown the tyrant Zimri and usurped his throne, the king's family was an old one. For hundreds of years they inbred because no one outside the clan was trusted with preserving the spectacular height and refined features that were its fame and great conceit. After a century or two, the men in the family—the only ones who counted, of course—could be judged from a distance as splendid and noble lords, even as their spines were becoming permanently bent from stooping to enter doorways or simply from lending an ear to ordinary folk, who generally came up to some point between their middle rib and armpit.

Beauties they were, these giants, but before long the elegant faces took on a strangeness caused by skin grown so transparent that the veins showed plainly, noses become so narrow and arched that it was a wonder air could pass through them, and ears curiously devoid of lobes. Dark eyes had evolved to a startling, inhuman blackness such that the difference between pupil and iris could no longer be discerned, and even the long upper lips of the men eventually ended in bloodless but altogether too pretty bows.

Speech that passed through these fine lips sounded lofty and nasal like buzzing bees, due to the constricted proboscises of the owners. In fact, the haughty noses were perpetually poised in an attitude of breathing some exquisite perfume of which lesser mortals were unaware, the wings of the nostrils having narrowed progressively until they, like the earlobes, ultimately disappeared.

Such was the ancestral breeding of Ahab the King, a man who had not glanced into a mirror for twenty years and who was, therefore, unmindful of what a constant scowl had done to his inherited comeliness.

Scarcely more charming was the young Ahaziah despite his curls and finery. The prince's customary reply to all questions and statements was a sonorous "Truly?", eyebrows raised clear to the hairline. His personal family consisted of a pair of alabaster-complected female cousins, neither of whom had thus far succeeded in producing any more elongated royalty.

The king was never unkind to his daughters-in-law, who were, after all, genteel young ladies, and even encouraged them to be fruitful by promising great reward. But when the two shyly hinted that they were not to be held accountable, the king was not a bit surprised. Ahab himself could abide none of his own wives. Many of them—as might be expected—were also kinswomen, others spoils of war, yet others goodwill offerings or acquired by what means no one recalled. Most of his women, however, the king had inherited from his father, the mighty Omri. The harem was a continual hotbed of quarrels and intrigues. The concubines, primarily a fat indolent lot, were forced to amuse themselves as best they could, and their favorite pastime was rivalry. Rivalry not for the king's affection—that was beyond hope—but for supremacy among themselves. None could call herself queen. The woman who had borne that title, the mother of Ahaziah, a supremely lovely cousin for whom Ahab had cared deeply, lay in one of the tombs at the bottom of the hill, gone in her youth. When it came to the king's attention, via a eunuch spy, that more than one wife prayed to her own particular gods for his swift demise so that her banished son might ride into Samaria and supplant the effete Ahaziah, Ahab reacted indifferently. He confided to his steward, Obadiah: "Their smiles are false, their caresses forced. They do not love me, not a one."

The steward, shocked to hear his master speak of love, could conceive of no reply. It had never occurred to him that the king, who smiled at no one, suffered for want of an artless sigh or a spontaneous dimple. Nor was he able to dissuade Ahab from finally sending all the aging odalisques packing, back to the cities and lands whence they had come, each dowry refunded twicefold. The king, as he was wont, put it simply: "They wished me dead so that they and their offspring might carry off my goods."

When the steward could not resist reminding the king that the women nonetheless had carried off half the treasury because of his decree, Ahab appeared unconcerned. "It comes very dear this peace of mind, but have I not gold enough left for a hundred men?"

To that, Obadiah could only nod solemnly, remembering the wondrous articles that had accompanied old Omri to his grave, the precious metals and gems grown now lusterless amid decayed flesh and grinning skulls. When it came Ahab's turn to join his sire, there would be no lack of treasure to pile around him. The frugal steward shuddered at the thought of so much wealth lost forever and even gazed wistfully at the king's gold-and-ebony walking stick, which very likely would be the last thing tossed in before the tomb was sealed.

This very item, gorgeous as it was, seemed an unlikely funerary object at that, as even the most disconsolate mourner could not fail to be moved to mirth in recollection of the unusual service the walking stick had seen. The king, under most circumstances, could get about very well without any aids, but this masterwork of a cane, meant to be a badge of rank, might have been a dead twig for all it was valued by its owner, who carried it with him on expeditions to the farms that were part of the family estates. In fact, the king was often called into consultation by his kinsman, as he had the knack of curing diseases in animals. It became a common sight to see ebony and gold prodding the udders of a cow or lifting up her tail. Earthworms were poked at, grain was stirred and grape clusters knocked down for inspection by a man who saw more beauty in a well-grown cabbage than in the costly article he held in his hand.

Once the harem had cleared out, Ahab's subjects were divided on why he had rid himself of his women. Some conjectured that he had lost his manhood. He was always referred to as "old Ben-Omri," most everyone having long since lost sight of the fact that he was only a little over forty years of age. Others, thinking he meant to acquire a new set of wives, began to wash their daughters and fine-comb their hair. When the king failed to act, rumors that he now consorted with she-devils spread, and people claimed to have heard shrieks of abandoned laughter from the summit at night. Others swore they heard nothing at all.

Not long after the incident of the concubines, the king announced his intent to get Ahaziah an additional spouse, a daughter of the King of Sidon and Tyre. The dandified young man, who wore copper armbands decorated with rosettes on his shining arms, objected to the union with a pagan princess who, in his eyes, was the daughter of a common merchant. It *was* a fact that the King of Tyre was not above dealing in lumber, and his subjects tended to be artisans who were never any help in time of war. Besides, the whole island of Tyre reeked of the famed scarlet dye that his subjects pro-

duced—it was a smell like that of rotting clams. When his father insisted that the alliance would guarantee the safety of Samaria by providing a cushion on the northern border, Ahaziah spat and said, "Let
the Tyrian keep his beggarly daughter!" Only when Ben-Omri
showed his son a sketch of the magnificent chariot that was to be part
of the dowry, did Ahaziah relent, as it was far superior to the one he
had been driving for the past few years.

It should be pointed out there were other madmen in Samaria besides the king. Notable among these was a strange person called
Elijah, an old man with golden hair and curious features—far odder
even than those of the Omrid dynasty—who appeared one day and
announced himself to be a messenger sent by the Lord of the Universe to straighten out the thinking of the Sons of Man. He went
about his mission with such single-minded purpose and such im-
patience with the existing foibles of those he planned to enlighten
that most dismissed him as an out-and-out fanatic. Nevertheless,
baffling and frightening things tended to occur wherever he went,
and little by little, this Elijah, prophet and wizard, accumulated a
substantial following. Because it was believed that Elijah's madness
stemmed from religious zeal, it was excused, and even admired.

Of course, the main object of the prophet's disapproval was the
king himself, whom Elijah denounced at every opportunity. But
Ahab seemed little disturbed by this bad publicity, remembering
that some of his forebears had received much worse. The fact that he
allowed the prophet to roam about in subversive freedom was, to
the Samaritans, only further proof of the king's eccentricity, as any
of his predecessors would have taken swift steps to silence Elijah.

And so Prince Ahaziah was not alone in his aversion to the marriage. Elijah made his way to the palace and confronted Ahab, who
was in his bath, concerning this marriage proposal. While amazed
and indignant, the king was relatively helpless in the slippery stone
vat.

After listening briefly to Ahab's acrimonious commentary on his
sentries, Elijah said slyly, "Perhaps I know how to make myself invisible."

"Very well, then do it now!" barked the king.

"The land is already overrun with idol worshippers," cried the prophet. "Would you invite them *all* here to marry the Sons of Israel and poison them with their licentious ways?"

The king snorted and said, "We cannot shut ourselves off from other nations. Who are we to despise their gods and customs. They will massacre us one day for such conceit, in spite of all my best efforts. Besides, you look to me like a foreigner yourself."

"Very true," admitted Elijah.

"How is it you have learned our tongue so well?"

"Impossible to explain," said Elijah after a moment's hesitation.

Quite suddenly, Ahab took hold of the queerly fashioned rod the prophet always carried. "You are said to be a wise man. Well, tell me this: What have I done to raise all of you up against me? Why do my people call me mad? Am I mad? I who have always done my duty without complaint."

"That, Ben-Omri," replied Elijah, "is sufficient to make any man mad. What a curious fellow you are. Once, they say, you were a comely and not unlearned youth, a true prince of your people. Now, I am bound to say, you have the appearance of a man on a diet of unripe fruit. Your wives were happy to be banished and your children content to be called bastards rather than receive a blessing from such as you, miserable mortal!"

Instead of protesting what he knew to be perfectly true, the king stared at the prophet with narrowed eyes.

"It is you who are a poor and pitiful creature," he said, "for you must truly be a lunatic to address your master in such a way. You are yourself an unlikely appearing fellow, if the truth be told. You are too ugly to have been sent by even the worst of my enemies. Yet someday I shall discover who you are and where you came from."

"Who I am," replied Elijah, "and how I came to be here are matters beyond your understanding. I tell you, unfortunate human, that my only master, the Lord of the Universe, has chosen your people to show the other nations how to avoid the destruction of your race. You have proven heedless and perverse, and he has grown weary of the lot of you. I expect that at any moment he will abandon you to your own devices and recall me to him."

"For that at least I thank him," said Ahab. "Other than that, I have no use for this master of yours, whoever he may be."

Although the water had grown cold, the king did not stir but continued to fix his gaze on Elijah, a man with hair the color of which he had never before seen. "Where is his domain, this lord of yours?"

The prophet pointed upward with his rod, a thing, in the king's opinion, he must surely have stolen, for it appeared to be made of precious metals and rock crystal. In fact, it had an impudent resemblance to a royal scepter amid the stars.

The king laughed. "Ah, but that is very far away! Farewell, you poor fool and trouble me no more."

"Where the woman comes from they throw tiny babes into the flaming bellies of idols," said Elijah. "What think you of this sort of madness?"

"The devil you say," murmured Ahab reflectively, for he had quite forgotten this practice of his neighbors to the north. "Let me tell you, the children of the Israelites aren't destined for any flames. Such things will occur over my dead body, I'll vow an oath!"

And so, the king and Ahaziah went to the winter palace at Jezreel to await the arrival of the Tyrian bride. There, the king looked forward to tending his herb garden, pulling out weeds for later planting. Ahab possessed a sorcerer's knowledge of herbs and their uses. The only occasions on which he had ever been observed looking contented and serene were when he knelt amid his plants, his hands black with earth.

Not once did the king try to imagine what sort of girl his son's betrothed might be. He had not so much as bothered to learn her name. He had only specified that King Ethbaal send him the tallest of his daughters. Other details he took for granted—to this extent did he trust in his own power and the awe in which neighboring rulers held him. Certainly, the King of Tyre would never dare send anything but the finest, since he knew that in one of Ahab's cities, Hazor, hundreds of stables and chariots and men dedicated to the business of war were ready at a moment's notice. The King of Tyre also knew, as everyone surely did, that even the cellars of Ahab's houses in Samaria and Jezreel were crammed with chariots. Almost daily, the king would go below to inspect them personally, and he was often heard to hiss and mutter as if communicating with those who had ridden them to the grave. Ahab sought comfort from his vehicles in good repair along with the banishment of the women. Whatever else the people of Tyre and Sidon did on their mollusk-littered shores or in their forests of cedar, the King of Israel declined to contemplate. He had his own troubles and left theirs to them. And Ahaziah, who had no interest in plants or the contraptions of war or any other practicality, had submitted after initial protestations, although he showed no signs that he was about to send the princess a gift as befitted a proper bridegroom.

But one night the king, being unable to sleep, went up to his storeroom and rummaged through the articles belonging to his dead queen. Tied up in a kerchief he found an anklet of silver bells whose sensuous tinkle caused a shiver to pass through his body. The king tried to recall the face of the woman who had worn the ornament, but nothing formed in his mind. Although the storeroom was cold and smelled of mildew and old clothes, the king took the shawl from his shoulders, wrapping in it the anklet and other pieces of jewelry which he intended to dispatch to the bride of Ahaziah. The king's old dog, which had followed him upstairs, began to whine and chew on the fringes of his master's hem. Ahab cursed him for a tiresome beast but, nevertheless, took him outside, whereupon the creature fell to running in a circle and howled like a jackal. The king aimed a pebble at him for silence, but to no avail. Shivering, he looked up at the clear winter sky and noticed how unusually large and close to the earth the stars appeared. Standing there in his courtyard, the scents of jasmine and heliotrope cloying in his nostrils, Ben-Omri felt the hairs rising on the back of his neck and imagined that he was being observed, and that the silvery beauty of the night was not of this world but only a searching illumination from above.

The town of Jezreel, where the king stayed the winter, was not unlike many others from Dan to Beersheba. It had the same dome-topped mud-brick dwellings and narrow streets plagued with beggars. Its only redeeming feature was that it commanded a splendid view of the beauteous Jezreel Valley, known for its rich farmlands and prosperous vineyards, where grapes turned to gold. For centuries, crashing battles had been fought on the open terrain, leaving it scattered with corroding armaments.

The people of Jezreel had witnessed much since the town was first founded, but nothing like the sight that passed through the market-place on a sun-drugged afternoon. It was first spotted from an upper-story window by some men who raised such a shout of en-thusiasm that the entire populace came out to see what the matter was. The main object of the men's excitement proved to be a chariot unlike any other ever seen in the valley. No clumsy war chariot, it was plated with a pale metal, neither gold nor silver. A scene depict-ing grotesque beings performing obscure rites had been hammered out on it, and it caught the sun in a blinding fashion. The chariot was being driven by a man wearing a foreign costume of vivid scarlet that was painful to the eye of those accustomed only to the subtle hues extracted from plants. He was receiving directions from none other than Ahaziah, riding alongside. The latter cursed fluently as he tried to prevent people from pulling the tail of his horse or laying their hands on the electrum chariot. The prince, fairly popular in this re-gion, was besieged by women begging for kisses, and a few of the bolder ones asked for even more. Mothers stood in doorways, their children hung out of windows, and men left the tavern, cups still in hand. All stretched their necks to catch a glimpse of the woman, who sat in the gleaming chariot, covered with a cloak of the stun-ning Tyrian hue. The cloak slipped a bit and a hand reached out to draw it together. The Jezreelites saw that the nails and palm of the hand were stained with henna, a fashion affected by those whose fingers touched nothing ordinary, who employed others to lift even their food and drink to their lips.

The townspeople had scarcely a chance to remark on this when they were confronted with a new spectacle—men and women on horseback and in garishly painted carts. The women wore a dresses of yellow with black stripes that, combined with their coarse, inky hair, gave them a singularly bestial appearance. They gazed back at the astonished Jezreelites with insolent, soot-rimmed eyes. Unlike the women, the men appeared to be individuals of rank and distinc-tion, although each was bedecked with odd charms and amulets. The men chanted in unison in their dialect and a few swung censers, sending vapors of strong incense in every direction. Judging from their haughty expressions, they disdained the very air around them.

The good citizens made the sign against the evil eye and bade their children not to look upon the woman in the chariot, who might, after all, be a sorceress. But, transfixed, the children looked on while their elders spat profusely and grew silent lest ill-intentioned spirits enter their bodies by way of the mouth.

There remained little doubt as to the sort of folk that had come to Jezreel.

Suddenly, the procession halted and everyone pressed closer to see what had gotten in the way. There, directly in the path of the chariot, stood Elijah the prophet. The crowd grew very lively then until the old man motioned for silence. He pointed his rod at the woman, saying in a loud voice: "Then you are she who has come to overthrow the House of Israel!"

The only reply that issued from inside the cloak was a low-pitched, full-bodied laugh that seemed to echo even in the open air. The people groaned and the prophet disappeared into the crowd.

The prince, face suffused with blood, could only bellow, "Worthless cattle, make way for this lady and her servants!"

This incident and certain other aspects of his intended frightened the young man. For example, when she finally showed him her face, she failed to lower her eyes like a proper virgin, preferring to watch the impact of her own flawless beauty. Yet even her face, in its perfection, was not without a sinister cast. Ahaziah could not help but stare at her until she made so bold as to snap her fingers under his nose to bring him out of his trance. He imagined he detected a clammy odor in spite of the quantities of frankincense and myrrh that the Tyrians had put into the atmosphere.

The prince vowed that nothing could induce him to marry this arrogant woman with her eerie entourage, alliance or no. So Ben-Omri, whose honor was at stake, saw that he had no choice but to marry the Tyrian himself. Incensed at his son's lack of filial duty and his own foul luck, he pitched his walking stick into the ground, where it quivered like a stuck knife. Nevertheless, he soon had his beard trimmed and his grimy gardener's fingernails pared.

In spite of his distrust of women, the king had to admit that the Princess Jezebel was exceedingly comely. Her eyes glistened like multicolored raindrops, and her olive skin was like greenish gold.

The initial sight of her affected him like a blow between the shoulder blades. He even thought it *winsome* when, on greeting him, she pulled up her skirt and danced around on one foot, displaying the silver anklet, which she had carefully polished. Far from being afraid of him, the young beauty gazed into the king's brilliant eyes as though they were mirrors, preening and smiling rapturously until little beads of sweat dripped from the latter's temples. In fact, the girl was on a level with Ben-Omri, who was as tall as a native Samaritan.

"By Baal," she was heard to chuckle, "you have no horns at that!" When told of the altered wedding plans, the princess shrugged as though it were nothing at all to her and the king appeared not to notice when she straightaway tossed him her cloak to carry as if he were one of her own attendants.

To her credit, the girl knew how to make poultices, which she applied to the king's bad leg. She kept his bed warm and refrained from cooking altogether. On the other hand, she wore scents of clove and sandalwood that made him sputter and cough all the more. Though pliable enough at first, this Jezebel soon began to display a strong and willful nature. When the king, irritated by her lynx-eyed handmaidens, insisted that she eat by herself, she got grease on her cheeks and bosom and threw bones under the table, and then would wipe her sticky fingers on the sleeves of her husband's robe. She even maintained the king's dog stank. The beast, for his part, could not abide her overwhelming perfumes and whimpered whenever she came near. In response she kicked him in the ribs, screaming, "Begone, you bag of worms!"

Jezebel's other habits included selecting some person at random, searching his head for lice, and squealing with glee if she found some. She was expert at cracking vermin between her long nails. She brazenly seized venerated graybeards by their whiskers and bleated, "Meeh, you old he-goat!" directly in their faces. Instead of rebuking his young wife, the king seemed genuinely amused at her antics. Even when she plucked off his tall, cylindrical hat, filled it with wine and drank from it, he only scowled a little and shook his head, remarking, "Oh, what a fierce beauty she is!"

Matters only grew worse. The queen became pregnant, threatening to populate the land with more of her kind. Having brought her priests and magicians with her, she insisted upon worshipping her own imported gods, erecting altars and groves willy-nilly. Everything she did or bought or commissioned was in typical terrible Phoenician taste. The palace was flooded with blatant imitations of Egyptian artistry that lacked the originals' beauty and grace. All that she found in Samaria the queen wanted to alter, and it irked her no end that she could do nothing about her husband's nose, which was curved and graceful in high Samaritan style.

The king, beset with his nameless malady, felt weak and powerless to oppose his Jezebel. His coughing spells became more frequent and his body seemed to be drawn toward the ground. Even his exotic nose became useless when his sinuses turned to stone.

The queen, with witchlike sagacity, knew his troubles were caused by the goat-hair shirts he wore, but never troubled to inform him. Instead, true to her fiendish character, his wife took advantage of the king's indispositions. She pulled his earlocks and poked fun at his black, hairy arms. She mixed vile-tasting concoctions for him to drink, claiming they were powerful medicines, and he, the herbalist, made no effort to determine their sources. Never once did the Phoenician woman flinch before his glittering, obsidian eye; in time, that eye took on a sort of film, and finally grew gentle in its weariness. All believed that the queen feared nothing and could stupefy the Prince of Darkness, himself.

One day the king was forced to entertain some foreign princes. The distinguished company, having heard tales of Jezebel's beauty and ferocity, pressed Ben-Omri to produce this notorious woman and let them see for themselves. His brain beclouded with wine, Ahab had neither the inclination nor the patience to amuse his allies himself, so he sent for the queen. He was long past any vanity of his wife's appearance or her temperament. He knew her to be a source of endless macabre stories and bawdy jokes, which made her better fit than he to amuse his guests.

When word came back that the queen could not be found, Ahab, concluded that his wife was merely out to vex him once again. He staggered up from his seat and vowed to return with the queen if he had to drag her by the hair.

He stumbled through the corridors, bellowing into every room, until his search brought him to the treasury. To his amazement, the king saw that the doors of the great chamber stood wide open and that someone had caused the torches to be lit. Only two men were allowed inside the treasury—himself and the steward, Obadiah, whom he had just left in the banquet hall. The king wore at his waist a ceremonial dagger, toward which his hand instinctively moved, thinking perhaps the very men who guarded the treasury had turned thieves. But apparently they had been sent away, because there, amid the splendor of riches, both booty and tribute, stood the queen, like one entranced. When Ben-Omri approached her, she seemed not to take notice of him, her eyes dazed by the sheen of gold.

Sobering up instantly, the king shook her by the shoulders, shouting, "You shall not have it! Gold is mischief and you have wrought enough as it is. This will never fall into your hands."

Jezebel only made a kind of chuckling sound and answered, "How not? I am young and you are old."

"Though you hasten my end by every means at your command, you shall still not have it. I shall take the gold with me and you shall see it nevermore," replied the king.

"Does a shroud then have pockets?" mocked his wife.

"Pockets!" hissed the king. "I shall one day show you the depth of my pockets! The earth swallows up everything, even gold. Yes, even that fair head on your shoulders must someday go down and what will avail you then? Will gold bring back your beauty when your face is withered and black?"

The queen was so young that her own end was beyond her imagination. Nevertheless, the king thought he glimpsed a darkening of those taunting eyes and her voice lacked its usual fine-honed edge when she cursed, "A stone in your belly! Spit pus and blood!"

She continued to curse as her husband shoved her from the treasury. Yet even as he heard himself wished every possible malevolence, the king felt his anger giving way to a strange sense of resignation. Since *his* heir was a wastrel and as unfit to be king as a man could conceivably be, this woman's children might yet sit on his throne and tell the whole world to go to the devil.

"Miser! Lousy Samaritan garlic-eater! Leprous scab! You should stink tomorrow like your grandfather does today!"

At this reference to his ancestor, Ahab was obliged to administer his queen just the merest blow to the side of her head, which quieted her considerably. And within the hour, she assembled her dwarfs and conjurers and put on the diversion for the guests that the king had requested.

Ahab the King, for his part, watched none of these goings-on and simply gazed at his own morose reflection in his wine goblet, the lines in his face deepening as his wife's exultant laughter assaulted his ears.

Lost in gloom, the king was startled when he felt a hot breath on his cheek and the queen's long hair falling about him as she proposed loudly enough for all to hear: "A riddle, my lord, to test your wit!"

"Begone," he muttered.

But she persisted. "An easy riddle for you, I promise. We would hear your answer."

"Yes, yes!" came the shout. "We would hear it!"

The queen began to recite:

> What will outlast stone and clay?
> What outshines the light of day?
> Silver, beryl, jasper, jade
> All are pale and cast in shade.
> For this bright thing a man will bleed
> And only death will dim his greed.
> Bread for hunger, water for thirst,
> By these things we live,
> But the other comes first.

"Your reply, my lord," cajoled the queen, her voice dripping honey. "Tell us now. What is it?"

Ben-Omri raised his head and his eyes, opaque and dark as bottomless waters, calmly regarded the painted, leering face of his consort as he said, "Love. It is love of which you speak."

Her hair whipped his face as she turned from him. "Old spoilsport."

Jezebel grew increasingly bold. Needing more property for a temple she was erecting to the goddess Ashtoreth, she stole her husband's golden seal and ordered the land of a vine grower in Jezreel named Naboth to be confiscated. Having dispatched this order, she dispatched the vintner for good measure. Later, she was spiteful enough to say that it was the king's own doing. This and other acts incensed the people of Samaria-Israel, but no one could think of any means to stop her. Finally Elijah went before the king and demanded he take action, but Ben-Omri seemed to have other things on his mind and absently murmured, "Who can puzzle out these young women?"

Ahab's apparent lack of concern so kindled the prophet's wrath that he cried, "Where the dogs licked the blood of Naboth, there will they lick your own! Accursed be Ahab and all the sons of Ahab forever more!"

Naturally, Elijah's foreboding sat badly with the king, but as he had grown rather accustomed to having bloody fortunes forecast for him, he turned his attention to more pressing matters. Ahab's old enemy, Ben-Hadad of Aram-Damascus, was drawing close to the hill of Samaria, and as always Ahab was making ready to push him back. The king was relieved at the notion of escaping his consort, if only for the duration of the fighting, for she pestered him day and night, promising to give him a miserable old age. So far she had presented him with two children who fortunately had not yet invented any tricks of their own.

On the day of his leavetaking, the queen, peevish as usual over some trifle, refused to kiss him farewell and slammed the shutters of her window when he called out in parting from the courtyard.

"Then may you be consumed, you treacherous she-ass!" bellowed the king, who turned to depart, bowed by the loneliness that had long ago turned his perverse old madman's heart to bitter wormwood. Even a man who lives atop a mountain needs more to sustain him than clear, bright air. For all he knew, before the day was spent, his own gore might be decorating the countryside. If, on the other hand, by some chance he should live, the king had it in mind to say a few words to his wife and take stronger measures with her in the future.

As the chariots of the hosts of Israel rumbled off in the direction of the foe, Ahab the King looked behind him once more and, imagining the prismatic eye of his queen observing him through the lattice, raised his fist and shouted, "Enough is enough!"

Over the din of wheels and horses, men and weapons, cymbals and trumpets, all combined in an unworldly uproar, the king's ear caught for a brief moment what seemed to be a woman's strident voice calling out, "Too late!"

Ben-Omri's fate had stalked him—his blood-smeared chariot and armor were washed in the pool of Samaria. Once laid to rest, the king ceased to be the subject of slander and was proclaimed a hero and savior of. Israel. Those who had once called him madman collected in respectful groups to see how the king's body fluid had tinted the water of the pool. At sunset, reflections from the sky seemed to alter the water to pure blood or perhaps the scarlet of Tyre. Nevertheless, someone stole the fatal arrow that had pierced Ahab's side and sold off bits of it for souvenirs.

In time, as the rains washed away every trace of Ben-Omri's demise, the old legends were resurrected and even embellished, until Ahab the King became a sort of demonic champion. Soon after him, the Samaritan kings were no more. The Assyrians swept out of the Mesopotamian plain like voracious locusts and denuded Samaria. The victorious Sargon II carried everything back to Khorsabad, his capital, including 27,000 Samaritans. Nevertheless, while these Israelites sat in exile on the banks of the Tigris River, the hill was not forgotten, and the eyes of little ones still widened at the mention of the name of Ahab.

When no Assyrian ears were present, it was surreptitiously whispered that all had not been plundered. What is interred with the dead cannot be so quickly snatched away. The House of Israel had not been destroyed—it only waited in anonymity. There were murmurs of golden breastplates and helmets and rings and armbands and diadems still resting on the withered corpses of the Omrid dynasty—all hidden in darkness to be reclaimed when Israel regained her might. But these whispers soon faded into nothingness, a silence that was to last a long time.

★ ★ ★

In 5686, the Christian year 1926, J. W. Hawkes of the Palestine Exploration Society added his tuneful whistle to the sounds of life that remained on the hill of Samaria. Where once curses and denunciations had rumbled like thunder, the wind now carried the gentle strains of "Molly Malone." In that very place where sundry pagans had offered up their incense and sacrifices, the Englishman set a match to his pipe and paced the summit, pondering where he would sink his shafts and dig his trenches.

During the twenties, the area known as Palestine or the Holy Land was not yet free of the peril of malaria, and frequent bloody skirmishes between the Arabs and the Jewish settlers from Europe also endangered archaeological expeditions. Hawkes, however, had brought along plenty of quinine and was thankful to find that the Arabs in the region near the mound were not only peaceful, but were delighted to indulge the English's mania for "treasure hunting.' The Arabs were, at first, hard put to understand the anxiety the professor displayed at the exuberance with which they attacked the earth and were amused at his version of their language. Women and children were put to work as well, carrying off in baskets on their heads the loosened dirt that later was carefully sifted to trap even the tiniest bead. This was supervised by Hawkes' wife, Alma, whose red-haired, freckled appearance caused a stir among the Arab females, who found it difficult to fathom why a man so energetic as Hawkes would have chosen such a thin, delicate partner.

One morning, the villagers from the nearby town of Nablus, who comprised most of the crew on the dig, appeared at the site but did not take up their implements. They had designated a spokesman, one Ibrahim, who respectfully advised the archaeologist: "Good sir, we are honest persons and can no longer accept your money. There is no treasure on this hill. Whoever advised your excellency that there was is mistaken. These men have told us that it was all taken away thousands of years ago."

Before Hawkes could get in a word, Ibrahim motioned to two men—strangers to the Englishman—who were taller than most of the Arabs by a head.

"Please, sir," continued Ibrahim, "we have brought to you these persons who are descended from those who lived here in bygone days. They are learned men and respected among their people. They will testify that you are wasting your time here."

The men, who, in spite of their Arab dress, resembled two European diplomats with well-kept beards and refined features, introduced themselves to be *Samerim,* or Samaritans, the remnant of Israel in Palestine.

"Why, they're Jews!" exclaimed Mrs. Hawkes.

Although she had made the comment in English, the Samaritans seemed to understand her and smiled tolerantly.

Hawkes, too, brightened. Even in a rustic place like Nablus, he associated Jews with enlightenment and cleverness. In his halting Arabic, he attempted to explain to all present that he had never hoped to find treasure, although he was truthfully not averse to the notion. His goal, and that of the Palestine Exploration Society, was to substantiate parts of the Bible. When he was rewarded for his speech with blank stares, Hawkes looked at the Samaritans, who stood with folded arms, and an idea came to him. He asked Alma to fetch his Old Testament, which contained the Hebrew and English versions. When she returned, Hawkes handed the book to one of the *Samerim,* who leafed through it while his counterpart looked over his shoulder. They politely shook their heads and returned the Bible to the archaeologist.

"You could not read it?" Hawkes wondered. "Why, it is your Torah, your holy book. It is Hebrew!"

"Ah, yes!" answered one of the strangers. "Unfortunately, it is written in the new Hebrew script in which we are not fluent."

"New Hebrew script," laughed Hawkes. "But this is ancient!"

"Not to a Samaritan," was the soft reply. Then, the one who had spoken knelt down and, with his finger, wrote in the soil the even more archaic Hebrew alphabet—borrowed from the Phoenicians—which the Jews had ceased using centuries ago. "This is how *our* Torah is written. The *Samerim* do not change," added the Samaritan with a gentle laugh of his own.

With that, the representatives of the "remnant of Israel" turned to the Arabs, telling them that the English wanted to learn the secrets of the hill from things that might be buried there, and that they should continue to cooperate because the English were guided by a holy book that had been revered by Mohammed.

The Samaritans bowed to the Hawkes in parting. As they turned to go, one of them glanced around in a kind of dismay and said, "Forgive this poor place" in the tone of a housewife apologizing for not having made the beds.

"What fine gentlemen," whispered Alma. "One of them reminds me of a portrait of Queen Victoria's Lord Melbourne. He has the exact same handsome, intelligent face."

Evidently the word of the Samaritans was good enough for the Arab diggers. They resumed their labor with a new vigor, now convinced that it was all for a noble cause, even though they remained of the opinion that all the English were a little mad.

The following day the Samaritans returned to the dig. At their arrival, the Arabs once again left off working. Ibrahim, the headman, threw down his pick and shouted, "By Allah, they have brought the boy with them!"

He beckoned wildly to Hawkes and Alma—who were up to their elbows in a tub of water washing pieces of pottery to reveal possible inscriptions—and grinned broadly as if to say, "Now you'll see something!"

The two Samaritans were accompanied by a teen-aged youth, whom they introduced as Naftali ben Yoram. One of the older men, the one Alma had likened to Lord Melbourne, began to make his salutations to the English couple, but Ibrahim, impatient with the Samaritan's elegant manners, broke in excitedly, telling the bewildered Hawkes that the boy was someone very special, a prince among his own people. All three Samaritans denied this in amusement. It required considerable explaining and gesturing, but Hawkes at last understood that this Naftali had been born with a caul and, therefore, according to local tradition, was gifted with powers given only to a few.

Ibrahim assured the archaeologist that the boy would be very lucky for Hawkes and his project, as he had already established a reputation in Nablus for being able to locate missing objects. Once in a while, when persuaded, the young Samaritan would "bend things with his will," and it was suspected that he could foretell the future, although modesty prevented him from doing so.

Hawkes sucked benignly on his pipe and tried to absorb what he was being told. It was difficult to get anything done when these odd people came around, but so far, the Samaritans were the most interesting discovery he had made since coming to the hill.

"Is this true?" Hawkes asked the boy in Arabic. "Can you tell the future?"

"No, sir," came the response in English. "This is not for me to do."

Alma clapped her hand together in delight. The Samaritans, apparently also quite taken with their prodigy, volunteered that Naftali had somehow picked up a little English on his own. In fact, the youth never forgot anything he heard or read. They added that if Hawkes, as a scientific Englishman, thought there was anything he could teach Naftali, the boy would be willing to serve him for nothing.

Intrigued, the Hawkes promised to put Naftali on the payroll. After the older Samaritans had gone, the professor slapped him on the back, saying, "We'll teach you English, m'lad, if you'll help us with Arabic." Then he added in that language, "Do you know what we are doing here?"

The thin, pale Naftali answered without hesitation. "You wish to know about that which is no more."

"Correct," said Hawkes. "Does such work interest you?"

"Very much," was the reply. "I would choose it a hundred times over the calling for which I am destined."

"What do they hope to make of you, lad?"

"A conjuror. A sorcerer."

Hawkes removed his pipe and stared at Naftali.

"You don't say!"

"Yes, sir," replied Naftali and then added quietly, "Your watch has stopped, sir."

And sure enough, it had. Years later, when Hawkes told anyone the story of Naftali the Samaritan, he would always say that he was never sure whether the strange lad had stopped the watch himself in order to impress Hawkes or if his sensitive ear had simply perceived that it was no longer ticking.

Yet Hawkes and Alma, even when they began to realize that the boy was unlike anyone they had ever known, were unable to fathom his secret. It was, together with the still-unearthed mysteries of the hill, shrouded, and endlessly waiting.

Even among his own people, Naftali was considered both a wonder and a freak. He and his sister were orphaned when they were
quite small, but fortunately, their mother had two brothers named
Efraim and Nessim, the same courtly men who had come to speak to
the English. The uncles were respected by everyone in the vicinity.
They had the duty of chanting the prayers during religious services,
as the Samaritan synagogues have not one cantor, but two. Of
course, this did not constitute their livelihood—the uncles were
goldsmiths, both of them fine artisans.

When Naftali was still very young, the brothers came to realize
that he was not what a lad of his years might be expected to be. These
inquisitive men were fascinated by the strange talents the boy came
to display and encouraged him to perform the unusual tricks he had
discovered that he could do. The uncles envisioned Naftali as a person of renown who would attract folk from great distances to witness his unusual powers. They told Naftali tales of famous magicians
and fortune-tellers throughout the east who had amassed great
wealth, even though the uncles were certain that they were actually
fakes. Naftali, clearly, was genuinely gifted. He needed no artifices
to perform his feats, and were he to explore the depth of his power,
there was no telling what he might achieve.

It was an interesting life the boy led for several years. He was taken
to see conjurors, soothsayers, hypnotists, Gypsies and even Indian
holy men, presumably to pick up knowledge from them all. In the
end, it was they who usually wound up astonished by him. Only he
among them could flatten a coin to a paper thinness by merely rubbing it with his finger or call out the design and number from a deck
of cards fifty out of fifty-two times. Both these accomplishments required tremendous concentration, but it was left to a man from Da-
mascus to reveal to Naftali the ultimate possibility of highly focused
energy. Bending metal and doing card tricks was all very impressive
and entertaining, but affecting the human will with one's own mental processes was quite another area of endeavor. From this man the
boy learned more than from all the rest, yet he never used the
knowledge he obtained. The notion of tampering with the minds of
others frightened him, and in any case the Damascene had warned
him that all those he knew who had ever done this had come to a bad
end.

And so Naftali absorbed this unusual education and followed these unlikely pursuits until he reached young manhood. As his uncles had predicted, people were already making their way to his house in search of the extraordinary. But now Naftali no longer cared to be singled out in this fashion and the curiosity of the people bored him exceedingly. In spite of his oddness, he still retained the yearnings of an ordinary young person.

When they saw how unhappy Naftali had become, Efraim and Nessim decided that perhaps a wife would cheer him up. But the people of Nablus, the town near the hill, had grown afraid of Naftali. It was rumored that he was under the influence of spirits, and nobody was willing to subject his daughter to a man possessed in this manner. In short, his superstitious people both revered and feared him. With perseverance, the uncles might have found a bride for Naftali, perhaps a Samaritan girl whose family lived far from Nablus, but when his uncles showed Naftali the gold, marriage became out of the question. Matters had arrived at this point, when the Englishman came to dig at Samaria.

This was the first he had heard of the treasure—the secret was so well kept. He was shocked that such things existed, and the sight of so vast a hoard left him speechless. The gold was still in the tomb with the kings, an expertly hidden burial place. But the brothers, aware of these new European treasure seekers, were worried that the site might be uncovered accidentally. Naftali having come of age, they had decided to show him everything and enlist his help in moving the wonderful objects to a place where the English would be less likely to dig. Of course, Naftali was pledged to silence on this subject for the rest of his days. He was allowed to reveal the secret to his future sons when they became men, but his wife was never to be told—no woman was ever to learn the secret of the Samaritans.

Naftali never forgot how his hands trembled as he removed the diadems from the pitiful skulls of those who were once masters of the hill. With what trepidation did he take the golden scepters from their bony fingers and lift the plates from their crumbling ribs. At the same time he marveled that his uncles, Efraim and Nessim, had no such qualms about their ghoulish task.

"Peace, my boy," he recalled one of them saying. "They are giving up to you what is yours. Only a dead man gives a crown to a living one—remember that."

The tomb with the royal skeletons was sealed, with the hope that it would never be reentered—even the uncles did not dare to transport the bones. The gold was placed in a hidden cave.

The reason Naftali was sent to work for the Englishman, was not, of course, to help but to spy on him. The uncles were concerned that the excavation should not venture too near the grave of the kings.

At first, the young man only reported that the professor had slow methods and proceeded with great care. At the rate he was going, it would take him a hundred years to get anywhere near the tomb. As time wore on, he left off worrying and immersed himself completely in the work. The uncles would have been dismayed had they suspected how fascinating and challenging Naftali had come to find the science of archaeology. It drove all thoughts of wizardry and magic from his mind. He also forgot the purpose for which he had been brought to the hill. Rather than being wary of Hawkes, he began to dream of escaping life in Nablus by following the professor and his wife to England, where he hoped to study and become a learned man.

Then, Naftali began to change—gradually at first. To the amazement of everyone on the dig, Naftali grew more than two head taller within a matter of three months' time. Previously, his eyesight had been somewhat weak, but he soon thought he was gazing at a new world, everything as sharp and clear as crystal. Naturally, he did not mind these changes. Nor did he object to the attention he began to attract. Knowing that previously he had been nothing much to remark about, he was gratified when Mrs. Hawkes and the Arab women began telling him that he had become a tall, handsome young man.

But even as his vision and appearance impoved, Naftali's emotional health began to deteriorate. At times, he was overcome with a weakness and moodiness that he was hard put to comprehend and, at other times, a restlessness that was even more difficult to bear. Some mornings he awoke to find that nothing on the hill looked familiar, that the trenches and mounds of earth were a disgusting and disorderly sight.

Little by little, strange fears and longings came to the Samaritan boy's mind until he could no longer be certain what he would do from one moment to the next. When he looked at his hands, they were unrecognizable, and his voice sounded gruff and alarmingly deep to his ears. His face he rarely dared to examine, for whenever he did, it was like gazing into the eyes of a stranger.

At length, Professor Hawkes began to be aware that the boy's formerly open and cheerful nature gave way, at times, to a sullen and imperious personality. On those occasions, Naftali refused to take orders and even presumed to tell Hawkes his own business. Yet Hawkes found it was hard to stay angry with the boy as, moments later, he would revert back to his charming affectionate ways. However Hawkes decided to teach him a lesson by sending him home for a few days when, to Hawkes' surprise, his protégé reported to the dig with an old rifle and cartridges, declaring that he could not understand how Hawkes could leave the hill so unprotected. Hawkes, knowing the Samaritans to be the most peaceful of people, had no inkling of how or where Naftali had gotten hold of the rifle. He told him not to return until it had been disposed of, as he wanted no firearms on his excavation.

A week or so later, Naftali, who up to that time had been in excellent health, was brought to Hawkes in great pain, spitting up blood. Following an unconscious spell, he came to, took a look at Hawkes and company and demanded to know why so many strangers had been allowed on his hill. After that, the young man was often ill, although the Italian doctor brought in to examine him could find no evident disorders.

Yet Hawkes kept Naftali on, as the young Samaritan had an amazing knowledge of the history of the area. Naftali was also helpful when it came to deciphering ancient writings. Hawkes would send his inscriptions to London for translations, and when the results were returned to him, he saw that the young fellow's "guesses" were, for the most part, absolutely correct. Naftali could read the ancient Hebrew alphabet with ease—too much ease, perhaps. Once, when Hawkes handed him a freshly unearthed clay tablet, Naftali scarcely glanced at it, dismissing it as a mere ancient shopping list.

To make matters worse, the English woman became infatuated with him. Just as Naftali was undergoing a change, so was Alma Hawkes. She was an intelligent woman but not single-mindedly driven, as was her husband; she was rather lonely on the dig. Naftali could sense this, but he hardly knew what to think when she began to grow coquettish and to cling to him at every opportunity. When he held himself aloof from her, Mrs. Hawkes turned pettish and sullen. It became increasingly difficult to work with her. Naftali fervently hoped that Hawkes would not notice his wife's behavior—an idle concern, since the professor kept his nose strictly to the ground. He was truly a very good man, but Naftali discovered himself growing resentful of the Englishman and his young wife.

At any rate, he was soon to be parted from them. The turning point was Naftali's discovery of what he believed was the true treasure of Samaria, something quite apart from the gold of the kings. This was the object that he called "the rod."

The minute he first noticed it in the ground, he knew that it was not made by his ancestors or any ancient man. It was of metal, he thought, or at least something that resembled platinum. Inscribed into this metal were strange characters that Naftali could not decipher. On the end of this stick or rod was a sort of bluish crystal, and inside the crystal were tiny filaments like those in light bulbs. These appeared to be made of gold. At first Naftali thought the rod was some sort of scepter, but something told him that was not the case. Part of him wanted to run over to Hawkes and show him this prize, but he simply could not do it. He decided it was his duty to show the object to the uncles first; so he covered up the rod and said nothing. The more he thought about it, the more convinced he became that he did not want the English to take the mysterious article away from Samaria to their own land.

A few days later, Naftali dug up the rod again with the intent to hide it inside his clothes and carry it off. The excavation was getting closer to the rod, and he realized he had to move it immediately before it was found by someone or, worse yet, accidentally damaged in the process.

And so Naftali uncovered it and gazed at its strangeness. Suddenly, as the sun glinted upon it, the thing grew warm in his hand and began to vibrate slightly. The little filaments in the crystal-like end grew fiery red, and a quiet voice came from the rod as from a wireless. It was not a language that Naftali had ever heard in all his travels. The voice frightened him terribly. He threw the rod to the ground and scooped earth over it, his heart beating so quickly he could scarcely breathe. It was all simply too much—this devilish article on top of everything else that had happened to him. He ran toward the Arabs babbling like a madman and then fell in a faint before Professor Hawkes.

By the time Naftali recovered, he had become the object of much attention. Hawkes wanted to know what had gotten into him, but the youth was at a loss for words. He was aware that the professor and his crew were staring at him as if he were a mistrusted stranger.

Although he disliked the idea of touching the rod again, Naftali realized that he had to remove it from the site right away. When night fell, he crept over to where it was hidden, every crunch of pebbles beneath his feet sounding like an earthquake. For the third time, he uncovered the rod and even found the courage to place it close to his ear, but this time it was silent. Though Naftali had an instinctive fear of the thing, he also had a burning curiosity about it. He knew his uncles would want him to show it to them first, since his purpose on the hill was that of an informer. But, clearly, this object had nothing to do with royal gold. What was it? What was the language that it spoke? Surely no one in Nablus would ever be able to answer these questions, but a scholar from an advanced nation like Hawkes might find a way to solve the mystery. There was no help for it. He had to show the rod to the Englishman. Naftali, holding it carefully, hardly knowing what it might do next, climbed the hill to Hawkes big tent.

When he called Hawkes by name, the professor told him to enter quietly because his wife was asleep. Naftali obeyed and, without a word, held the rod out to Hawkes. As the young man's eyes shifted from the rod to the Englishman, he saw the archaeologist's mouth had fallen open with horror. Naftali glanced down and perceived, to his own terror, that his entire body was giving off a green light. His face, he knew, must look to Hawkes like that of a demon.

"What are you?" Hawkes asked him. He could barely speak.

"Listen to me, Professor," Naftali began, but before he could explain, the rod seemed to crackle like fat in a fire and then, suddenly, to chatter like a flock of birds. Somehow Naftali knew it was not the sound of birds, but of voices, perhaps human, speaking swiftly all together. Faintly colored lights began to dance around the tent. Naftali forgot his own eerie appearance as he watched these beautiful swirling spots. The rod was causing the sparkles, of course, and it also continued to speak but now in a single, demanding voice that seemed to be asking, in its own tongue, the same question Hawkes had posed: "What are you?"

When Naftali took his eyes from those lights, he saw that Hawkes had gotten hold of a gun and had it trained on him. Alma Hawkes had awakened by this time, and her hands were clutched to her face in alarm. Naftali was dismayed to see his friends suddenly afraid of him. He wanted to explain to them that this was no trick and, in fact, was none of his doing whatsoever.

But Hawkes said, "If you move, I'll shoot you."

At that moment Mrs. Hawkes jumped from her cot and shouted, "No! Don't harm him. It's Naftali, for the love of God!"

Naftali moved toward her to touch her arm and reassure her that there was nothing to be feared from him, but as soon as he came in contact with her flesh, she shrieked with pain as though she had been burned.

And so, that most gentle of men, J. W. Hawkes, lost his head and shot Naftali in the side. Naftali saw the blood but, curiously, felt nothing. Certain that the professor would fire again if he did not leave immediately, Naftali fled from the tent, still green and dripping blood, the unworldly rod still glowing and buzzing in his hand.

He hid himself, after a time, and examined the damage done to his body. It was painful to breathe, but he was nonetheless breathing, so Naftali concluded that the bullet had passed through his side, breaking a rib but not lodging in his flesh. Even the bleeding did not look serious, although his side was beginning to hurt a great deal. The rod, for its part, had grown cold and silent.

Dr. Edward Reisman, born in Warsaw, educated in Berlin and newly liberated from Treblinka, was illegally smuggled into Palestine in 1946, during the British blockade. As soon as his feet touched the soil of the homeland of his people, the young archaeologist was more or less drafted into the Jewish underground, the Irgun, and was trained to be a fighter.

Unlike most concentration camp survivors, Reisman knew how to make himself understood in both Hebrew and Arabic, so he was given special assignments. When the fighting was over and he had grown older, it sometimes gave the professor heart palpitations to remember how he had risked his neck every few days in acts of sabotage and smuggling that would cost him a long spell behind bars if he were caught. But, in those days, Reisman had the idea that God, if He existed, had saved him from the gas chambers for some purpose. So, with the help of the Almighty, he turned to mayhem, bombing, and firing on military vehicles, doing to the befuddled British everything he had dreamed of doing to the Nazis.

One day, some Tommies burst in on a meeting a few of Reisman's group were holding in anticipation of a boatload of illegals coming in that night. The Irgun was supposed to create a diversion of some type to take attention from the landing. A contact was scheduled to meet them at a certain address to bring them explosives, but the British got there first.

Reisman jumped through a window and ran down the street, but the soldiers fired on him. He fell down to avoid being hit, convinced he was done for, but the next thing he knew, there was an explosion and the street behind him grew black with smoke. An Arab, of all people, pulled Reisman off the pavement and onto the back of a waiting lorry.

Reisman was coughing too hard to speak, but he pointed at his rescuer's clothing. A dark stain was spreading across the Arab's chest and Reisman thought he had been shot. But the Arab only laughed and said in good Hebrew that his blood must be 90 proof. Around his neck, like an old-fashioned milkmaid, the man had hung two bottles of whiskey on a cord and hidden them in his loose robe.

The professor-turned-terrorist saw his rescuer many times after that. He was a very famous fellow in the area. The Jews called him the Magician, as did the British. He could get his hands on anything from guns to Guinness.

The Magician and Reisman became quite friendly for a time and worked together on several "jobs." Of course, the Magician was no Arab at all, although he usually dressed the part, but a Samaritan, the first Reisman had ever seen. His real name was Naftali. Reisman kept quiet about his own past. Being a freedom fighter had become his whole existence and he wasn't sure he would ever go back to archaeology. In fact, Reisman had long ago forgotten what it meant to live a peaceful life of any sort.

Some of the comrades in the Irgun were originally kibbutzniks, meaning they had lived on a collective farm. They had heard there was going to be a dance at their kibbutz and invited Reisman to come along. The refugee was unable to recall how many years had passed since he had last danced, but the idea rather appealed to him and he agreed to go. He even persuaded the Magician, Naftali, to come with him. He knew the people on the kibbutz would get a charge out of seeing him.

Reisman was right. When the Magician walked into the dance, the musicians nearly stopped playing. People just stood there with their mouths hanging open. It was as though the Messiah himself had just been announced. None of them had ever seen a man like this before: unbelievably tall and handsome, dressed in an outfit that was like an Arab's yet more old-fashioned. When Naftali flashed them one of his smiles, Reisman could sense the hearts of the girls melting like wax.

Reisman, taking advantage of the presence of pretty women, joined the dancing. But not Naftali. He leaned his long frame against a wall and watched the goings-on in his aloof, amused way. Some girls brought him refreshments and began to flirt with him, but he seemed to only tolerate them, although with dignity. No one, of course, thought of urging him to dance. For such a person an act as ordinary and frivolous as dancing the hora was unthinkable.

Later, after the musicians had put away their instruments for the night, the whole group sat around a great fire and began to sing songs and tell stories. When someone got up the nerve to ask Naftali if he knew any stories, to Reisman's surprise, he said he did. And what stories! He completely captivated his audience in a very short time. Naturally, many were already familiar with his tales, which were mainly recounts of famous Biblical military exploits. Yet, as Naftali narrated them, they become contemporary, as if they had occurred only yesterday. And he added information that Reisman knew had never been written in the Old Testament. Finally, someone begged him for a song, something of his own people. And so he sang, in a deep and exceedingly pleasant voice a Hebrew melody with oddly stilted phrases. It had something to do with the moon being down and covered with clouds and women wailing and tearing their garments because Israel was lost. But Naftali the Samaritan sang that Israel would never be lost, that the watchmen were wakeful and the guardians steadfast of heart. That made sense to Reisman because the word *Samaritans* in Hebrew is *Shomeronim*, which means watchers or guardians. But the last part of the song puzzled Reisman. Naftali's words were to the effect that the moon might well be covered with clouds and the sun covered with blood, for the watchmen had a great secret that was more radiant than the moon and more dazzling than the sun, a secret that would someday take away the darkness that was over Israel.

It was somehow not a shock to the professor when Naftali showed him the gold bullion. When Reisman asked him where it had come from, Naftali merely shook his head and said that gold was a wicked substance and ought not to have so much power in the world. But now it had the power to buy guns and ammunition and that, Reisman supposed, was what the Magician did with his golden bars.

Edward Reisman eventually took up the much-raveled thread of his life. Ironically, after Israel gained her independence, he took a position at a university in England. Reisman married an Englishwoman, had a family and never mentioned his days with the Irgun.

The professor, an expert in Semitic languages, both ancient and modern, rarely did any fieldwork. He taught his classes and, of course, did translations of texts that were sent to him by other archaeologists. Having been rootless so much of his young life, Edward had no affinity for travel and only occasionally attended a conference or went on holiday to the south of France with his wife and children.

Many years later, long after Reisman had established his career at the university, he was invited to a cocktail party—one of many, to be sure, but this one turned out to be rather special. The reason was that J. W. Hawkes was in attendance. Reismán had no cause to anticipate meeting the retired excavator. The old man had never made any spectacular discoveries, nor achieved any degree of renown. All the same, he was an old-timer in the circle of British archaeologists, known mainly for his ability to spin a good yarn.

At this particular party Hawkes, glass in hand, was holding forth as usual. Reisman, who could not be considered a good mixer, stood by himself against a wall, catching drifts of conversation from several groups. Suddenly Hawkes' voice boomed out.

"'Get off my dig!' I told him. 'I'll have no firearms on this hill.' He'd gone rogue on me, you see. Pity, too. Brilliant lad, in his way. Alma and I were going to bring him back with us, see to it he got an education. But he had other ideas, this Naftali. Yes, indeed, very different ideas."

Naftali! Reisman had not heard that name in twenty years. Had Hawkes and his wife actually known the same man who had befriended *him* so long ago?

Hawkes turned his head as Reisman tapped him on the shoulder. "Excuse me, Professor, but I simply couldn't help overhearing you mention someone called Naftali. I once knew a man by that name, a Samaritan from Nablus. Could the person you spoke of have been a Samaritan as well?"

Reisman was taken aback by the confusion he read on Hawkes' craggy face. The elderly woman next to the professor, whom Reisman presumed to be Hawkes' wife, actually looked frightened.

Professor Hawkes cleared his throat with a loud *harrumph*.

"Foreigner yourself, are you?' he asked.

"Yes. My name is Edward Reisman."

"Oh, yes. Read your articles in the journals. Good stuff, some of it."

Someone politely vacated a chair next to Hawkes and Reisman sat down. "Was your Naftali a Samaritan?" he repeated.

"He was," replied the old man with some indignation, "and a bloody scoundrel to boot. Disappeared for good one day, he did, but not without taking something of value with him. All our Arab diggers thought so, too. The beggar wouldn't have run off otherwise. Well, it can't be helped now, can it? Still, I've wondered all these many years what the boy found that was so important. God knows I never uncovered anything of significance on Samaria myself. It must have been gold—Naftali would never have left unless there was a temptation too great for him to resist."

"We thought Naftali was dead," said Alma Hawkes, a faded red-head with skin as pale and transparent as air-mail stationery.

Old Hawkes shot a glance at his wife. "Nonsense! Why should he be dead? This young man here said he knew him, didn't he? Well, Reisner, suppose you tell your story. Where'd you come across that wily devil? Didn't make off with your wallet or something, did he?"

Edward narrated a much-abridged account of his meeting with the Samaritan. He was careful to minimize his own involvement in their exploits. He told the truth about Naftali's wartime deeds, but did not mention the gold bars he had seen in Naftali's possession on the day of their parting.

J. W. Hawkes shook his head skeptically.

"A terrorist, eh. I can't believe it."

"Naftali was a gentle boy," insisted Alma. "He wouldn't have hurt a fly."

The old archaeologist once again gave his wife an impatient look.

"High-strung is what he was," Hawkes said.

"I believe I heard you say you'd ordered him off your dig for carrying a gun," Reisman told him.

"He'd lost his mind by then, poor bugger."

"It was the hill, you see," said Mrs. Hawkes.

"The hill?" echoed Reisman.

"Something there," said the old lady, almost in a whisper, "something there took hold of Naftali."

Hawkes snorted. "You mean he took hold of something there, something belonging to me—or at least the people of Great Britain. You knew him, you say. Did he ever mention anything about working for me?"

"No, I can't say he did."

"Of course he wouldn't admit to stealing anything, I suppose," Hawkes added rather hopefully.

"Naftali very often commandeered things during the war in Palestine, but somehow . . ."

"Somehow you can't believe he'd steal anything for his own benefit," said Alma.

"No."

"Neither do I," declared the old woman.

By this time any other listeners had lost track of what was being discussed and had wandered away. Only the Hawkes and Edward remained. The elderly couple were practically glowering at one another, as if about to launch the thousandth installment of an argument that had begun years ago.

"Well, why didn't he come back, then?" the archaeologist asked his wife. "Always treated him well, hadn't I? Everything that happened was the lad's fault and you know it. His entire tribe or whatever you call them lived near the excavation. He had no cause to go off if he was innocent."

Alma turned to Reisman and said in a voice that sounded terribly weary, "Naftali left because he was in love with me. I wasn't so very old back in the twenties, you know. Oh, you know how it is. Young boys get crushes on older women. It wasn't Naftali's fault, really. He and I were constantly thrown together. You see, Naftali worked mainly with me. I taught him to speak English. In fact, Naftali was really the only person I could talk to on that dig. My husband was busy with other things and I didn't know much Arabic. But he was an odd boy. There's no question about that. The Arab workmen used to say that he had certain gifts, strange powers. I saw proof of it myself. Do you know that once when I was feeling depressed, Naftali bent the prongs of a fork to amuse me. But he never actually touched that fork in any way. I'm glad he grew to be a courageous man who fought for what he believed in. He loved his people and their history, and I imagine it pleased him no end when Israel was declared a state, ruled by her own people as in ancient times." She turned her face to her husband. "You ought to be glad, too, J.W. Very glad."

"Sentimental fools, women are," Hawkes grumbled. "We're probably talking about the chap who blew up the King David Hotel."

"I don't think so," said Reisman. "Anyway, he may very well not have lived to see Israel's independence. I lost track of him before the fighting had actually stopped. Naftali may have been killed, or died since of some illness if he survived the war. Or perhaps he is back in Nablus, where he was born, the patriarch of a large, Biblical clan."

Alma Hawkes wagged her head sadly. "I doubt it. Naftali was always a solitary person. People shied away from him because they were superstitious. They thought he was possessed. If he was capable of stealing anything from our dig, it would have been in order to get away, to make another life in a place where nobody knew him. Poor Naftali, so handsome and clever, but really quite mad at the end."

"Now you're making some sense, Alma," said Hawkes. "The lad exhibited serious mental disorders. You see, Reisner, the strain of his so-called 'gift' was too much for him."

"I can see him now," said Alma, "an old man wandering about on that hill of his, lonely as an owl." The fragile-looking woman sighed deeply. "Oh, how he frightened us. It was simply too horrible."

Reisman was about to ask just what had been so horrible, but he changed his mind. Something told him that the topic was best not explored, that the old man and his wife had long since erected a wall around it. The look in their eyes made it plain that this was one of those matters upon which married couples affix a seal of silence, something that would make them lifelong conspirators no matter how they might disagree on everything else.

But, as sometimes happens, a long-buried memory, once resurrected, can turn into a rather lively ghost. Not a month after his talk with the Hawkes, Edward Reisman happened to be paging through an issue of National Geographic when he noticed an article about Samaritans living in the vicinity of Nablus, Jordan. As might be expected, there were several excellent color photographs, one showing Passover rites being held on Mount Gerizim. In that picture one man stood out in the group, just as he'd always done. No, there could never be a mistake in identifying Naftali.

Then, suddenly, the 1967 war between Israel and the Arab nations broke out. Reisman pored over the papers for news of the
fighting and watched the telly every evening, waiting for footage
taken in the Middle East. When headlines proclaiming an Israeli
victory appeared, Reisman, like other Jews the world over,
breathed a sigh of relief. When he read that the territory constitut-
ing the West Bank of the Jordan River had been captured and occupied, he could only think of the Magician and how thrilled he
must be to live under the jurisdiction of a people who, like his own,
revered the Torah and were part of that homogeneous group called
the Children of Israel.

But the suspicions of Professor Hawkes preyed on his mind, too.
Soon all Reisman could think about were those ingots he had seen
and how many golden objects had to be melted down to make up
bars that size. He recalled stories of peasants and shepherds in Egypt
and other places in the Middle East who had discovered caches of
priceless relics and had sold them off little by little over periods of
time—sometimes over decades—so as not to arouse too much notice. Even though such artifacts went to private collectors more often than not, at least they remained intact. But to destroy them, to
melt them down! The more he thought about it, the more Reisman
became convinced that J.W. Hawkes was right to believe Naftali
had betrayed him. Where else could the Magician have gotten so
much gold? Edward Reisman made up his mind to buy a plane ticket. If there *had* been a Samaritan treasure, there might still be some
left.

And so he made his way to Nablus. Finding Naftali was relatively
easy. The man seemed to be well known in the area, something that
hardly surprised Reisman. It was the rest that would be difficult.
Reisman had encountered situations in his life where his courage
was put to test, and he knew that he was no coward. Yet it made him
tremble to think that very shortly he would accuse Naftali of being a
thief.

Reisman saw at once that Naftali had changed very little. At first
he enviously attributed the Samaritan's youthful looks to a simple,
spartan diet. The archaeologist began to realize that Naftali looked
even younger than himself, although when he had known him during the late forties, he had clearly been Reisman's senior.

As it turned out, Naftali of the magnificent appearance had never married and was living with his sister in a small, whitewashed house. The sister, Leila, was also very tall, dressed in black and could be called handsome except that her cheeks bore traces of smallpox. She spoke only Arabic and, after initial greetings, did not attempt to enter into conversation with the men.

The modest surroundings came as a surprise to Reisman, who had expected to find that Naftali had grown rich.

"How wonderful it is to see you again," said Naftali, his teeth bright in his tanned face.

"I would have come sooner," replied the professor, "only I . . ."

"Wasn't certain that I was still alive," finished the Samaritan. "But then you saw me in the magazine. How marvelous. So you live in England, do you? Once, going to England was my heart's desire, but then . . . things happened."

After a few whiskeys, Naftali turned pensive and tapped his long fingers on the table. They had quite exhausted the subject of their wartime escapades. With the tapping of those fingers, Reisman's heart plummeted into his stomach. It was then that he first noticed the ring.

The object appeared to be large and heavy, made of gold infused with a little iron for rosiness in the manner of Eastern jewelry from Biblical times to the present. It was beyond value. Reisman knew that no modern man owned such a ring unless he had first taken the risk of breaking a glass case in a museum or, as the Samaritan had surely done, taken it from the ancient earth.

The archaeologist knew he had no choice but to ask where the ring had come from, but before he could think of a way of broaching the subject, the Samaritan looked him in the eye and said simply, "I am not long for this world, Little Edward."

"Nonsense," said Reisman. "You look wonderful." No one had, of course, called Reisman by his nickname since the Jerusalem days. It made him feel strangely young and vulnerable to have the Magician use it now.

"Bum ticker, you know," said Naftali, pointing to his chest as if the whole affair were only too tiresome. "My burdens are too heavy for me to bear any longer."

"I can see." Reisman replied. Then, indicating the ring, asked, "What are you going to do about it?"

"What is it, Little Edward?"

"Naftali, I want to be perfectly honest with you. This is not purely a social call. Some months ago in London I had a conversation with a man named Hawkes and his wife, Alma. Do you remember them?"

The Samaritan sighed. "Ah, the Hawkes. But what have you to do with them?"

"Nothing, except that J. W. Hawkes and I are colleagues, fellow archaeologists."

Naftali smiled. "Are you worried about my ring? It's of no consequence—only a cleverly crafted fake."

"Either that or you are," said Reisman. "Who in the devil would invest that much gold in a false artifact? But then you always knew how to get gold, eh, Magician?"

The two men turned their heads at the tinkling sound of Leila's bangles.

"Excuse me. Yousef is here with the brothers."

Naftali tapped his forehead in the gesture of having forgotten something. "The brothers already!" He turned back to Reisman. "Yousef is my cousin, a very sociable fellow, much more than I am, I'm afraid. He often acts as go-between."

"Go-between?"

"Yes. When people wish to see me, they ask him and he makes the arrangements."

While Naftali and "the brothers" wore the traditional Samaritan garb of turban and loose-fitting cotton robe, Yousef wore a pair of baggy trousers and a red plaid shirt, and puffed away on a cigarette. When introduced to Reisman, he gave a sort of "hello sucker" smile, which suggested to Reisman that Yousef was an operator, not above taking a tip for making "arrangements."

All three of the newcomers bowed to Naftali, and Reisman was amazed to see the brothers kiss Naftali's hand.

Naftali shrugged at Reisman.

The formalities having been observed, the brothers began talking excitedly to Naftali simultaneously. When Naftali joined in, it sounded, to Reisman's ears, like a machine-gun burst of Arabic out of which he could make no sense.

"What is the trouble?" he asked Yousef, who was keeping at Reisman's side out of the way.

"Oh, much, much difficulty. Very bad feelings. These men are brothers and they have been quarreling ever since their father died. The family has a lot of sheep. Also some goats. The elder brother believes the herd belongs to him. If his brother wishes to continue to stay on, he must work for hire only, and not expect to share in the profits from the stock. The younger brother disagrees. He says there are too many sheep and goats for one man and that the other brother should give him a few head so that he can begin his own herd. There, do you hear? The older brother has called the younger a communist! He claims his little brother has gotten such ideas because his wife is one of the Samaritans from Holon—you know, the Israeli Samaritans over there on the other side."

"Fascinating," murmured Reisman. "But what has Naftali to do with their problems?"

"He must tell them what to do."

"Why him?"

"Why not?" replied Yousef, flipping his cigarette butt out of the open window.

Naftali had succeeded in calming the parties down.

"I dislike to hear of these troubles between sons of the same father," he said, addressing the men more slowly so that Reisman could now understand without using Yousef as interpreter. "It is unwise for brothers to make bad blood, for in time of disaster, where does a man go for help but to his own brother?" Naftali pointed a finger at the younger of the two. "Why are you arguing? You know that your brother has come into his rightful inheritance as the eldest. Not so much as one lamb belongs to you, as sure as I am a Samaritan."

Yousef winked and elbowed Reisman vigorously in the ribs as if urging him to pay closer attention to some tremendous feat Naftali was about to perform.

"Now then," continued Naftali, "the younger brother can work for the older for wages, if it pleases him, but I do not like this. More arguments, I think." He addressed the older Samaritan. "I shall tell you what you must do. If your brother is a cinder in your eye, pluck out the cinder. Do not give him even one goat. Instead, you shall sell some of the herd and give your brother enough money to start him in his own business. However, it must be another business altogether. No, he shall not be a shepherd. Then he will not be able to say to himself, 'My brother still has more stock than I do because, being the elder, he was more fortunate.' No, he will look to his own merchandise and ever after have no more thought for sheep and goats."

The two brothers glanced at one another. It was evident that they had not given this solution any previous thought.

"Of course," said the elder, slowly, "I have never been known as a stingy man. But how could I allow my brother to take what is lawfully mine? However . . . to set him up in business . . . now that is another matter."

"It is your duty as eldest," the younger brother declared.

"Do not presume to tell me my duty! But, being a generous fellow, it would give me pleasure. Yes, it is my pleasure to finance my little brother in a business of his own! Naturally, I had thought of this plan myself, but, you know, the boy with his socialist ideas . . . Did I think he would go into business?"

"What are you talking about?" cried his brother. He stretched his hands out to Naftali. "What shall I do, my lord? It is all I hear from him—communist, socialist, anarchist! He does not even know the meanings of these words. To tell you the truth, my lord, I spit on business. My family have always been shepherds; we never soiled our hands with merchandise. Still, I will do as you say. My wife, fortunately, comes from a family that knows only commerce. She will run everything and do very well, I promise you."

"Well, thank God," said Naftali. "And let us have no more political talk between you. What has it all got to do with making a livelihood?"

That, apparently, was the end of the interview. The brothers backed out of the house salaaming and bowing. Yousef clapped Reisman on the back and said good-bye to his cousin. Reisman was impressed. He had never seen a problem solved so quickly and neatly. "Does this sort of thing happen often here?" he asked Naftali.

"Several times a week."

"Are you some sort of judge among your people?"

"No need for a judge. But, Little Edward, I believe before we were interrupted, that we were talking about gold."

Reisman sat down. "Will you talk about it? Will you tell me the truth?"

The Samaritan poured a couple more drinks. "Yes. Why should I deceive you, my old friend?"

Reisman leaned forward. "Except that I must warn you that what you are about to tell me may put you in jail. Do you understand that, Naftali?"

Naftali's black eyes shone abnormally. "Little Edward, have you changed so much?"

"I haven't changed a hair."

"Nor have I. Yet you suspect me of being a thief, a grave-robber, something like that, eh?"

"Well, are you?"

"No," said the Samaritan. "The gold belonged to me. It would have belonged to my sons, except that I have no sons. Times have changed, Little Edward. Israel exists once again, but my family line is soon to die out. There is only my poor self, Leila, my sister, who is only a woman and also without a son, and that rascal Yousef, a distant cousin who has seen too many American films." Naftali thought for a moment. "You owe me your life, Little Edward."

Reisman's face colored at this unexpected reminder. It was true, several times over.

"Yes," he said. "That makes this difficult."

"No, it is not a difficulty. You see, in a way, that makes you my son. And as my son, I am permitted to tell you my secret. All my secrets, in fact."

And so he began. "When I made my way back to this place after the war of liberation, my uncles—those I told you of long ago— were overjoyed to see me still alive.

"I explained to them that I had been driven away by the Englishman, Hawkes. Of course, they had guessed as much and told me that the gossip in Nablus had been that my disappearance had had something to do with Hawkes' wife. That solution suited me as well as any, and I neither confirmed nor denied it. After twenty years my alleged love affair had lost its importance, in any case.

"To my astonishment, it turned out that I had returned to my people in glory instead of in disgrace, as I had expected. Stories concerning my wartime adventures had been written up in the newspapers. My family had seen these articles and had clipped them out. They knew that I had to be the so-called Magician and were both delighted and amused that I had been able to trick the British into believing that I was an Arab and on their side.

"I was also informed that my mentor, Professor Hawkes, had quit the area soon after I had gone. I might say that I could hardly blame him. His association with me had been a trying experience for him. I always knew that he never meant to kill me. The poor professor was simply another victim of the ancient curse of the hill—neither the first nor the last.

"When my uncles presented the ring to me, shortly after my return, I was shocked. I thought it was the genuine ring from the cave. They assured me that it was only a copy they had fashioned, but that I should have it for a talisman.

" 'You must know, Naftali,' one of them said, 'that you are the first man in all the centuries since the collapse of the kingdom of Samaria fit to wear a ring such as this one. We Samaritans have grown to be a weak nation and none of us are fighters any longer. But you have the blood of the Old Ones in your veins and their great spirit in your heart. It is a wonderful thing and has given a new hope to our people.'

"At first I did not want to accept the beautiful ring. I confessed to my uncles that I had betrayed their trust by stealing some of the treasure of the kings to help the Jewish cause. And you know, they were glad that I had done it. It pleased them enormously that a little of that long-hidden gold had at last done some good.

"'Besides,' they added, 'it was yours. It was always yours—as surely as you are a Samaritan.'

"Now I must tell you about the rod, the splendid thing that I discovered on Professor Hawkes' excavation during the twenties. Before I disappeared from Nablus, I hid it in the cave with the gold, but it is no longer there. What became of this mysterious rod is a tale. Little Edward, you will think me completely mad when you hear about that rod.

"Once, I had the idea it was the cause of all my misfortune. If it remained in the dark, out of the way, I assumed it would hurt no one. But, of course, I was very much mistaken. It was never the rod but the hill itself that was my enemy. The rod was a very valuable thing. Had I known to whom I should show it, what might not be different today. There you are, Little Edward, the old masters' wealth was nothing but a heap of metal made by people just as ignorant in their ways as we are in ours. But that rod . . . yes, that was the true treasure of the Samaritans. That was worth all the gold on earth."

Naftali emitted a long sigh, a moan perhaps, and Reisman put his hands to his skull and squeezed, trying to absorb what he was being told. The room was hot and full of shadows. The caged bird in the corner had been covered for the night. Naftali's sister had turned off the light in the kitchen and had gone to bed. Reisman felt unutterably weary and a little drunk, but the Samaritan appeared quite fresh and alert, claims to heart trouble notwithstanding. It may have been the poor light, but Reisman thought Naftali looked even more youthful than he had when the evening began. When he removed his turban, black curls barely touched with gray, moistened by the perspiration that had given his remarkably unlined neck a soft sheen, tumbled about his shoulders. As Naftali wiped the perspiration with his turban, the ring seemed to wink at Reisman with the motion.

"Shall we have another, old boy?" Naftali asked with a flash of his enviable teeth. Not only were they still white, none of them were missing. Probably never even had a filling, Reisman thought fleetingly.

"The whiskey's gone," the archaeologist muttered.

"So it is. Well, there's more where that came from."

Naftali took another bottle from the cupboard and lowered himself back into his chair. He glanced at Reisman rather slyly, then grasped the bottle with both hands. Naftali stared at it so intensely that the veins stood out in his forehead. Suddenly the cork popped out of the bottle with a dull report.

"How in the world—"

Naftali laughed. "Magic, old boy, only magic."

Reisman laughed too, not at the trick but at the Samaritan's accent. Despite all his years in England, Reisman had never managed to lose his Mittel-European speech patterns, but Naftali had the sound of an Oxford don. For a man that clever to have remained in a small town like Nablus all these years meant that he must have a damned good reason for doing so.

Naftali leaned forward. "Little Edward," he said, using the only name he had ever called Reisman, "do you believe in other worlds?"

"Is this your way of changing the subject?" Reisman wanted to know.

"That, my friend, is the subject on which I am about to embark. There is even evidence to uphold my testimony. I am sure there still exist old newspapers that report, in part, what took place here on August 15, 1965. I myself read about the sightings in a Jordanian newspaper from Amman. For you see, Little Edward, that night a few persons in Nablus saw something in the sky that could not be explained; but they were better prepared to guess what it was than those who had seen it thousands of years ago had been.

"I myself did not see the object that was described in the papers. I was at home, preparing for bed, when I heard Leila conversing with someone who had come to see us. I thought perhaps that people had come with some dispute for me to settle, and I was ready to ask her to tell them to return in the morning.

"When I looked through the curtains, I saw that there were two very tall men with my sister, but it was not possible that they could be Samaritans. Although they looked like foreigners, dressed in dark business suits and ties, they were speaking Arabic. But Arabs they were not. They could have been Scandinavians or Germans, their coloring was so fair, and they resembled one another closely enough to be twins.

"The strange thing was that Leila does not usually admit unknown persons into the house so readily, but she seemed quite relaxed with the men. When I came into the room, she smiled in a contented way and sat down in a chair.

"I asked them what they wanted. They replied that they wanted to speak with me and that I ought to sit down and be more comfortable. Seeing no reason not to, I complied, thinking at the same time how odd their voices sounded. I looked at my sister near me and saw that her eyes were closed as though she had fallen asleep.

"Ah, to call those twins strangers is an understatement! Their skin was deadly white and their eyes curiously shaped with very large pupils. Their light hair was very long, but they had taken pains to dress most conservatively in new and expensive-looking clothing.

"Yet it was only when I glanced at their shoes that I suspected that something was amiss. There was nothing extraordinary about those shoes except that they were absolutely spotless. The men, you see, had presumably just walked through the dusty streets of Nablus and up the earthen path to this house, yet their shoes had remained as clean as if they had been removed from shoe boxes only seconds before.

" 'You have put my sister to sleep,' I said to them. 'Why is that?'

"'It is necessary,' one of the replied. 'Do not be frightened of us. We have not come to do any harm here.'

"I told them I was not frightened of them, but that *they* looked ill at ease. At that, they glanced at one another and then smiled. Their lips were extremely thin, almost non-existent, and their teeth appeared to be very white and sharp.

"'Where have you come from?' I asked.

"'Far away.'

"'Are you messengers?' I asked them and they nodded simultaneously, evidently much pleased that I was not afraid and seemed to understand their purpose. In the newspaper article I read later, it stated that a guard, seeing their startling vehicle, fired at it with his gun out of terror.

"One of these 'twins' began to stroll about the room, touching and examining everything with great interest. The other, it seemed, wanted only to have a proper look at me and was not shy about his curiosity. I must admit I observed him very closely in return. Despite their unusual faces, the two were not actually ugly or sinister in any way.

"'Are you a real man?' the one nearer to me said.

"'You must know that I am,' I answered him, surprised at such a question.

"'Then why is your light different?'

"'What light?'

"'The light that surrounds you. Every human has this light, but yours is not the same as the others. A great deal of energy emanates from you. Why is this?'

"'I know not what you speak of,' I told him. 'I assure you that I am as much a man as you would appear to be if you deigned to walk on the ground as everyone else does. Why have you come here?'

"'Our master has sent us to talk with you. We have been searching for you a long time.'

"'But why?'

"'You ought to know yourself! You signaled us or, at least, commanded someone else to do so. We did not know your position for a long time, but we calculated it at last.'

"'My position? What position do you mean?'

"'Your position in the galaxy. Your distance from the sun. Yet you are only a man from the green planet, after all. How could you have reached us when no man here has the means by which to do so? This we are not able to understand.'

"'I do not recall contacting you,' I told him, 'nor can I think why I would have wanted to. But I am glad that you have returned, o men from the stars.'

"'Returned?' he echoed. 'We have not been here before.'

"'But you have! Long ago. Do you not know? It is written that you—or others like you—were in this very place.'

"'Where is this written? Where?'

"'Accept my word, it is written and remembered.'

"The twins, or angels, looked at one another for a long time. I think they communicated without speaking, for their expressions changed rapidly.

"Then the angel closest to me did a curious thing. He removed from his pocket a small round object, which immediately lit up in his hand. He spoke to this little ball, but not in Arabic. I had heard this language before, but I understood not a word. After a few moments, he placed the object near his ear, appeared to listen carefully, then restored the ball to his pocket.

"'You spoke the truth,' he informed me. 'The machines have told it; they remember all. We have, indeed, been here before but were resolved never to return because the inhabitants of this place were an altogether unworthy and unintelligent species. We even experimented with interbreeding with you to improve your race, but it was of little use. The negative outweighed the positive and nothing was achieved.'

"'Tell me,' I said, an idea coming to me, 'what are you called in your own tongue?'

"'I am a *maloch*, a messenger, as you guessed.'

"'Then there is no question that you were here before, for your very name, *maloch*, is still used today by our people to describe ones such as yourselves. You are the *malochim*.'

"The angel shook his head in wonder. 'How is it you recall these things? You are a very primitive people and have no way of—'

"'We are fond of remembering,' I interrupted him. 'I think, too, that your blood did have some effect. Some of the people who came from here became great intellects. One of them, a man called Einstein, devised a theory about the universe that enabled others to invent a way to destroy the earth in less . . . in a very brief . . .'

"The man from the stars made a knowing face. 'I was right. It was futile. Of what use is that—to destroy yourselves? Nothing but evil. Listen to me, man with the bright light, I have questioned others in this area. You are the master of this place. If you did not contact us, who did? The signal was as clear as from our own instruments. This is a matter of great interest, otherwise we would not have troubled to come. It is a simple matter for our kind to journey here, but we do not like what we see. When our business is done, we will quickly depart. What has sprung up on your world is a dreadful thing to behold, an abomination to all intelligent beings.'

"'You are right,' I agreed. He seemed overwhelmed to hear me say it.

"'You know this?'

"'Yes, it is known. Yet there is much good here.'

"'Where is it to be found?'

"'If you were not so afraid,' I told the twins, 'and did not plan to depart so quickly, you would find there is good.'

"Then I described the object I had found on the hill more than thirty years before. The angel knew at once what I was speaking of.

"In the corner of the room, the silent messenger had discovered a music box and, having known enough to wind the spring, was now listening to its tinkling sound, holding it away from him as though it might momentarily explode.

"'You came upon a very old thing,' said the stranger I had been speaking to. 'No longer in use. But it is ours. It must have been left here; of that I am certain. You must give it back. It is of no use to your people at all.'

"'Then why do you want it back?'

"The angel gave me an impatient look. No doubt he thought me merely another crafty and ill-intentioned human. 'You must give it back,' he repeated. 'It is of no use.'

"'I expect it is. That is, if one were to discover its uses.'

"'And who will discover those uses? The ones who found the means to destroy their own planet? Never! Give it back I tell you, for your own good. Do not trifle with this thing.'

"'Can you force me to return it?' I asked of him.

"'Yes!' he answered emphatically. Then he was silent a moment and said more softly, 'No.'

"I smiled at him. 'Ah, you cannot put me to sleep like my sister, nor get information from me in the same way you did the others in Nablus.'

"He shook his head. 'No. You are very strong.'

"'Nor, I think, will you use violence against me, for that would make you as barbarous as the inhabitants of our planet. It is unnecessary, in any event. I will give you back your rod, your instrument, but will you grant me a favor?'

"The other angel came over, still holding the music box. He was obviously now enchanted with it.

"'I know not what this means,' said the first angel, his apparent superior.

"'I mean to say—do you have the power to help me?'

"'What do you want of us?' he asked coldly.

"'I ask that you restore the kingdom of my people just as you found it in ancient times,' I said, 'and protect it from now on from all enemies. If it grows evil beyond your tolerance, you may abandon it again. But if good remains, you must watch over it, as do those of my people who are still alive. You see, our vigil has been too long, and we have barely survived it. Can you give us back our land, which is now ruled by others, while we are still here to witness it?'

"'Why should we meddle in this petty thing?' the angel said, looking at his comrade.

"I did not know how to reply to him. Perhaps he did see it as insignificant and not worthy of any bother.

"'Out of pity,' I finally said. 'From compassion. And because you have intervened before. I know. That is written too.'

"'Is it?' said the angel, not disinterested. 'If so, it must have been very long ago.'

"'Yes, very.'

"'There was one time,' he said, carefully, 'not so long ago, when the evil . . . not here in this place, but on your planet . . . were horrors never before seen. Never, I tell you. Some of us thought that perhaps your entire world had gone mad, and a few of us even proposed to putting an end to it. But our master, the Lord of the Universe, would not agree to it, and after a time, we elected simply to let you destroy one another, as we knew you surely would.'

"'You should have done something,' I told him, 'something to help.'

"'Perhaps,' he admitted, surprisingly enough. 'Some of us suggested that, too. But no one knew what to do. Nevertheless, our master then sent two other messengers to a place . . . I cannot think of its name. A place so beautiful the messengers could scarcely believe their eyes when they witnessed the horrors committed amid the splendid foliage. Yes, this place where you live cannot compare with those lands—flat, rockless fields with the wheat moving in a slow wind. The messengers said that one would have thought it the most peaceful spot in the universe. They were quite taken with it at the start.'

"'Poland,' said the previously silent angel with the music box, simply. 'It was called Poland.'

"'Yes, Poland. It was terrible. There was a place where the messengers saw so much death and suffering that they could not take in the enormity of it. Huge numbers of little children were slain and burnt to ashes each day. I joined the messengers our master had sent.

We were so grieved by the sight that we decided to go to these wretched humans and ask them how we might help to halt the killing of their little ones. We quickly learned their language, as we have learned yours. In order not to frighten the poor people, we dressed in their native garments and asked them what might be done. We told them we were a peaceful race and detested violence, but that we were willing to fight for them if necessary. These people needed only to point out their enemies, all of them, and we would punish them for their dreadful deeds. And do you know what those poor foolish men did? They laughed at our messengers and made great sport of them. They laughed at their clothing and at the color of their hair. Some, admittedly, did not laugh, but they were afraid of our intentions and ran away to hide. But most of the others thought it a wonderful joke and never left off laughing until the messengers went away, despairing of them.'

"I stared at the angel as one transfixed, but I managed to say despite the fact that I felt I was about to weep, 'These messengers—were they tall beings like yourselves with yellow hair? Did they put on striped clothing with yellow star badges?'

"'Yes! Exactly so.'

"'Small wonder that they laughed, even despite their pain,' I told him, 'They mistook your messengers for their own captors, many of whom were pale, tall men with fair hair. Yes, it was both a great joke and a great misfortune . . . Yet you are a good race, God be thanked. Now go and tell your master that the time has come to intervene on behalf of the House of Israel, as in olden times. But depend on your own understanding and do not ask the guidance of men.'

"And so I took them to the cave that night and gave them their magical rod, and then a wonderful thing happened in that cave. The messengers, the angels, saw the gold, and ignored it. That was a marvelous moment. They cared nothing for the treasure—they neither admired it nor coveted it. They were the first to come to Samaria only wanting what was rightfully their own. That is not quite true. They did want something more, and they asked for it most politely: the music box, a simple, charming toy. That was all."

Reisman's head was throbbing. He downed his refilled glass with one gulp, took off his glasses and wiped them slowly with his handkerchief.

"I have never told this to anyone," said the Samaritan, "nor should I have told you, perhaps. I can see that you do not believe me."

Reisman placed his palms upward in the age-old Jewish gesture of resignation. "Tonight I can believe anything. But *I* am not a creature from outer space, and caves filled with ancient treasure interest *me* enormously. So does the idea of a so-called man of science trying to kill a young native boy. What is the truth about Hawkes??"

"He saw me with the rod. I tried to show it to him, but the strange thing frightened the professor and his wife. They thought it had something to do with me." Naftali pulled his djellabah up to his chest. He lifted his arm, exposing an ugly mass of scar tissue that looked to Reisman as if it had only formed recently, it was still so purplish. Naftali talked nonchalantly about the hole that Hawkes had put into his side, but Edward's father had been a physician and had taught his son something of anatomy. Reisman found it astonishing that the Samaritan was still alive. Normally, a bullet in that area would pierce a lung and perhaps other vital organs, with death quickly ensuing. He had personally seen bullet wounds on the living and the dead during his days with the Irgun, but Naftali's injury looked different. In his head Reisman could hear his father saying in Polish, 'Trauma from a pointed object.'

"Damned thing never healed properly," said Naftali. "Looks like bloody hell."

"You probably never had it properly attended to. You simply ran away, didn't you, wound and all."

"Yes. When I returned, I learned that Hawkes claimed I had stolen something from the dig. Stolen! I would have done anything for the Hawkes. I wanted to go to England, remember? I wanted to become an archaeologist, a modern man with a love for the past. But I was destined to become something else."

"Until he met me, Hawkes thought you were dead," Reisman told Naftali, but his friend just stared at something across the room. Evidently the Samaritan had nothing more to say concerning the perfidy of his former sponsor.

"Naftali," began Reisman, "about the gold—the so-called treasure. Is it of any great significance?"

"Tutankhamen's tomb would have looked a pauper's grave in comparison."

"Who exactly was this treasure buried with?"

The Samaritan held out the hand with the ring. "Here. You can read it, can't you?"

Reisman adjusted his glasses and peered at the gleaming object. Sweat broke out all over his body. "AHAB MELECH ISRAEL," he whispered hoarsely. "Ahab the King of Israel . . . My God, Naftali—this is your secret? How can you call yourself a modern man? You must have known that such a tomb would have been the find of the century! The husband of Jezebel. I can't believe it! Why in God's holy name—"

Reisman mopped his face. He actually felt ill, on the verge of vomiting. He was about the ask the Samaritan how he could have kept from reporting such a marvelous thing to the world when suddenly it all seemed clear. He was sitting across the table from the man who considered himself the heir of the ruler whose signet ring he wore. What's more, Naftali was not alone in this delusion; Reisman had seen the evidence just an hour ago. How in the world had Naftali managed to convince the Samaritans that he was their rightful king? Certainly, it had to be a lot of rot. It was impossible for a dynasty to survive—in anonymity yet—for nearly 3,000 years. Rubbish! One might as well believe there was still a Romanov czar somewhere.

"Naftali, you must give it up. This is the twentieth century. What you and your family have been hoarding for so long rightfully belongs in a museum for everyone to admire—in an Israeli museum. There are international laws now; nobody can simply come and take away the treasures of another nation. Those days are over, at least among the peoples of the civilized world. If there's anything left of that tomb, you must show it to me. Together, somehow, we can think of a way—"

"To keep me out of jail?" finished the Samaritan.

"Well, yes! Do you think I want you arrested?"

"I know what you want," said Naftali. "Pretty things on display in tidy museums for ignorant people to ogle."

"How little you understand," Reisman argued. "I want to know more about *them!* The gold has nothing to do with it. I want to see the cup Ahab drank from, his worn-out sandals, letters he received. I want him to be real, not just a character in an absorbing tale. I want to see Jezebel's earbobs, the stuff she used to paint her eyes, a lock of her . . ."

A muscle twitched in Naftali's cheek. "What?" he said, in a puzzled sort of way.

"Jezebel, Queen Jezebel, man! Don't tell me you don't know her."

"Eesabel," the Samaritan murmured, giving the name its correct pronunciation. "You mean Eesabel."

"Yes," breathed Reisman, hardly daring to go on. "Was there anything . . . have you seen something that might have belonged to her?"

"No!" Naftali snapped indignantly as Edward drew back, startled. "How could such a thing be? Do you suppose they would have buried her, the dreadful foreign woman, with *him?*"

"Why not?" asked Reisman with a soft chuckle. "They were both reprobates. A perfect match."

Naftali glowered at him. "How do you know this? From a story in a book, eh? What do you know of the king's troubles from a distance of thousands of years? It was all her doing, I tell you! He was not to blame. He was a decent man, he . . ."

This time Reisman laughed aloud. "What? Ahab?"

Naftali slammed his glass on the table. "He did his duty!"

"All right," said Reisman. "All right."

"Archaeologists!" Naftali got up and went to the window as if to draw in a breath of fresh air. He stared out into the night.

What is he looking at, Reisman wondered. Is he expecting another shipload of aliens?

But the Samaritan remarked quietly, "J. W. Hawkes was full of theories, too. The ancients lived this way, did things that way, must have done, could have been. Mostly nonsense! The simplest Arab on the dig could have set him straight on what the ancients were like because when I was a boy, life here was no different from a dozen centuries before. But Hawkes couldn't see it. To him, we—the Arabs and Samaritans—were the primitives and our ancestors the civilized ones. Hawkes would have agreed with you about Ahab. He too knew all about him. But Naftali knows more."

"I daresay," replied Reisman with some archness of his own. "You've had the privilege of touching his property. Perhaps had you allowed poor old Hawkes a peek at it, he might have changed his infamous theories to coincide with your own."

"I have no theories," said Naftali, unruffled this time. "I have seen the face of Ahab and this is how I judge him. What a turn that death mask, with its sorrowful nobility, would have given Professor Hawkes, and you too, come to think of it."

"Then show it to me, by all that's holy!"

Naftali turned back to look at Reisman. "It's too late, Little Edward."

Reisman sprang up with a dexterity no one would have imagined he possessed and grabbed the Samaritan by the neck-opening of his robe. "What does that mean? I haven't come all this way to play games with you. What have you done?"

Naftali extricated himself gently. "How violent you are. I would have thought you'd given that up by now. I, myself, once enjoyed a bit of fighting, but now I abhor all violence. That's what I mean by too late—too late for the peoples of the civilized world. Thanks to a not-so-civilized war that was fought here recently, even I cannot show you the cave now. It was blown up, Little Edward, blown up in the fighting. A rocket or something, I don't know. A direct hit. A ton of rock and earth has obliterated everything and has probably crushed the wealth of the old masters of the hill."

"But you know where the site is, Naftali! You could still show the experts where to dig!"

"Not I," said the Samaritan. "That I can never do."

"For pity's sake, what are you afraid of, man? Some ancient curse? You call yourself my friend, tell me the story every archaeologist wants to hear, and then refuse to help me do what you must know is the proper thing. What's the matter with you, can you please tell me that?"

"No," said Naftali, putting his hand on Reisman's arm. "I cannot tell you what is the matter with me. I don't know, myself. Or perhaps I do and cannot accept it. Little Edward, if you wish to search for the treasure, you must do it without me. Maybe luck will be on your side. As your friend, I wish you well. But," and at this he stood rigidly, "Naftali ben Yoram has a covenant with the dead, and he cannot betray them."

Reisman groaned and put his head in his hands. He sank back into his chair, rubbing his temples.

"What can I say to you?" he nearly sobbed. "Damn it all to hell! I can see that you'll never change your mind. That's why you people, you Samaritans, are still here. Because you don't change."

Naftali helped the archaeologist to his feet. "Come now. You need to rest. Your bed is ready for you."

"Never change, never change," repeated Reisman in the voice of a man who has stumbled on a theory so mind-boggling that he must say it out loud many times before he can credit it, himself.

"There's a good fellow. Here we go." Naftali's bedroom, which Reisman was to share, was clean and sparsely furnished, like the sleeping quarters of a monk. Above the Samaritan's bed, like an icon, hung a portrait of Moshe Dayan, complete with eyepatch. Reisman wanted to laugh but he was too weary. He murmured a goodnight to his friend and lay down on the cot Naftali's sister had provided, but even though he guessed that he had drunk enough to put him out for two days, sleep eluded Edward Reisman.

In his youth, Reisman had been impressed with the Magician to the point of hero worship. Now he realized he had never known the man. A few feet away, Naftali stirred in his own bed. Was he able to calmly sleep after what he had divulged? Indeed, was the fellow sane or mad? Were his fantastic stories just imaginative lies, or could so many incredible things actually have happened to one man? Reisman had no idea. There was no way for him to judge the truth. Perhaps there had never been a treasure at all. After all, of what value was the word of a person who claimed to have spoken with extraterrestrial beings? The story about the cave having been blown up seemed a shade too convenient. Reisman could imagine himself going back to England and asking the university to sponsor an excavation on the strength of the evidence he had heard from Naftali—they would think *him* mad as well! In this way did Reisman attempt to dissuade himself of the Samaritan's credibility. But the more he discounted it, the more convinced he became that the mysterious Naftali had never been a liar in his life. He even grew ashamed of the manner in which he had invaded the Samaritan's privacy, armed with suspicions and accusations, ready to turn the place upside down because of an old man's self-serving tale and something glittering he had seen long ago.

Through the piece of cheesecloth that was nailed over the open window against bugs, Edward Reisman watched the stars glow with a clarity he remembered but hadn't noticed anywhere since he'd left Israel twenty years ago. Squinting in the dark, he could make out the features of the Samaritan, his proud nose like the beautifully carved prow of some weathered vessel. In his sleep, Naftali no longer appeared youthful but looked more like the old man he surely must be. Reisman, too, felt old—he blamed the whiskey, but when he glanced at the stars again, they were blurred. His tears were not for some treasure that might exist but that he would never see. No, the lost years of his youth were bore down on him, all that time wasted in places where terror and unspeakable acts were the daily bill of fare. The highlight of that youth had been his arrival in the Promised Land and his association with the Magician. And now the courageous Magician had lost his youth too, although his inner vitality and charm seemed to create the illusion of it when he chose. Perhaps he did it by magic.

As though tuned in to Reisman's thoughts, Naftali suddenly rose up, took something from his bedstand and appeared to place it in his mouth. Was it a pill, something to do with the heart condition he had mentioned?

"Are you all right, Naftali?" Reisman asked.

"Still awake, Little Edward? Brooding, no doubt. Look on the bright side, can't you? I'm sure that you have a perfectly lovely wife and marvelous children. Go home to them and let them be your consolation. I would if I were you, you know. Oh, yes. But I have not been fortunate, not a bit."

"Some would give a great deal to see what you have seen."

"Ah, the gold again! Keep in mind that, had you seen it, it might have consumed your life."

Even in his fuzzy-minded state, Reisman knew that Naftali was right. Surely, having discovered King Tut's treasure, Howard Carter's remaining years must have been one long anticlimax. How odd that he had never before viewed it that way.

"Go to sleep," the Samaritan advised. "You have seen more than you know."

"Tomorrow I'm counting on you to take me sight-seeing," said Reisman. "Don't worry. I'll play the ignorant tourist. All your secrets are safe with me. Let's get some rest."

"Let them rest who are able," said the Samaritan, but he lowered his head.

Eventually, during the course of that night in Nablus, Edward Reisman dreamed. He was taken back to a kibbutz in the year 1947 where there was music and dancing. Naftali was there too, the instant center of attention. The music and gaiety gave way to a silence that was brief, perhaps only the fraction of a second, but it was not to be missed. In the eyes of the people at that party, Edward saw once again the look he had noticed years before, but now he knew it for what it truly was. It was the momentary collective sighting of a ghost, not a frightening specter, but someone who was alien but somehow hauntingly familiar, the memory of whom was locked away in some sort of genetic file, a racial recollection that had been treasured for as long as a pile of golden objects had rested beneath the earth.

The Last of Rafaela

N O TEARS, DEAREST QUEEN," said Apollodorus the Sicilian to a sniffling Cleopatra. "They stab your servant to the heart. He will return some day."

"I hope not," intoned the Serpent of the Nile while leering at the audience, which responded with scattered cackles. Rosamund Peters left something to be desired in an actress, but she was an undisputed stunner in her scanty, transparent costumes. "But I can't help crying, all the same." Rosamund whipped what looked like a white handkerchief out of her cleavage and dabbed at her false lashes.

Backstage, John Drummer, the director, gnashed his teeth. He had expressly forbidden Rosamund to carry a handkerchief, claiming his research of the ancient Egyptian lifestyle had failed to uncover mention of this article. Actually, Drummer's intuition had warned him that the damned girl would be tempted to use it as a prop for some damaging bit of business. On this last night, however, it seemed Rosamund was determined to have her way.

"Don't do it, Rosie, you little bitch," the director pleaded to himself.

Yet there it was—a distinct burlesque honk as the Queen of Egypt held the hanky to her delicate nose. She then unfurled it and waved broadly, her gesture more in keeping with surrender than valediction. The audience laughed.

Two Roman soldiers drew their swords and presented them to the departing conqueror standing on the "deck" of his one-dimensional ship.

"'Ail Caesar!" they cried.

Byron Clement, the only well-known actor in the show, dutifully held up his hand and smiled at his fellow thespians as the curtain came down. When it came time to take bows, Clement received by far the heartiest applause. His Julius Caesar had been the quintessence of world-weary charm. Actually, Clement had simply played the part using his normal approach to life. By and large, his most successful roles had been those for which he had done no conscious acting but had behaved like Byron Clement the everyday man. Every critic in London had given him highest marks, but none had much liked this production of *Caesar and Cleopatra* otherwise. Some felt Shaw was becoming dated, but most blamed Rosamund Peters, "the Cleopatra who sank her own barge," as one wag put it. No sparks were generated between her and Clement, and their collaboration, if it could be called that, had run only six weeks.

In fact, Cleopatra was now on the run to her dressing room with John Drummer giving chase. She pushed past Clement, nearly cracking his papier-mâché breastplate. Clement wisely ducked out of Drummer's way as the latter caught the young actress by her asp-encircled arm.

"Ruddy cow!" snarled the director. "You've managed to sabotage even closing night. You played the whole evening like an escapee from a chorus line. And why, in God's name, did you have to blow your nose like that? It sounded like a bloody trumpet blast!"

Rosamund wrenched herself free of Drummer's grasp, only to have him pursue her into the dressing room before she was able to slam the door in his face. Even Clement followed and stood in the open doorway. He was joined by Rex Quigley, the company's Apollodorus, a good-looking youngster, over six feet tall, whose abbreviated tunic exposed a pair of extremely hairy legs.

Clement, whose large black eyes were usually full of mischief, was himself only of medium height. He was an impressive man, nonetheless, with a rosy complexion that still showed a minimum of wrinkles and sags despite his sixty years. Once Clement had been considered one of the most handsome men in England.

Miss Peters snatched off her wig and tossed it on a chair. "It got a laugh, didn't it? I thought this stupid play was supposed to be comedy."

"Stand by," Clement said to Quigley. "We may be needed to prevent an actresscide."

Drummer clutched at his sparse beard, perhaps only to keep his hands off Rosamund's throat.

"A comedy, not a farce! Which is what you've made it for six weeks. I wish Shaw himself were here to tell you how fucking awful you've been."

"He hates me," Rosamund pointed out unnecessarily to the men at the door. "He told me I couldn't have a sodding handkerchief when Shaw wrote one in right at the end. 'She waves her handkerchief to Caesar,' it says. I'll wager Drummer didn't even read the whole play."

Rosamund plopped down, brimming with self-righteous indignation, and slathered cold cream onto her face. Having thought of something more to say, she turned on the men, a smeared painting spouting cockney, which she frequently lapsed into when offstage.

"Here," she said, "I'll tell you what's really wrong with this croaking play—no sex, that's what! I mean, not even a lousy peck on the chops between Caesar and Cleopatra. Clement here told me those two had a kid together. How could that happen if he don't even kiss her in four bleedin' acts and then just ups and leaves, I'd like to know? Why didn't you think of that, Mr. John Bloody Drummer, eh? That's why this show is closing—it's all talk. People don't pay good money to watch a history lesson with no love scenes. I'll bet you George B. Shaw was no more than an old faggot, hisself. Ask Clement there. He knew him!"

Clement's eyebrows flew upward. The venerated playwright had once been pointed out to him years ago, but he had never actually met Shaw.

"Not true," he drawled, "but I once acted with Garrick at the Old Globe before it burned down."

"Well, it shows!" the actress declared. "You're the best damned actor I've ever seen." She drew a bead on Drummer. "Why don't you ask him what he thinks? He's been around, hasn't he? He's even been seen on the telly. Come on, Ducks, tell old fuzzy face here you wouldn't have minded giving me a little nip or two for the sake of the play."

"My dear, I would have been delighted," laughed Byron Clement. "By George, Drummer, the girl's got a point. In this, her wisdom exceeds that of Shaw."

"How dare you try to get him on your side," Drummer hissed at his nemesis. "Isn't it enough you've got the producer kissing your arse? Don't you know you've done Clement out of a job, out of a part he was born to play? You and you alone have shut down this play—make no mistake about it!"

"Easy, old man," said Clement. "The audience liked her well enough."

"All the tit-fanciers, certainly! The only thing she projects beyond the footlights is her nipples."

"He don't like tits, see," rejoined Rosamund, "because he don't like girls."

"She needs killing," said Drummer. "Badly. And I need a drink. If anyone wants me, I'll be at the Four Swans."

The director stalked out. Clement and Quigley also took embarrassed leave of the fiery Rosamund as she threatened to strip bare before their very eyes.

"Well, that's that," muttered Clement. "Time to pack up and go home."

The days were gone when Byron Clement had a dressing room of his own. He had shared this one with Quigley, which he hadn't minded in the least. The lad was a good sort and usually talked football instead of theater. But tonight Quigley was in a post-mortem mood.

"I say, Clement, what do you think?" Rex piped up as they began to remove their Roman trappings. "Was I right or wrong in telling Drummer that Apollodorus ought to be played like a queer? You know, with a lisp and all. Drummer, of course, wanted him done straight, a romantic fool who has half an eye on the queen. But, I ask you, who but a flaming queer would have carried on like this Apollodorus chap?"

Clement gave Quigley a long look, finding it hard to imagine the boy camping it. "Too late now, I'd say."

"Too bloody right," said Quigley emphatically. "It might have done something for the play, actually. Faggots seem to go over well these days. Every show's got at least one written in."

Quigley rubbed off his makeup with a rough towel and began washing his face. "Listen," he burbled, "I'm going over to the Swans to argue with Drummer for a while. Nothing bucks him up like a good squabble."

"I thought John was very cruel to Rosamund," Clement said.

"Peters is a cunt."

"Is she? I wonder."

"I don't. She's a merciless scene-stealer. Tonight she stepped on all my lines. Are you coming with me or what?"

"No, I think I'll toddle on home. At my age, closings tend to be depressing as hell."

"Well, I'll be off, then," said young Rex, extending his hand. "I hope to work with you again one day. You were a better Caesar than old Julius himself. Even when I was a kid I liked your films, especially the war ones. So long, Clement."

Clement wished Quigley farewell and echoed the sentiment about working together in the future. Nice fellow, Quigley. He didn't imagine many young people recalled his old movies, which in most cases was just as well.

Clement had just begun to peel off his Roman wig when there came a knock at the door. Probably the actors who played Rufio and Britannus wanting to urge him on to the Four Swans.

"Come in," Clement invited with a heartiness he did not feel.

The mirror before him showed none other than Rosamund Peters in blue jeans and jumper. She sat down wearily and began massaging her bare toes. Devoid of makeup and bristling eyelashes, she now looked more properly the teenage queen she had been attempting to portray for six inglorious weeks. Outside of rehearsals and the actual performances, this little Cleo of his had never been known to waste a word on him. Now suddenly she seemed to want to chat him up.

"Going out?" asked Rosamund.

"Going home to bed."

"Me too. Look here, Mr. Clement, I'll come right out with it. I know you never liked me much."

"Who says so?"

"Still, you've always been nice to me. Just you. Why?"

"Oh, I don't know. Perhaps you remind me of my old mum."

The girl sighed. "That old lady in pants, Drummer, is right. I was the worst Cleopatra in the history of the English stage."

"You're young," said Clement kindly. "You can learn. I thought you showed some comic talent and were a highly decorative presence for sure."

Rosamund laughed softly. "You're a real gentleman, you know that? Not like some in this sodding theater. I like your real hair. It's kind of cute. The thing is, sir, I've come to ask a favor of you."

"Hmm?" said Clement, hardly daring to wonder what it might be.

"Now that the play is done with, I've been asked to a weekend in the country. At Lord St. Giles' place, actually."

"Really?" was Clement's comment. Lord St. Giles was the producer of *Caesar and Cleopatra*. It was he who had wanted Rosamund cast in her role over Drummer's objections. No doubt the girl was St. Giles' cup of tea. Unfortunately, G. B. Shaw had never written a part for a creature blessed with physical qualities alone.

"There's going to be a Hollywood bloke there who's interested in me for a flick," Rosamund went on. "Only I can't bear to show up by myself."

"Why in heaven's name not?"

"I'm scared," the girl admitted. "I'll have to talk posh the whole time. It's hard enough to do it for a few hours on stage, but for an entire weekend—no bloody way! The invitation said I could bring a guest. If you went with me—as my date, so to speak—you could do most of the talking. Nobody talks nicer than you, not even a blinking lord. Will you do it, then?"

Clement couldn't help smiling. What a child the girl was to believe that talking "posh" would lead anyone to mistake her for a woman of refinement.

"My dear, what nonsense! An old man like me for an escort—I'd only be in your way. If you go alone, you might meet some well-heeled young eligible in that crowd, perhaps even the chap from America—who knows? Anyway, Americans don't talk posh."

"But they expect the British to!" wailed Rosamund.

"Oh, I don't know—Michael Caine did all right, didn't he?"

"Michael Caine is a good actor," Rosamund noted dourly.

Clement saw her point. "Rosamund," he said, "did it ever occur to you that I might have been asked to that party myself—on my own, that is?"

"Of course you were. I never said you weren't. Then I suppose you've got someone lined up to go with."

"As a matter of fact, I don't."

"Good," said Rosamund brightly. "Then there really is no reason why we can't go together, is there? I'll be on my best behavior. I won't disgrace you or anything."

"I'm not afraid of that, my dear," said Clement. "Oh—why not? I'll be glad to take you. Only we'll have to take the train. I haven't a car."

"We can rent one," suggested Rosamund, visibly relieved. "I'll even drive. I'm one hell of a driver, actually."

"I shouldn't be surprised," said Byron Clement. "Very well, Rosamund, we'll rent a lovely car and arrive in style. Now pop off and let me get changed. Call me tomorrow at home and we'll work out the details."

"No," said Rosamund. "You can ring me like a proper date. It's bad enough I had to beg you to go with me. Now that it's settled, you've got to do the ringing up."

Clement sighed. "Oh, very well. What's your phone number?"

Rosamund seized Clement's eye pencil and scrawled the number on the mirror. "There you are, my lovely lad," she chirped, apparently no longer thinking it necessary to call him "sir" now that they had paired off for the party.

"Thank you, Rosamund. Now both the sweeper and I have your number. Good night."

The girl was about to leave, but then hesitated. "I'm sorry, Clement."

"Oh, I'll wipe it off!" said the actor good-naturedly.

"No, I mean about the play. You were tremendously good in your part—so good that I felt like an awkward dolt every time we had a scene together. Any road, Drummer said—"

"Never you mind what Drummer said. You just go on home and get some rest. Take the advice of an old trouper: When you get bad notices or a play shuts down, you simply forget it—don't think about it. It's the only way, believe me."

"Well, it certainly wasn't *your* fault that matters turned out the way they did. Perhaps I can make it up to you one day."

On that promissory note, Rosamund Peters left Clement about his business.

True to her word, Rosamund proved herself a devil behind the wheel. Clement couldn't recall when he'd been so nervous as a passenger. The girl talked his ear off, as well, but she had turned herself out very prettily, smelled divine and had the grace to not flirt with him just because they were members of the opposite sex alone in a car. Somehow, during this motor trip, Byron Clement managed to accustom himself to Miss Rosamund Peters and he began to think of her as verging on human. He felt he now knew everything that had happened to her, good or bad, in her young life. She had been raised by her mother, her father having died when she was young. She had hated school and had always dreamed of being in the movies. En route to this goal, Rosamund had managed to land some small stage roles, but supported herself by being a magazine model, not surprising considering the good looks of this ravishing green-eyed redhead.

Rosamund told Clement she was sure she would have enjoyed his movies had she seen any of them, which she was unable to recall ever having done. Clement assured her that she had probably watched him on the telly, but that he would have looked too young for her to recognize him now.

"I wonder," said Rosamund, "if you were as kind then as you are now."

"Men seldom are kind in their youth."

"What about women?"

"Oh, they only grow worse."

"Is that why you never remarried?" (Clement had told Rosamund that his wife, Sylvia, had died two years ago.)

"I probably shall one day. I fancy I'm the hearth-and-slippers type —or will be any day now."

"Well," the girl took her eyes off the road and gave him an apprais-ing look, "you'd better not wait too long."

Clement looked back. "Now suppose you tell me the real reason you want me to escort you to this gathering. I'm not so green as I'm cabbage-looking, you know."

"I need a date, but it can't be anybody young. I don't want St. Giles to get jealous, but I don't want his wife to become suspicious and chuck me out, either."

"Aha! So now I've become what is known as a beard, a decoy. Odd role at my age, I must say. Are you in love with St. Giles? He's old enough to be your father."

"Don't go passing judgment," said Rosamund. "You're older than he is and nobody'd be ashamed to be seen with you." Rosa-mund tossed her head. "Of course I love him. Being a peer of the realm has nothing to do with it. He's close to getting divorced, and my guess is that this weekend should clinch it. His wife'll be there and so will I and Alec will be comparing us the whole time."

"A contest you can hardly lose, eh?" observed the actor. "Have you ever met Lady St. Giles?"

"No. Have you?"

"Society is not my milieu."

"Well, it could be mine. I rather fancy having a great house in the country to give parties in."

"Parties aside, the country can be awfully dull if you're city-bred," Clement reminded Rosamund. "Well, this is nice! I'm bringing you to a weekend bash so you can steal the hostess's hus-band. Poor lady. I feel I'm doing a bad turn to someone who's done me no harm."

"Don't talk rubbish, Clement," scoffed Miss Peters. "You were going anyway. Besides, Alec told me that Lady St. Giles wanted you to come especially. It seems you're her favorite actor."

"Am I? That makes it even worse. I don't recall Lady St. Giles ever coming to see the play. Did she?"

"Alec's wife hasn't gone anywhere for ages. She had a nervous collapse—something like that. Simply stays in the country and vegetates."

Clement groaned. "Wonderful. Rosamund, I hope you know what you're doing. As for me, I'm becoming terribly depressed."

"Don't be so dramatic."

"What else is an actor good for?" murmured Clement, staring out the side window. Rural England whizzed by. How fast was she going?

"Carry on all you like," Rosamund told him. "You don't fool me one bit. Look at you, past your prime, as it were, and still handsome. My guess is, you looked a rare treat in your day and used to lay them out what glanced your way. Don't tell me in all that time you were never unfaithful to your wife because I wouldn't believe it."

"You'd do well not to believe it," replied Clement quietly.

"I thought so!" said the girl triumphantly. "You're all alike. But it's nothing to me, I'll have you know. My mum never raised me to expect men to be angels. I don't blame myself Alec's marriage is dead because I didn't kill it. It's not my fault Alec doesn't love his old lady. What's more, she doesn't care for him either."

"According to him."

"Well, he bleeding ought to know, hadn't he?"

Clement had to concede there was some logic in this.

"When I was your age, I thought love was simple—you know, cut and dried, black or white. Later on, I found out that love is possibly the most complicated matter on earth." Clement studied Rosamund's profile. "You know, you rather remind me of someone I once . . . never mind. It's all too long ago."

"So I'm your type, am I?" said the girl, falling into good humor once again. "You're rather dishy yourself. Knock a few years off you and I would have had a bit of a job choosing between you and St. Giles."

"I've a feeling money would have carried the day," said the actor.

"You don't know everything," Rosamund replied. "Old school tie you've got round your neck there, is it?" she said, joking.

"Harrow."

"You mean you really went there?"

"Of course. Why would I be wearing the tie otherwise?"

"'Cause it looks smashing with your blue blazer, I suppose. How come if your old dad had the lolly to send you to Harrow you became an actor?"

"It was an unfortunate accident. You know, you really are a terrible girl," said Clement, but he was smiling.

"Look, there's the turn-off," said Rosamund. "We'll see the house soon if I'm not mistaken. Crikey, I bet I look a mess."

"You look fit to eat," answered Clement. "Or fit to kill."

Rosamund took the car down a bumpy little road. As usually happens with manor houses in the middle of nowhere, the St. Giles mansion suddenly popped into view, a huge, lone edifice sprouting tall Elizabethan chimneys, and surrounded by endless fields.

"Last night I dreamt I went to Manderly again," quipped Clement with a glance at the driver, who, not being literary-minded, failed to see the jest.

"Good God, it's a palace!" cried Rosamund. "Clement, I'm scared. Suddenly I've got stage fright."

Rosamund guided the car toward the parking area near what was once a carriage house. She switched off the engine and smoothed her hair, rather shakily, Clement thought. Rosamund gave Clement a weak version of her sardonic little smirk.

"I suppose you're going to turn traitor and desert me now. Just as well. Even you're not a convincing enough actor to pretend to be my admirer."

"Perhaps I do admire you in a way," Clement said. "You know what you want and don't hesitate to go after it. You've got nerve, I'll say that for you. Come on, let's get our things."

Clement took their bags out of the boot. He handed Rosamund her case, although he was fairly sure she expected him to carry it. Then something overhead caught his eye. In one of the upper story windows, he noticed the figure of a woman looking down at them. Clement's eyesight was good, but he squinted in disbelief. It couldn't be. There must be some mistake. But Clement knew it was she. Had he not seen her, he would have sensed her presence somehow.

"Bless my soul," whispered the actor. "It's Rafaela."

"Where?"

"Up there. In the window." But the figure had gone.

"I don't see anyone," said Rosamund impatiently. "And who's this Rafaela?"

"That's what we must find out," answered Byron Clement.

Among the weekenders was, naturally, Mr. John Drummer, Rosamund's arch foe. Alec had insisted on inviting him, the girl told Clement. Only he'd best keep out of her path if he knew what was good for him. Drummer seemed only too glad to oblige. He didn't greet Clement until Rosamund was led off by St. Giles. Clement, thankfully, had been handed a drink by that time. Drummer was already the worse for several cocktails. Of Lady St. Giles, whom Clement longed to meet, there was still no sign. No doubt she was biding her time, planning an entrance. Or perhaps the idea of any sort of entrance overwhelmed the woman. And Rafaela? Even Rafaela must eventually appear. How was it possible? Clement reminded himself that if men could land on the moon, Rafaela Livi could surface in the English countryside.

"I can't believe it," said Drummer. "You and Rosie the Terrible arriving together. What gives?"

"I needed a thrill," Clement told him. "Devilish exciting she is behind the wheel."

"She's Alec St. Giles' bit on the side, in case you haven't heard. So much for his taste, what?"

Clement sipped his scotch. "Somehow I have the feeling his taste is better than one imagines. Look here, John, take my advice and be nice to Rosamund this weekend. Two good things might come of it. One being that St. Giles will let you direct his next production."

"Some hope of that with Rosamund on the horizon," grumbled the director.

"Business is not Rosamund's area of authority. We leave her in charge of pleasure. Number two is that Rosie might become the next Lady St. Giles and retire from the stage. Or if things go wonderfully well here, Rosamund might even go to Hollywood. Is that far enough away, do you think?"

"Heaven isn't that provident," said Drummer.

"In that case, I intend to give providence a helping hand."

"What are you talking about, Clement? Do you mean to say you're here to help that damned girl land herself a ruddy lord?"

"Right on. For this service to the British theater I shall deserve a knighthood at least. Excuse me. Duty beckons."

In fact, Rosamund was wildly trying to get Clement's attention from across the room.

Clement joined her. "Where's his nibs?"

"Entertaining his guests. Come with me. I've got something to show you!"

Rosamund pulled Clement after her down a corridor and into the library.

"He brings me in here to give me a squeeze and what do I see? That!"

Over the fireplace hung a portrait in oil of a young woman with auburn hair and striking, decidedly un-English features. She wore a gown of cream-colored satin and thousands of pounds worth of diamonds and emeralds. Most women who pose for such paintings bedecked in like fashion come off looking fairly smug, but in this case, the artist had seen a wistfulness and captured it perfectly.

"Dead beautiful, isn't she?" said Rosamund gloomily. "Lady St. Giles herself. Looks a bit like me, doesn't she?"

"A good deal like you, I would say," ventured Clement.

"What a kick in the arse! I never expected this."

"I can see you didn't," said the actor, trying not to grin. "Actually, men quite often choose mistresses who resemble their wives. I believe it's a hopeful sign."

"As regards what?" demanded the girl.

"Everything." Clement stepped closer to the painting. "Ah, Rafaela, Rafaela, *tu sei molto bella!*"

"Here, what's this? You're speaking Eyetalian. Alec's *wife* is Eyetalian! You knew it all along!"

Clement shook his head. "I didn't know a thing. But I do know this lady. And she knows me. Rosamund, go and mingle. And for God's sake, don't create any scenes. I've something I must do."

"Where're you going, then?"

"Upstairs," said Byron Clement. "I think I'm wanted upstairs."

He found the right room because the door was open. Rafaela sat on her bed looking expectant, a handkerchief crumpled in her hand. She looked older, certainly, than when Clement had seen her last, but still wonderfully lovely. To a man of sixty, a pretty woman in her forties can seem an appealing young girl. Rafaela stood up and held out her hand to him.

"Clement, I thought you would never come up. How good it is to see you!"

"Rafaela, you nearly gave me heart failure." Clement pressed her hand between his two. "Why haven't we met before this? How could you be in England—God knows how long—without looking me up?"

"I was afraid to see you," explained Rafaela.

Clement noted the fine lines around her eyes. He fought an urge to kiss them.

"Why, in heaven's name?"

"I thought perhaps you wouldn't care to remember me."

The actor blew out his breath. "What a silly notion. And you were always such a sensible creature."

"Sit down, Clement, please. You'll find I speak English very much better now. Ah, you haven't your black curls any longer!"

"To have any sort of hair is a blessing at my age."

"But your eyes haven't changed. How I admired them—*gli occhi belli*. Too bloody marvelous—that's what Moira Belmont said you were. Who is that charming young girl you came with?"

"I came with Cleopatra, otherwise known as Rosamund Peters."

"Does she love you very much this Rosamund?"

Clement was startled. "Me! Come now, Rafaela!"

"I've always thought of you as irresistible. Even fatal. I haven't been well, Clement. Not for a long time. I've become rather like my uncle Claudio, a recluse. That's how I met Alec. He came to Rome to do a documentary about my uncle."

"I didn't know you had an uncle worth filming."

"I never told you about him," said Rafaela. "I kept some secrets from you, Clement. Did you watch *The Appian Way* on the telly last week?"

"I was at the theater that night."

"I saw it. It was the night I decided I must see you again no matter what, perhaps talk with you a little. I'm not embarrassing you, I hope. Do you still hate *The Appian Way*?"

"I confess I now find it hard to dislike any film that has my young face in it . . . Rafaela, I have something I must tell you. Only I don't know how I *can* tell you. It's actually none of my business when it comes down to it."

"Never mind. I want to talk about Rome. Do you ever think of it . . . Cinecittà . . . Hollywood on the Tiber?"

"Damnedest place I've ever seen in my life," said Byron Clement.

★ ★ ★

During the fifties there was always a set recalling the glories of ancient Rome on the lot of Cinecittà, the Italian film studio. From picture to picture it was altered in various ways—new diaphanous hangings, different furniture—but basically it was composed of a great deal of ersatz white marble. Amid the pillars and in the sunken baths, the Rome of the Caesars flourished once again, but this time, instead of Latin, the populace spoke a Babel of tongues in diverse accents. This was the era of the epic, the blockbuster, when the movies were made of lavish costumes, gigantic props and glaring inconsistencies that no one seemed concerned about. In the same scene, it was not uncommon to hear a father, played by a plummy-voiced Briton, addressing his son, who responded in flat Americanese, while the daughter, an Italian or French starlet, struggled to make herself understood in what passed for English. The mother's English might sound mid-Atlantic but, very often, what one heard failed to match the movement of her lips.

All these ingredients—and then some—promised to be present in "the spectacle to end all spectacles," the much-touted film *The Appian Way*, which began rehearsal one lovely day in April. Before it was finished, another April was to pass, hundreds of thousands of dollars were to be spent and some 60,000 Italians were to find employment as extras.

The cast—for the main, American and British—already knew

their lines, but some of them were meeting for the first time. On one end of the set, forming a sort of impromptu London club, were gathered a few elderly English character men who had, over the years, appeared in countless stage and screen productions together. They talked, predictably, of old triumphs and fiascos, events mellowed by the patina of humor that past experiences tend to acquire. A few of these actors had known Henry Irving and Herbert Beerbohm Tree, and had carried spears in the shadow of the great Ellen Terry. When they were born, Queen Victoria still had some twenty-odd years to go in her long reign.

The director, a stocky American of Jewish descent with anxious eyes and spiky gray hair named David Prince, drank coffee and kept glancing at his watch.

"Where the hell is Clement?" he asked his assistant for the third time. "Did you phone his bungalow?"

"He ain't there, I'm telling you. Either he's still in London or on his way."

"Too many people in this picture," said Prince. "A regular circus. How we gonna keep track of 'em all?"

"Search me. What does this Clement look like, anyway?"

"Dark fella about my size. Fortyish, different-looking. Hey, don't you ever go to the movies?"

"Not if I can help it," smirked JoJo, the assistant. "That Livi babe's not here yet, either."

Prince shrugged. "She's not on the schedule for today."

"You wanted her to be here to meet Clement, remember? God, I hope she knows some English."

"She better. The boys at the top swore to me she can talk pretty good. They know I don't work with anybody doesn't understand what I'm saying. This Livi, though—ever see her picture? Wow! She's a cute one, I'm telling you."

"Italian dames are knockouts," agreed the assistant, "but who the hell can understand 'em? I ain't seen one yet who didn't need subtitles under her tits."

"So where the devil is Clement?" David Prince repeated to no one in particular.

Prince liked to have the full cast present on the first day of run-throughs so that everyone could check out everybody else and get a feel for the other actors they had to contend with in the movie. Sometimes, the director made a speech, briefly stating his aims. Today Prince had no statement prepared. Being on location, he felt the phantom breath of the bigwigs at Diadem Pictures down his neck, spurring him on to get going with this damned expensive picture before it ruined the studio altogether.

Nevertheless, protocol demanded that nothing could begin until the arrival of Byron Clement, one of the stars of the film. Clement, who was English, and Allen Shields, the American heartthrob, were the leading men of *The Appian Way*, the ones who would wind up with the beautiful girls.

This billing order, however, had never been made clear to one of the beauties, a curvaceous, full-lipped Roman named Rafaela Livi. Her arrival on the set caused the stir it was bound to. Rafaela wore a yellow cotton dress whose neckline dipped low enough to show off the artificial tan she had acquired for the film and allow a good view of the healthy breasts that were de rigueur for Italian starlets. *The Appian Way,* in which she was to play the slave-girl Barbara, was Rafaela's first picture, indeed, her first acting venture. She was twenty-three years old and had not long ago been the winner of the Miss Rome beauty contest. Rafaela was so stunning that her photograph began to appear in papers throughout the world. Quite naturally, she came to the attention of Hollywood and Diadem Pictures, which was looking for a new face to play the uninspiring role of Barbara, the lovely captive who wins the heart of her snooty, aristocratic master. Rafaela Livi made a lot of people at Diadem happy when it was discovered she spoke English very well and would require no coaching or dubbing. Whether or not she had any acting ability, no one had troubled to find out.

Rafaela knew no one on the set, not even any of the Italian technicians. She was not a part of the Roman film community, nor had she ever dated a celebrity. Before walking away with the beauty prize, Rafaela had attended university where she was an honor student. Her goal had once been to become a linguist, but that had all changed suddenly. Lured by the excitement and glamour of the movie industry, she was now placed among foreigners, seasoned performers who would surely ridicule her when she began to speak her lines in their language. Although she knew she was not rehearsing that day, Rafaela's palms were sweaty and her mouth kept drying up. She wished she had her costume on so that she would at least look like an actress. She had no idea what to say to anyone, but everybody kept staring at her and she wanted them to stop.

"*Guarda chi si vede!*" Rafaela heard one of her countrymen say. "Look who's here!" and then "*Lollobrigida è meno bella di essa.*" In the eyes of that beholder, she came out ahead of "La Lollo."

But Rafaela was not comforted. She was suddenly sure she had made a horrible mistake in giving up her studies. Her parents had begged her not to become involved with the cinema. She recalled their pleading, and tears welled up in her beautiful hazel eyes. "God gave you your beauty to please one man," her mother had told her, "not for thousands to leer at." The parents had reminded her that the Livis were an ancient Roman family, most of them scholars and teachers.

Rafaela was far from being the female lead of *The Appian Way*. That distinction, she knew, belonged to an English lady called Moira Belmont, who sat in a canvas chair that had her name printed on its back. Miss Belmont was blonde and fair, beautiful in a regal way, yet her expression was neither cold nor haughty. She seemed to be acquainted with everyone and laughed at remarks that were made to her. Will I ever be like that, wondered Rafaela, confident and admired? Will I ever be perfectly at home among all this, or is *The Appian Way* going to be the first and last of Rafaela Livi, actress?

She saw that a wiry young man was coming toward her. He had a clipboard in his hand and a pencil behind one ear.

"Miss Livi?" he asked.

"Yes?" said Rafaela expectantly.

"I'm JoJo, Mr. Prince's assistant. He wants to see you, but right now he's looking for another guy. Not that you look like a guy or anything. You look like a zillion bucks. Just hold tight, will you?"

"Yes?" said Rafaela, not having understood a word. Was everyone here going to speak as rapidly as this young man with the haircut that looked like the business end of a brush?

Moira Belmont's laughter once again drifted toward Rafaela. She seemed nice, someone who might be approachable. Moira Belmont, no doubt, knew the answer to a question that was on Rafaela's mind.

When Rafaela introduced herself, the English woman warmly invited her to pull up a chair. "It's your first time, isn't it?" Moira guessed. "I could tell from the look on your face when you walked on the set."

"I don't belong here," Rafaela heard herself saying. "It's crazy."

"Don't worry—everything will be fine. I started out in provincial theaters with no heat in the dressing rooms. You've never known an English winter, have you? The damp creeps into your bones and stays there. Your debut beats mine any day, believe me! Brazen it out. We've all had to at one time or another. Even those relics over there, venerable as they are." Moira indicated the club members. "You do understand what I'm saying, I hope."

Rafaela smiled. "Yes, yes. You pronounce very well. All the English pronounce very well."

"Oh, you've never been to England—I can see that!"

"The gentlemen you speak over there—they are very good players, no?"

"They're wonderful, even though I think one or two of them might have been knighted by Queen Victoria."

"They *are* very old," admitted Rafaela. "Eh, which one is mine?"

"Yours?"

"Which one he acts my lover?"

"Oh, you mean your costar! Not one of them, surely. They're all senators or something. Your lover is Byron Clement, I'm positive."

"Who is he?"

"He's late, that's who he is," said Moira. "Some delay or another. I wish he'd hurry, the old dear, before David's ulcer perforates."

"Ah, another old," sighed Rafaela.

"No, no, I didn't mean that. Clement's no kid, but he's far from decrepit. I think you'll be pleasantly surprised—oh, look! There he is, your lover-boy . . . and there's mine as well."

"Dio!" breathed Rafaela. "What a beautiful man!"

Actually, it was an apt description of either of the two men who were now making their way over cables and past the cameras and equipment that stood everywhere. Rafaela had been so busy wondering who her own love interest in the movie would be that she had failed to notice that the main star, Allen Shields, had also not been present. Of course, Rafaela knew who Shields was; few people in the Western Hemisphere were unfamiliar with his handsome face. Shields had been wandering about the "gardens" having several cigarettes. He never liked to appear on the set a moment before he had to; although he had been in the business for twenty years, his insecurities were perhaps as great as Rafaela's own when it came to acting. Shields pointed in the direction of Moira and Rafaela, who rose to greet the men. When they all stood face to face, their combined beauty was enough to stop a heart. Merely by standing in each other's company, these four people created the sort of radiant tableau that only Hollywood in its heyday could arrange. Even the jaded old actors who had seen everybody worth looking at on several continents were moved to cease their conversation and stare.

When Rafaela was introduced, Allen Shields only said, "Hiya, kid!" and winked, but Byron Clement shook her hand as if meeting Rafaela was the most important thing he would do all day. When Rafaela looked back on it, she knew she began to love him at that moment, her hand in his, those great dark eyes crinkling slightly about the corners as he said, "I'm delighted to meet you" in a voice of black velvet. Rafaela could only nod dumbly. Men like these were outside her experience, although she was not sure what made them so special. Rome, after all, was full of attractive men, so many that one almost took them for granted. Yet they tended to walk a little bowed, somehow defeated, not like these two strangers, who held their heads as though they bore invisible crowns.

It was only after a few moments that Rafaela realized that Allen Shields' profile, although cameo-perfect, was a bit puffy about the eyes, and that he had a speck of tobacco stuck to his lower lip. He had the dullish skin of a heavy smoker. If his looks were his fortune, Shields did not seem to be taking very good care of the capital.

Byron Clement was also not what he seemed at first glance. His were the sort of features that changed constantly, depending on the angle one viewed him from. Rafaela became confused. One moment Clement's nose was too long and sharp, and the next instant it was absolutely right. His dark eyes with their black lashes, striking Rafaela as doelike when serious, could be made to snap with mischief or smolder with something resembling ardor with such lightning speed that Rafaela began to grow hypnotized watching the varying expressions, no longer hearing what was being said. Suddenly, a sad-eyed man with a gap-toothed, elfin grin burst upon them.

"The brothers Gracchus! Wonderful, wonderful. Now that you kids have all said hello, maybe we can get going here. Whattya say?"

Rafaela, getting her first look at David Prince, marveled at how anyone could appear so comic and yet so tragic at the same time. The man seemed elderly, yet he fairly crackled with energy. Around him there would never be any doubt as to who was in charge.

"I say you're a prince of a fellow," quipped Allen Shields.

The director groaned. "For wit he ain't known," he explained to Rafaela about Shields. "How you doing, doll? I'm David Prince."

"How do you do?" said Rafaela carefully.

Prince's grin expanded. "Did you hear that? I couldn't have said it better myself. Terrific. You got any questions, honey, I'm your man."

"I have one now," said Rafaela, aware that everyone was smiling at her. "Which is which?"

"Come again?" said the director.

"Who is who? I forget."

"Of course you do, my dear, " said Byron Clement with a laugh. "I can barely remember it myself. I'm Tiberius—Shields is Gaius."

"Gaius Sempronius Gracchus at your service, ma'am," Shields drawled in the voice of a western cowboy. "I got a question. How come brother Tiberius got to go to that Eton school or whatever and I didn't?"

"Mater liked me best," retorted Clement.

"You know this story?" Prince asked of Rafaela. "This Gracchus Brothers business?"

"I know it. It's Roman history, no? Little children learn in school how Cornelia, the mamma, tell everybody her sons are the family jewels."

David Prince covered his eyes. "I wouldn't touch that one with a ten-foot pole."

"Me neither," said Shields gleefully. "How about you, Moira?"

Moira Belmont made a wry face. "Innuendo before lunch gives me headache every time."

"Did I say something wrong?" Rafaela wanted to know.

Clement tried to look somber, but the devilish look in his eyes gave him away. "No, no, you explained it wonderfully well. I like my character much better now. In fact, I like everything a good deal better."

"Let's get the hell to work," said David Prince. "Every time the second hand on my watch goes around, God knows how many thousands of bucks go down the drain. With pressure like that they still expect art."

"*Ars gratia pecuniam,*" said Byron Clement. Only Rafaela smiled, even though she was the last one of the group to comprehend just how true "art for money's sake" was of the movie industry.

It was determined that Allen Shields should run over to wardrobe for fittings and that Rafaela, as long as she was here, might as well have the light man check her for her best angles. Moira and Clement would do a run-through—the scene where she tells him she can't marry him because she's in love with his younger brother, Gaius.

While Prince was having a peek at the set through his viewfinder, Moira said, "Byron, what happened to you earlier? You had me worried."

"I woke up feeling rotten. Some sort of bug, I expect."

"How do you feel now?"

"Relieved," murmured the actor.

"I know what you mean. She's more than you thought, isn't she?"

"The prospect of playing opposite Miss Rome didn't exactly set me on fire. At least this one has possibilities."

"What gorgeous, sparkly eyed redhead doesn't?" commented Moira with a little catlike smile.

"Surely her hair isn't red," Clement differed. "It's auburn. Definitely auburn."

"Drank it all in, didn't you? Byron, old soul, your charm has far too much candlepower. Miss Rome, for all her cleavage, is a bit of an ingenue. If you're too kind, she's bound to misunderstand."

"Why, Moira, you astonish me," said Clement.

"Do I? The trouble is," Moira went on, "that you really are kind. That'll make it interesting, anyway."

That evening Rafaela was invited to a party, a celebration of the launching of *The Appian Way*. She was even consulted as to where the gathering should take place. Rafaela was careful to choose a nightclub that catered to tourists, where one could find the sort of Italian culture the latter were prepared to experience and where the offbeat night people of Rome would not be encountered.

Rafaela felt somehow that she was expected to sit next to Byron Clement but avoided doing so for reasons not altogether clear to herself. She had the overwhelming suspicion that such proximity to the charming actor would reduce her to a blushing, stammering idiot. God forbid, he might even get the idea of asking her to dance. Rafaela trembled a little at the thought of it. She was bound to make a fool of herself. Surely her palms would perspire, and Clement would know her for the green schoolgirl she was at heart, instead of the glamorous beauty queen she was touted to be. How could she bear the onslaught of those unnerving eyes while clumsily having to converse in English? David Prince urged Rafaela into the chair next to his and she took it gratefully. There was something about the bombastic director that she found reassuring, even familiar. Rafaela knew exactly what it was.

The orchestra played, but no one in the group seemed inclined to dance. Byron Clement placidly smoked his pipe, and every so often a sonorous remark from him drifted her way. Well, thank God actors were talkers, not dancers, thought Rafaela. A rotund tenor appeared to sing a group of Neapolitan-type songs. He had a big, silvery voice and Rafaela began to relax as the beauty of his tone washed over her. Suddenly, among these strangers, she felt proud to be Italian, proud of the language and the lovely, sensuous music that was part of her heritage. At the same time, Rafaela found she was unable to stop stealing glances at Byron Clement. This was easy to do now as the actor had turned to present his exotic profile to her. She wondered briefly what types of songs the British liked. She, herself, knew only "Greensleeves" and bits and pieces of Gilbert and Sullivan in English. But these tunes were very old ones and probably ignored these days, just as the pop-culture Italians sneered at "Non

Ti Scordar di Me," which dated back to the war, when it was put on everybody's lips by Beniamino Gigli. Rafaela loved this piece and requested it when the tenor pointed to her and asked "la bella signorina" what she wanted to hear. Rafaela saw that Clement was staring at her now. His eloquent eyes seemed to smile, or perhaps they were full of taunting. The message they telegraphed across the long table seemed to be "Any day now you will have to kiss me before the cameras and tonight you haven't the courage to come near me."

"Great voice," observed David Prince, applauding. "If this guy looked more like Mario Lanza, I'd give him my card." The director winked at Rafaela, the sorrowful half of his countenance enlivened by the wine.

Rafaela clapped loudly with the rest and dutifully blew the singer a kiss for his recognition of her. Out of the corner of her vision, she noticed Clement wiping his brow with a napkin. It really was warm in the club. Rafaela, too, felt the heat. She took a hanky from her purse and dabbed at the sheen on her throat and bosom.

Prince observed this act with a benign leer. "You sure are a cute little tomato," he told Rafaela. "Also, you're one helluva lucky kid. No acting experience whatsoever and you got a part in the biggest picture of the decade. All right, *Camille* it's not, but it's a pretty damn visible role for a gal who hasn't paid her dues. But, kid, take it from old Prince, everybody's gotta pay their dues sooner or later."

Rafaela thought she knew what he meant. "You are saying, pretty cute tomato is not everything. I know this myself. Better to look like Anna Magnani—*che stupenda!*—to have a face so full of passion and eyes that have seen too much. This is the face of a great actress, eh? I know I have not this face now, but perhaps I can find it. I want to be an actress. That is why I enter in the beauty contest. I want to study, to work very hard—to pay the dues, as you say."

"Where did a little girl like you learn such good English?" asked Prince, staring at her in wonder.

When Rafaela told him, he asked, "What does your old man do for a living?"

"My father? He is a professor of Latin and Greek."

"You don't say! What does he think of you getting into the movies?"

Rafaela made a thumbs-down gesture, at which the director nodded.

"Smart guy, your old man. But you seem like a kid with a little *tsechel* of your own. That's a Jewish word. It means 'good sense.' I guess you don't get to meet a lot of Jewish people in Italy. To me, the Italians look Jewish. A Jew could hide in this country and never be spotted."

"There are Jews everywhere," said Rafaela Livi. "I know. I am one of them."

The director's eyebrows flew up in genuine surprise. "You're joking, I hope."

Rafaela shook her head. "It's true. Professor Falco is not even my real father, although he and his wife have care for me since I am a child. My parents were killed during the war. My father was a professor too, a friend of Falco family. He beg them to save me and they did. They are Catholic people, but they did not have me baptize out of respect for my mother and father. Now I have disappoint them very much, of course. Maybe my Jewish parents would have been disappoint, also."

"Listen, Rafaela," said Prince, his face now totally serious. "It's a good thing I'm the one you told this to. Don't tell anybody else. The studio wouldn't like it to get out."

"But the studio big boss, they all have the Jewish names!" said Rafaela with a laugh.

"That's just it," Prince went on. "Everybody knows it's the Jews who are putting out the pictures. Behind the scenes is one thing, but Jewish pusses—even pretty ones like yours—plastered across the wide screen is too much. It's going too far—you know what I mean? Soon John Q. Public starts to gripe that the Jews control the film industry—which is true, make no mistake—but it's a helluva lot easier to swallow the fact when they give you Robert Taylor and Joan Crawford to look at. Capish?"

"There are no Jewish stars in America?" Rafaela said, a crease forming between her eyebrows.

"Well, sure," conceded the director. "They're all over, but they've changed their names and they don't look Jewish. Years ago I met a guy named Ricardo Cortez. This was in the twenties. Cortez's studio was grooming him as a sort of rival for Valentino—you know, the Latin-lover type—but somehow Ricardo didn't catch on. No wonder—his real moniker was Jacob Krantz and he was born in Vienna. Some Latin lover! I think he quit films and became a stockbroker later on. You see, those bedroom eyes of his were really Jewish eyes, maybe a little sexy but too sad and too smart. People spot those things. Then there's Edward G. Robinson. He's kind of the exception to the rule. If I were a goy, I'd think he looked just like my Jewish boss at work, but go figure. The public likes him. Of course, he's one heckuvan actor, Robinson. But he's a man. For you, it's not the same. You're a leading-lady type, not the comic relief like that Jewish girl, Joan Blondell. If this Jewish stuff were to leak out, it would be a disaster for your career. Hell, you ain't even got a career yet! When they see you in *The Appian Way*, no one will say, 'Gee, what a doll.' What they'll do is whisper in each other's ears, 'She's Jewish, you know.' And the answer will be what? 'You can always tell, can't you?'" Prince leaned over and pointedly hissed these last words in Rafaela's ear.

Rafaela digested this in gloomy silence. Finally she said, "This must change. Hitler is dead, no?"

David Prince snorted. "Hitler had a big mouth, but there are tons of folks out there who quietly believe just what he did. Take my advice, honey. Keep mum on this one. What's the word? Yeah, *silenzio*. No spilla the beans."

At the other end of the table, Byron Clement was reluctantly involved in a different sort of conversation with JoJo, Prince's young assistant. Actually, JoJo was a relation of the director, a cousin not quite far enough removed to suit Prince a good deal of the time.

"God, I can't believe it," marveled JoJo. "You're *the* scary guy! Dad used to screen a movie of yours at my birthday parties when I was a kid. *Laugh Clown Kill*—what a title! I couldn't remember your name, but, man, you sure scared the shit out of us with that damn clown."

"You mean you saw the awful thing more than once?"

"We loved it!" protested JoJo. "A circus picture where all the performers get bumped off one by one is a surefire hit with any kid. Too bad the elephant stomped on you at the end. Dad said it knocked out any chance of a sequel."

"That was the idea, I think."

"Dad's in the business, too," the assistant explained.

"The whole family, eh," mused Clement. "My forebears ped-dled used clothes in Whitechapel."

"Yeah?" JoJo was thoughtful. "I think my family used to do that too, before movies were invented. Anyway, why *did* you kill all those other circus people? I never did get that—I mean, they were supposed to be your friends. The trapeze dame was in love with you, for Chrissake!"

"I don't know," confessed the actor, struggling to suppress a belch. "I tried to analyze it myself at the time, but couldn't get a clue. Just went off my nut, I suppose. The part of the murderous clown—the director's explanation, at the time, was that I became a homi-cidal maniac because everybody laughed at me."

"Hell, clowns want people to laugh!"

"Not if they're really paranoid-schizophrenics," said Byron Cle-ment.

JoJo seemed to mull this over momentarily. "You know what Dad said about you? He said he thought you looked like a Yid to him."

"Oh?" said Clement.

"Yeah. Dad was never wrong when it came to actors. Well, are you or aren't you?"

"An actor or a Yid?"

"Come on, off the record, you know."

"Can't *you* tell, JoJo? Aren't you a chip off the old block? Dad wouldn't have asked, JoJo, he would simply have *known*." Clement rose rather unsteadily. "Excuse me, son. I think I need to take the air. We'll discuss this some other time."

"Hey, man," the assistant called to Clement's back, "no offense, really. I'm your biggest fan!" To no one in particular he added, "He's drunk. The guy's drunk."

No sooner had Rafaela noticed Clement's absence than the eve-ning grew at once flat and dull. Added to that, her talk with David Prince had depressed her spirit. Unused to anti-Semitism in any form, Rafaela hardly knew what to think about the things he had said. Oh, there had been that terrible time during the war, but all that had happened to a bewildered child, a young girl with whom Rafaela could scarcely identify, even barely remember. Until this evening, it had never occurred to her that she had anything to hide, a secret that must be kept from public knowledge. It had been a long time since Rafaela had been a part of the Jewish community or practiced the religion in any way, yet the idea that David Prince assumed she would take his counsel and deny her Jewishness for all time both affronted and confused her. Would Prince refute his own identity so readily? Looking at the director, Rafaela decided he could never get away with it in any case, while she was able to pass for an Italian though she had no Italian blood whatsoever. She recalled her real mother telling her that, for the hundreds of years that the two Jewish families, the Livis and Giordanos, had resided in Italy, there was no record of anybody connected with them marrying outside the faith. Even as a little girl, Rafaela had been impressed by so much steadfastness and fidelity to an ideal that she, of course, had not really understood.

Suddenly, Rafaela understood it much better. She felt, all at once, that she had nothing in common with anyone at her table, not even the Jew, Prince—especially Prince. She wanted only to go home. Allen Shields asked her to dance, but Rafaela pleaded a headache. Later on, she decided she was probably the only woman to have refused the star anything in his lifetime. She said her good-byes and hurried out into the fresh air.

The spring night had turned chilly and it was about to rain. Rafaela had neglected to bring a sweater or coat. She knew that to go from heat into cold dressed so inadequately was risky. It would be just her luck to catch a cold now that she needed all her resources for the film. Hopefully, a taxi would come by right away. Rafaela crossed her arms over her chest, shivering. Behind some shrubbery a few feet away, she heard the unmistakable sounds of someone being sick.

Rafaela Livi had been raised never to turn away from distress or to mind her own business when there was a chance she might be needed. And so she waded into the bushes. Concealed there, seated on a marble bench with his head in his hands, was none other than the magnificent Byron Clement.

"Oh!" cried Rafaela with no less commiseration than if she had come upon the actor's hacked-to-pieces corpse.

"I expect you think I've had too much vino," said Clement.

"No, no, not at all. I saw you drink very little."

"Oh, you did, did you? And here I thought I was beneath your notice."

Rafaela sat down beside Clement. "I believe you are ill. Don't worry. I will take you home."

"With you?"

"Don't make jokes. Can you bear to ride in a taxi? They are driving very wild here, I'm afraid."

"I feel a bit better now," said Clement, "but since my Italian is nonexistant, I'd better take advantage of your offer."

Rafaela helped the Englishman to his feet. He was trembling. Clement leaned against a tree while Rafaela found a taxi. She admonished the driver to take it easy. "This man is very sick," she told him, but she could see the cabby did not believe her. Not much older than Rafaela, he responded with a rude sound.

"You better put your papa to bed."

Byron Clement was staying in a bungalow on the outskirts of the city. It was probably owned by Cinecittà and was quite nice. In the light, Rafaela saw how awful the actor looked and that his teeth were chattering. She felt his forehead.

"You have fever," she told him. "Go into bed at once."

Clement nodded wearily and disappeared into another room. When he came back, he was wearing pajamas and a robe.

"Well," he said, "thank you very much, Rafaela. You've been very kind. If I weren't a walking plague, I'd kiss your hand."

"Maybe I must stay with you," replied the girl. "Only a little while, until you are asleep."

"What a good sort of girl you are."

"You are very far from home. Go in bed now. I will sit with you."

"But will you be able to get home yourself?"

"You have a telephone. I will call another taxi. Don't worry. The nights of Rome are very long. Some people are just starting the evening. *La dolce vita,* we call it—play all night and sleep all day."

Clement seemed only too glad to be in bed. He seemed very pale and complained of being unable to get warm. What if he needs a doctor? wondered Rafaela. She hunted up an extra blanket and pulled all the bedclothes up to the actor's chin. He watched her with the sort of resigned helplessness with which a suffering child might regard its mother.

"Odd, isn't it," Clement said, "how different people are from what one imagines."

"You speak about me, no? What did you imagine?"

"I don't really know. I suppose I thought you might be a pain in the neck, an ornamental encumbrance—vain, ambitious, a typical starlet. In my mind I endowed you with every attribute except that of humanity. You're also a bit shy. You must get over that, you know."

"What means this *shy*? Afraid, no?"

"Not exactly. Perhaps *reticent* is the word—fearful of what might happen."

"Your voice is very fine to hear," commented Rafaela. "How you learn to talk so good?"

"Well," said Clement, "one talks *well*."

"Ah! Now you see. I am fearful my English. Of strange men I am only reticent."

"A quick study, aren't you," said the actor. "Well, you're right. Someone in your shape can't be too careful. If my name really were Gracchus, I'd command that little minx, Barbara, to hop into bed and lend me some heat. If I were to stop shaking, I might get some sleep. Can you take a hint, Rafaela?"

Rafaela did as she was asked. This evening I was afraid to talk to him, she thought, and now I am in his bed. He will get better and I will become ill and that will be my reward. Yet she put her arm around the actor and held him until she knew he was asleep, all the while studying the back of his head. Even Clement's neck managed to be handsome, and his ears were neat and small. Unable to decide what to do next, Rafaela got up and switched off all the lights except a small lamp in one corner. Then she lay back down on the bed and listened to Clement's breathing until she, too, fell asleep.

Rafaela awoke feeling half frozen. To her dismay she saw that a bleak light was filtering through the shutters and she was aware of the steady pinging of rain on the window. *"O, Dio!"* she said out loud.

She had slept all night with a man, with Clement, whom she barely knew. Yet Rafaela had never gotten under the covers. That, of course, was why she was shivering. Her dress was a crumpled disaster. How could she walk down the street or even enter a taxi looking like this? Nevertheless, Rafaela thought she had better leave at once before it got too light. If she was very quiet, Clement would never notice her going. The actor's back was still turned away from her. Rafaela heard not so much as a single snore. How could a man sleep so silently? Was it possible he was dead?

She tiptoed around to the other side of the bed and peered at Clement's face. Yes, thank God, he was breathing! In fact, he looked very good even though a lot of dark whiskers had sprouted on his face overnight.

Rafaela knew she had no business being in the man's room at this hour—or any other. If this were to leak out, the scandal rags that had so often printed the pictures of her in a swimsuit would have a field day with her. Her adopted parents would certainly disown her. They were already furious with Rafaela for having moved into her own little flat. Ever since the beauty contest, Rafaela knew they could no longer live together in peace.

Why am I thinking like this? Rafaela asked herself. I am innocent and have nothing to fear. This man needed my help and may still need someone to tend to him. I cannot simply steal away and leave him alone.

Rafaela's teeth chattered, perhaps making enough noise to awaken Clement, for he suddenly opened his eyes.

"Rafaela!" he said. "What's the matter?"

"Are you well?" she managed to ask.

"Yes. I feel much better now."

"Good. I must go now, really. It's morning, you know."

"Nonsense," replied Clement, his voice deep and thick with sleep. "It's barely dawn—and raining, too! You look cold, Rafaela. For heaven's sake get into bed. We can sleep for hours yet."

"No, no, I can't. I should have gone last night, but—"

"You fell asleep worrying about me," finished Clement. "Look here, stop being so silly and come to bed where it's warm. You're quite safe with me. Do you think I would molest someone who's nursed me so faithfully? Come on. And take off your dress or it will be all wrinkled."

"My dress *is* wrinkled," said Rafaela in a small voice. She felt exhausted, as though she hadn't slept at all. Somehow, the last thing she wanted to do was go out into the damp chill. Rafaela's nose prickled inside and she stifled a sneeze. She must get warm right away, although she certainly had no intention of removing her dress.

Once under the blankets, Rafaela found that her side of the bed was very cold, indeed. There was no heat in the room at all, of course. In Italy, one was lucky to get heat even in winter and here it was already April. If only she could move a little closer to Clement, who had had all night to warm up his side. Rafaela was not actually frightened of the actor. He was obviously a person of refinement and Rafaela knew that people with roguish expressions were usually quite kind. But a man was a man, after all, a creature notoriously susceptible to temptation. ot that Rafaela's upbringing permitted her to do anything that might be construed as bold, much less seductive—if one did not count how she dressed. (That was a kind of occupational uniform: Italian starlets had to look like bombshells, not nuns. They represented the legendary heat and passion of Italy, although, according to the old code, their behavior had to be monitored by old women in prim hairstyles and stark, black dresses.)

As if in response to Rafaela's shivering, the Englishman turned over in his sleep and snuggled up close to her. Rafaela held her breath in anticipation of what would follow, but nothing happened. The actor slept on, his faint snores muffled by her hair. His body was like a stove. Rafaela soon dozed off herself, filled with a happiness that refused to allow any further consideration of the impropriety of being where she was.

Rafaela woke to the rattling of china. Byron Clement stood at the window, fully dressed, sipping what Rafaela knew had to be tea.

"What time is it?" she asked.

Clement turned around, raising his eyebrows in the comical way that had so charmed Rafaela the previous day.

"It doesn't matter, does it? No work today for us and it's left off raining too. We've got the whole day before us."

The Italian girl groaned and sat up. "Don't look on me," she begged. "Everything is a disaster."

"Rubbish," scoffed the actor. "Youngsters always look good in the morning. Tea?"

"Yes, please." Rafaela knew that the mascara she had not removed last night had by now made raccoonlike circles under her eyes, and her carefully arranged hairstyle had become unpinned and probably dangled wildly à la Medusa. Nevertheless, Clement seemed to be regarding her with as much admiration as there had been yesterday.

"Perhaps you might show me Rome," he said. "Or would that bore you too terribly?"

"Surely you make the joke," said Rafaela wryly, unable to believe that such a riveting person worried about boring anybody. "And I think you are still sick. Maybe you stay in bed this day, eh?"

"With you, gladly."

"Signore, please!" cried Rafaela. "I am not what I seem to be."

The actor laughed. "Who the devil is? Calm yourself, my dear. I was only speaking facetiously."

But Rafaela's cheeks were hot. "What is wrong with me that you forget to speak with respect? Tell me this. I stay in your room, yes, but this doesn't mean I am the—"

"All right, all right." Clement seated himself at her feet. "What a temper you people have. I beg your pardon, Rafaela. There is nothing at all wrong with you. Respectability surrounds you like a powerful aura."

"What?"

"What? What?" mimicked the actor, eyes brilliant with naughtiness. "Can't you force yourself to flirt a little—at least for the sake of my pride, that is? I'm not that old, am I? No, don't answer that." Clement held up his hands as if to shield himself.

"I can't answer," said Rafaela. "I don't know how old you are."

"I'm forty-two. Do you know what forty is, Rafaela? It's the old age of youth and the youth of old age."

Rafaela smiled. "Bravo. Did you invent this?"

"Alas, no. I'm not that clever. I make a living repeating other people's well-turned phrases."

"No matter," replied the girl, "for you have the *occhi belli*—the beautiful eyes. With eyes like this a man can even be without a tongue."

Rafaela's compliment seemed to silence Clement momentarily. Suddenly he sprang up.

"Come on, my girl! No more hanging about here. The glory of Rome awaits us."

"But I have no coat."

"Wear one of mine, then."

Rafaela gulped her tea. She would prefer to pass such a morning as this luxuriating in a cozy bed, but the idea of going out in chilly weather protected by this man's coat appealed to her enormously. Am I in love with him so soon? she wondered. What was it about him? What another man probably couldn't have accomplished using all his wiles, Clement had managed in spite of an upset stomach.

She sighed. "You must not go out."

"Yes, I must," said Clement firmly "I feel fit and ready for anything. But only if you are at my side. Otherwise I shall go right back to being ill. Are you with me?"

"Why not?" said Rafaela, but she knew perfectly well why not. It struck her that although she had met Byron Clement only yesterday, she seemed to be irremediably stuck to him as metal filings on a magnet. But, of course, the starlet said nothing of this. Her English wasn't up to it, in any event.

It was David Prince's method to film all the scenes requiring one set, even if they were out of sequence in the movie. It was a bit confusing for the cast but economized on set construction. That is how Tiberius Gracchus and Barbara came to do their first love scene before they had even been cinematically introduced.

In the script, the slave girl, brought to Rome in chains following the defeat of her country, toils away in the house of Gaius Gracchus as handmaiden to his wife, played by Moira Belmont. Barbara, believing that Gaius caused her brother's death, plans to gain revenge by killing Moira's baby when it is born. But Moira, dying in childbirth, stuns Rafaela/Barbara by making her promise to care for the child as though it were her own. Rafaela thought the whole plot was like an opera without singing.

In the scene being shot, Rafaela had just left the expiring Moira (who recovers later because Rafaela nurses her back to health using the medical remedies of her homeland) to go out into the courtyard to have a good cry. There she encounters her master's brother, Tiberius, who has, unknown to Barbara, admired her for some time.

The lights burn and the cameras turn.

Byron Clement, gorgeously robed, with his black hair arranged Roman-fashion, comes upon Rafaela in the moonlight. The girl is garbed in a revealing slave costume. Her hair is sexily disarranged. She sobs, her half-exposed breasts heaving.

> TIBERIUS: Barbara, what is the trouble? Has someone hurt you?
>
> BARBARA: Someone must have or I would not be here at all.
>
> TIBERIUS: Perhaps you will not always be a slave.
>
> BARBARA: How will I be free while I have no country, while my people are in chains? Even today I saw my father being driven through the streets with some others like a herd of beasts.
>
> TIBERIUS: Are you certain it was your father?
>
> BARBARA: I know it was he! I called to him, and I know that he saw me. Oh, my lord Tiberius, I take you for a kind man, but I cannot hope that you could understand what lies in my heart this night.
>
> TIBERIUS (lifting her chin): Then let me tell you what is in my own. You think me kind, although I know you hate the Romans. It is my pleasure to be kind to you, beautiful Barbara. If I were to buy you from Gaius, would you be kind to me as well?
>
> BARBARA: I care not who is my master. I have no more regard for one Roman than for another. Say no more, please, my lord. Do not add to my unhappiness.
>
> TIBERIUS: You wish me to be silent. Then silence me with a kiss.

Clement then took Rafaela in his arms and kissed her with a good show of lust. That was the trouble.

"Cut!" yelled Prince. "It was great until the kiss. No saliva,

Byron. You know better than that. I don't blame you for getting carried away, but let's put a rein on it." He called over his shoulder. "Check their makeup and we'll do it again."

"What does he mean?" Rafaela asked Clement.

"He wants me to kiss you as if you were my ruddy sister," grumbled the actor.

"All right," said the director. "Say your last speech, Byron, and give us a smooch that'll pass the censors."

Clement repeated his lines, took hold of Rafaela and chastely pressed his lips to hers. According to direction, she pushed him away, yet in this tight shot, the all-seeing camera picked up a certain look in her eyes and a little throat spasm that would pleasantly surprise Prince as he later viewed the rushes.

"Cut! Print that one."

David Prince patted Rafaela's shoulder. "Great going, kid. I understood every word."

"I didn't expect this part would come so soon," Rafaela told him.

Prince chuckled. "Baby, I've learned from experience that it's best to get the love scenes over with before the actors start to hate each other."

On her way to wardrobe, Rafaela was approached by JoJo, who announced, "Mail call!" and handed her an envelope. It was addressed to her in care of Cinecittà in what was a truly fine Italian hand, full of flourishes and curlicues. Rafaela tore the envelope and read:

My Dear Miss Livi,

I am not accustomed to write to film stars, but in this case, I feel I must make an exception. Today I read the newspaper, as I do every morning. There was an article about the making of a new motion picture, The Appian Way, a story I would normally pass over, but your name and photograph leapt out at me. It was not only your beauty that astonished me, but also the notion that I still have a relation on this earth when I thought I had lost all who were kin to me.

Miss Livi, there is no doubt in my mind that you must surely be the daughter of my poor murdered sister, Francesca, and her husband, Mauro Livi. I believe we met when you were very young, but later

on, I moved away from Rome to take a position in another city. I
feel sure you have forgotten all about me and I, of course, assumed
you had perished along with Francesca and Mauro.

From your picture, I see so much of your lovely mother in your face.
I long to see you in person, if only to convince myself that you are
real. Is it possible for us to meet? If so, ring me at my flat. I am always
at home. I am once again living in Rome. I returned when the war
ended.

Sincerely,
Claudio Giordano

There was a telephone number and address. Rafaela was amazed.
She failed to recall ever having seen her mother's brother, but she
remembered his name having been mentioned. Yes, Uncle Claudio was a journalist who worked for a paper in Bari. He was right—
Rafaela had forgotten him. To be truthful, she did not have much
desire to see him now. Her uncle wrote that he could always be
reached at home. That surely meant he had no job and perhaps
figured that Rafaela, being in the movies, had money to burn.
Rafaela at once felt guilty for thinking such thoughts. She was Claudio Giordano's only living relative. By the same token, he was also
hers. For the sake of her mother's memory, she owed him at least a
visit and even financial help if he required it. Rafaela put the letter in
her purse and resolved to call her uncle that afternoon.
    "Fan mail?" Byron Clement startled her by inquiring. "A propo-
sal of marriage perhaps?"
    "No, no. Not this time." Rafaela did not mention that she had
received quite a number of letters recently, most of them indecent
proposals from men with twisted minds. Rafaela's face grew a little
flushed as she remembered how Clement had first kissed her in their
scene. She had been startled by the intensity of that kiss and yet
wanted it to go on forever. Now, as he spoke, his deep voice stirred
her in an unsettling way. Rafaela understood that Byron Clement
meant to make love to her in the immediate future and that, if she
gave him the chance, she would not likely find a reason to resist. She
felt certain that the actor, with his wavy hair and unwavering eyes,

had made equally quick progress with other leading ladies. Rafaela
was overcome by a sense of being sucked into the decadent lifestyle
the Falcos had so dreaded—how quickly it had happened to her they
would never know. A part of her was tempted to tell the Englishman
to let her alone, that she was not there for his convenience. Yet, at
the same time, Rafaela had an urge to confide in him about the letter. Doing neither, she regarded him in glum silence.

"Rafaela," Clement said, "I so enjoyed our sightseeing tour yesterday. Shall we watch each other eat lunch?"

"I'm sorry," said Rafaela, looking somewhere else. "I plan to go
to the market."

"The market! Whatever for?"

Rafaela tapped her forehead with her palm. "How do you say, to
buy the dress, the shoes?"

"Shopping. You want to go shopping. Oh, I see. But, if you do get
hungry, I'll be at the Café di Napoli. Off you go, my dear."

Rafaela gave him a quick half-smile and hurried away. She nearly
ran over Moira Belmont.

"What have you done to Byron?" murmured the actress. "He
looks terribly disappointed."

"He does?" was all Rafaela could think to say.

"You see, he's just come from the long, bleak English winter. He
longs for a bit of spring—*primavera*, as you say. And you are as pretty
as a tree full of apple blossoms."

"Always pretty," said Rafaela, almost bitterly. "What good is
pretty."

"You're learning, aren't you?" the English woman remarked. "It
gets you a lot but never enough. Anyway, at the risk of appearing a
dreadful busybody, let me warn you that unless you keep right on
disappointing Mr. Byron Clement, he's sure to make you regret the
day he ever came to Rome."

"Veni, vidi, vici, you mean," said Rafaela.

"Mincemeat of the heart is what I mean."

"You must think him very cruel."

Moira shook her head. "I think him too bloody marvelous, just as
you do. What woman can resist that look—intelligent kindness, I
believe it's called? And those eyes—deliciously wicked one mo-

ment and soulful as a child the next. The man is a definite menace."

"I think you want me to know that Byron has a wife in England."

"Oh, he told you that, did he?"

This time Rafaela shook her head. "But I somehow know it and he knows that I know."

"Well, that's good anyway."

"You say that no woman can resist—but you resist, no? Why is that?"

"Oh," said the blonde actress with a sigh, "I suppose it's because I never fall for anyone that human."

Clement was exactly where he had promised to be. He was smoking his pipe, and there was nothing before him but a glass of wine. If it wasn't for that pipe and the tweed jacket he wore, thought Rafaela, he would look like any virile good-looking Italian. Nevertheless, Rafaela thought Clement an odd-looking Englishman, for there was certainly nothing Northern about him except the rosiness of his skin.

Byron Clement rose at once. He appeared surprised to see Rafaela, a thing that astonished her. "Well, this is nice," he said. "I haven't eaten yet. I hope you haven't."

Rafaela sat down in the chair Clement offered. She felt out of breath. "May I have some wine?" she said.

"You may have anything in the world. Couldn't you find the right dress?"

"What?—oh, no." Rafaela took a long look at the wonderful face before her and decided to stop pretending. "I was too unhappy to buy a dress. I only walk about and think how much I want to be with you."

Clement covered her hands with his own. "Then why didn't you come at once? Never mind—I don't care why."

"But I must tell you," persisted Rafaela. "I was afraid—afraid of you. Because you know how to make me love you. For it is a simple thing, perhaps a game. But I don't know such games."

Clement laughed. "You adorable creature, bless you for speaking English so well. What would I do with you otherwise? Here I am a man nearly twice your age and you know so much of my language and I so little of yours.

"Rafaela, my lamb, my pet, a man doesn't play games that make him as miserable as I felt when it seemed you were avoiding me today. Has it ever occurred to you that your power might be greater than mine?"

"I don't think so," said Rafaela with conviction.

"Are you very hungry?"

"Not at all. I don't want anything."

"Shall we go off by ourselves for a bit? I feel like a walk." Clement tapped out the bowl of his pipe and put it in his pocket.

Rafaela took the actor's arm. How different this was from the respectful distance they had kept on Sunday during the sightseeing. What had happened? Had something occurred during the filming? Perhaps that kiss that was supposed to have been only make-believe had changed everything. Rafaela felt that a magic spell had been worked on them overnight, mysteriously converting two strangers from different worlds into lovers even as they remained virtual strangers. Rafaela was so awed by this idea that she clung to the Englishman in silence. Having relinquished any illusion of control, she now knew what it meant to walk on air.

"Where shall we go, sweetheart?" Clement asked.

He does look both intelligent and kind at the same time, thought Rafaela, just as Moira Belmont noticed. His eyes weren't challenging anymore, but mild and indulgent. It seemed to Rafaela that the actor's lips, sensuous and finely marked, looked just like those on Etruscan statues.

"I know a beautiful garden," she said. "We can walk there."

"It's you who are beautiful," said Byron Clement. "*Molto bella.* Everyone is staring at you."

"Ah!" said Rafaela suddenly. "I forget. We must be careful the paparazzi."

"What?"

"They take the picture for the *giornale*, the, the . . . "

"You mean the newspapers."

"Oh, yes! They know me. I am what you call—girl of the moment. They take your picture with me."

"I see. Well, well." Clement laughed.

"In England there are no paparazzi? Do they not snap you?"

"I believe there are such creatures," admitted the actor. "But they don't want my picture. Most Britons tend not to make a fuss over actors—that sort of thing is reserved for royalty. No, I must confess that I am definitely not a person of the moment."

"But you are big star," insisted the girl.

"No, Rafaela, only a working actor. Tell the truth—you never heard of me before I came here."

"There is much I don't know."

"You'd heard of Allen Shields, I'll bet. Now *he's* a star."

"Why him and not you? Beside you, he is nothing."

"You're too kind," said Clement fondly. "Of course, Shields is an American. Some people say there are more stars in America than actors. Anyway, you have to admit he's a handsome chap. My luck to have to stand next to him for most of the picture."

Rafaela smiled. "You are comic. I like you very much."

"Do you? Come to think of it, I do very well in *The Appian Way*, don't I? I'm the only one who gets to make love to you. Had I known that earlier, the producers could have gotten me a sight cheaper, I can tell you."

"I hear the film costs much more than any other."

"Oh, I believe that!" said Clement. "It'll probably do well at the box office with all the advance publicity. But that won't make it less of a stinker, will it?"

Rafaela came to a halt. "Clement, what do you mean? Will the picture be no good?"

"The costumes will be stupendous."

"But Clement, why will it not be a good film?"

"Because the whole thing is a pretentious lot of artificial nonsense —just like every other costume epic. False dialogue, inhuman characters, just a show of ostentation without any real heart. But you weren't to know that, were you, Rafaela? Poor darling, I shouldn't have said all that. It's your first film, your first part."

"I was sure it would be wonderful," sighed the girl. "I was afraid that I would be the one to ruin it."

Clement put his arm around her. "Don't worry, we'll make our end come out right. I promise. There'll be nothing false between us. Meanwhile, why don't you call me Byron?"

"I like your other name better. Clement—this means full of mercy, no? The name of a pope."

"So it is. I never thought of that."

Seated in the garden, Rafaela began to protest against the vigor of the actor's kisses. There was no Prince to curb him now. "Clement, stop. You're biting me!"

"I want to do everything to you. Do you want to go to bed with me, Rafaela?"

"I can't go to bed with you anymore. I know that you are married. How can I forget this?"

"Of course you can't," said Clement, smoothing back Rafaela's hair, which was becoming quite tousled from his passionate efforts. "Neither can I, really. Am I frightening you?"

"No. It is you who are shaky."

"That's because I don't know what I'm doing. Believe me, this isn't a habit, a game, as you say. I haven't always been the best husband, but I've been a faithful one. Sylvia and I have been married for nearly twenty years. How can I make a young person like you understand the complex reasons people stay married to each other? I don't understand it very well myself. Sylvia and I have come to the point where we realize we are about to grow old together and can't decide whether we can stomach the idea or not. I asked her to come to Italy with me. She gave a lot of excuses why she couldn't go, but I know she didn't really want to. She'd rather be near her friends. I believe they bore her less than I do. And you know, I was relieved when Sylvia decided not to come. I told myself that a vacation from each other would do us both good, perhaps change things for the better. Then I met you. I feel I can do just about anything now— make a bad picture with a happy heart, make a fool of myself over a young girl and feel like a king doing it. Just watch me. You've suddenly changed my whole point of view. There's something about you—everything about you—that appeals to me tremendously. I don't want a vacation, I just want you. Do you know what you want?"

"No," answered Rafaela. "I mean, I don't know what to do."

"Would you rather stay just friends?"

"Yes. I think it will be best. I am not the girl for what you need."

"You've never been with a man, have you? You're a sweet little virgin, a box of unopened chocolates in the most divine wrapping."

"What are you saying?" Rafaela gave Clement a little shove. "Of course I am the virgin. What do you expect? In Italy every woman is the virgin until she marries."

"Every last one?"

"Well, who can say. But this I can tell you. I can't make love with you, because if I do, the man I marry sometime, someday, he will know and he will get crazy. He will ask me questions forever about how I can do this to him, why I didn't wait. What will I say? That an Englishman with a wife wanted to have a vacation with me?"

Clement was staring at her, but Rafaela saw something like approval in his eyes. Well, at least he knows I'm no fool, she thought, not a toy to be played with and then discarded. All the same, she found herself feeling unaccountably sorry for the actor, as though she'd done something to hurt him. Rafaela threw her arms about Clement's neck and pressed her face close to his.

"It's all right," he said. "There, there now, it's all right."

In the evening, Rafaela went to visit her uncle.

Claudio Giordano lived in a spacious enough apartment, but a profusion of books and papers made it appear crowded. The uncle proved to be a small man, somewhat shorter than Rafaela, but trim and orderly in his appearance. He had a sallow, small-featured face and dark, almond eyes surrounded by yellowish whites. His goatee was neatly kept, but he had wiry, gray hair that seemed to spring energetically from his scalp, exposing a high, scholarly forehead. Rafaela thought her uncle looked more like a mandarin than a Jew. She half expected him to begin spouting Chinese, but, of course, he spoke a professorial Italian, his voice pleasant and cultured.

Giordano did not seem to want to let go of Rafaela's hand.

"Forgive me," he said. "I am overcome. How lovely you are! However did it happen? Your poor mother had a pleasantly pretty face with much the same features, but on you they look different. You fairly blaze with beauty, don't you? A happy genetic coincidence, a profound statement on the evolution of our species is what you are. None of us, neither the Giordanos nor the Livis, have really been known for anything but brains, and here you are in the cinema. Sit down, sit down! My eyes must grow accustomed to you. It's rather gloomy in here, as you see, and you are the noonday sun come to call."

Rafaela laughed. "Are you a poet, Uncle?"

"No, only a writer of prose. Not even pretty prose."

"I thought so," said the girl. "This looks like a writer's home."

"I'm afraid you're right. What looks like disorder to you happens to be my filing system. My cleaning woman won't come anymore. Gave up, that's what. Yes, everything is in its proper place, but very dusty now, so mind your dress and gloves."

Giordano served some wine, and Rafaela, relaxed in the funny little man's presence, gave him a synopsis of her life since the war.

"And these people, the Falcos," said her uncle, "were they good to you?"

"Oh, yes. I became their daughter. Now, however, we are estranged over the film business. The Falcos find it undignified and can't understand why I've entered such a profession. One might have thought I'd taken to the streets. I hope you don't take this view, Uncle Claudio."

"No, but I can comprehend your foster parents' concern. I don't go to the pictures, but I understand that some of the people connected with them have unsavory reputations. Your beauty is bound to attract this sort, I'm afraid. You are a living, breathing challenge to some puffed-up Don Giovanni—"

"No, no," said Rafaela. "It isn't like that!"

"Ah," sighed Giordano, "perhaps not. Well, if you want to be a film actress, then that is what you must be by all means."

Rafaela played with her gloves. "I can't tell you how important it is to me. After Mamma and Papa left, I thought for a long time they would return. When they didn't and never wrote, I began to realize they were dead. I was no baby, no fool. I knew who killed them. I didn't feel safe either. I believed that someone would come to take me away next, that I'd be killed too. Wasn't I a Jew, after all? I felt it was stamped on my brow for all to see—Jew, Jew. I was afraid to die. I'm still afraid. Perhaps that's why I want to be in films. There I'll be immortalized. At least I won't disappear forever without a trace."

"It is a kind of magic," Giordano agreed. "I'm glad you've found the thing that makes you happy."

"I'm not so happy," said Rafaela with a deprecating little laugh. "What about you, Uncle? Have you no family at all besides me?"

"My wife died five years ago. We had no children. I keep myself busy by writing books. That is it."

"What sort of books?"

"Memoirs of my experiences during the war."

"Ah," said Rafaela, having hoped for something more interesting. Nevertheless, she liked this new-found relative. He seemed lively, not at all boring. But how well did books about war experiences sell? Surely there were a great many of those nowadays. Rafaela, having decided that Giordano was not the sort to ask for charity, made up her mind to offer assistance.

The starlet remained longer with her uncle than she had expected to. He had been decidedly a pleasant surprise. She liked the simpatico expression on his face, the way he rolled his keen little eyes as he spoke. Before taking her leave, she said, "Uncle, is there anything I can do for you?"

"Yes," answered Giordano. "You can come back soon."

"Is that all? Are you sure?"

Uncle Claudio laughed. "It's a great deal to ask of a film star."

"I'm not a film star," Rafaela told him, "only a working actress. Actually, I'm more like a fish out of water. Perhaps you'd like to have dinner with me sometime. I could introduce you to Professore and Signora Falco, too. You are just the sort of person to win their approval."

Giordano took her hand. "My dear, you are very kind. However, I must tell you that I cannot accept. I never leave this flat. I haven't left in five years, perhaps more."

"Not once?" Rafaela asked in disbelief.

"No. It's a dreadful phobia. Next time, I'll tell you all about it."

Rafaela assured Giordano that she would see him next week. Perhaps I'll even bring Clement, she thought. But then she remembered that Clement was an Englishman without Italian.

"Uncle Claudio, do you speak English?"

"Sorry, no," the writer said, "even though my books are printed in English. German is my second language. Yes, in German I can manage very well."

"Is it possible to borrow one of your books?"

"You may have any of them with my compliments. Here, wait. I'll give you my first one. I warn you, it isn't very nice reading. It may give you bad dreams."

"I'm used to those," said Rafaela.

"Nightmares pass but the world remains," said Claudio Giordano. He took up his pen and wrote something in a book and gave it to Rafaela.

She noticed that her uncle had blue numbers on his arm, a tattoo so ugly it made Rafaela wince.

Giordano's book was called *Nadir* and had a picture of barbed wire on the cover. Inside, the author had inscribed: "To my lovely niece, Rafaela—May your dreams be beautiful all your life."

Rafaela noted that the work had gone through several printings—evidently it *was* popular. She also discovered how Claudio Giordano had spent the war years. He had been an inmate of Auschwitz concentration camp. *Nadir* was the account of his survival.

Rafaela spent half the night reading *Nadir,* even though she had an early call in the morning. Fascinated, horrified, she simply couldn't put the book down. Her uncle wrote in a lucid, uncomplicated style, but he was clearly a genius. No detail had eluded the little man during his sojourn in that awful place. He communicated it all movingly, brilliantly, but curiously, without a hint of bitterness. It was as if Claudio Giordano saw his suffering as the unpleasant occupational hazard of being the chronicler of that particular hell called Auschwitz. Rafaela read until her eyes could take no more. Through his book, she got to know her uncle very fast and began to love him that very night.

The following day she took the book along and read between takes, hoping perversely that David Prince would notice so that she could say, "This book is by my uncle. He suffered a great deal because he is a Jew, yet he doesn't hesitate to proclaim who he is." But Prince paid no attention to anything but the filming. When Byron Clement came to sit with her, Rafaela dropped *Nadir* into her bag.

In her last scene of the day, Rafaela/Barbara was being taken from her father's house by the victorious Romans. She fought and cursed them with such inspiration and fire that the whole set broke into applause. Clement folded her into his arms in full view of everyone.

"You were marvelous," he said and added, "I love you, Rafaela."

Of course, Rafaela loved Clement too, but for some weeks she tried very hard to remain only on friendly terms with him. Occasionally, they went walking together or to a nightclub in the evening, but for the most part, they socialized in the company of other members of the cast and crew. Rafaela found this situation pleasant at times, but more often, very trying. Although she had been the one to resist having an affair, Rafaela found that she was having difficulty keeping her hands off Clement, wanting to touch him all the time. Decorum prevented her from doing this, but she came to greatly enjoy dancing with the actor. At least that way she could be in his arms with impunity, although Rafaela was not so stupid or naive as to believe the others did not suspect that something was going on between them. Meanwhile, Clement's burning looks would reduce Rafaela to weak-kneed giddiness.

Eventually the paparazzi struck. Rafaela, looking through the paper, came upon a photo taken in some club in which she was gazing at Clement with such rapture that it caused her to blush for shame. Rafaela wondered if the picture would find its way to England.

It was not until Clement's accident, however, that Rafaela decided to abandon her virtuous resolve. The actor was not expected to drive his own chariot in the movie, but when the vehicle was stationary, it was Clement who held the reins. Just as the shot was being set up, a kite landed on a roof, shrieking loudly. A high-strung horse reared and plunged forward, causing the unwary actor to be thrown from the chariot and dragged a few yards before the horse could be stopped. Clement had not been able to let go because the leather straps were wound around his hands.

Rafaela revealed herself by screaming more shrilly than the kite and running out to chase after Clement, but she didn't care. The scraped and bleeding actor was not seriously injured. It was he who had to murmur soothing words to his shaken little darling.

The script had to be revised in order to allow Byron Clement to wear the bandages that showed outside his costumes. On the day of the mishap, though, the doctor sent him home and said he needed looking after. Once again, Rafaela volunteered to play nurse and this time, nobody was surprised or ventured a comment when she left in a car with Clement.

That is, until Allen Shields broke the silence. "If Byron doesn't walk in here in a couple of days, it won't be because he fell out of a chariot. I'm telling you, those limeys fuck 'em with their accents first."

"What about Rafaela's accent?" Moira Belmont wanted to know.

David Prince gave Shields a disapproving look. "Come on, she's a nice little girl. She fell in love with the guy, that's all."

"He's nuts about *her,* you mean," JoJo put in. "Gee, I hope Clement's okay. You guys ever see him in *Laugh Clown Kill?* What a performance."

"Byron was in a picture called *Laugh Clown Kill?*" said an incredulous Moira.

Allen Shields laughed. "Yeah, his first film under his Diadem contract. Goes to show you what this studio has done for Clement's career. Man, he deserves better."

"He's working, isn't he?" said JoJo, loyal to the family business.

"Byron did some wonderful work in England," Moira told them. "Some people think he's the best screen actor we've got."

"This is his last picture under the contract," said Prince. "Clement told me he wasn't going to renew, and I don't blame him. Diadem never used him right. He could have been big in the right parts, but they buried him. Now, Warner Brothers used to make intelligent pictures—they woulda known what to do with an actor like Clement. They coulda made another Claude Rains out of him. I mean, the guy looks ten times better than Rains anyway and his voice is just as good. When did Diadem ever make an intelligent picture? The film's in the can, and everybody there asks if it's stupid

enough for the public. Shit, all Diadem is famous for is technicolor
so bright it makes you blind. But I got news for all you folks: Diadem
is gonna try to bribe Clement to renew after this, bribe him and beg
him. The rushes are telling me a story I never expected. Clement is
jumping clear off the screen and the girl right with him. Their scenes
are so hot I smell smoke. Even without Rafaela, Byron Clement is in
incredible form. He's fought to make a human being out of god-
damn Tiberius Gracchus, and he's done it in spades. Somebody's
going to nominate our boy for a gold statue if I know anything about
this game."

"I hope so," said Moira. "It'd be a pity for all that inspiration to go
to waste. God knows where he'll find it next."

"Hey, Dave," said Shields, "are we gonna do anymore here? I
could use a beer."

"We can shoot a few feet around Byron. These extras are getting
paid, accident or no accident. Check the light, JoJo."

"Light's good," JoJo said. "We got about an hour left, I'd say."

"Okay gang," said Prince, "enough vacationing in sunny Italy.
Let's make a movie."

"Man, that Belmont's a cynical dame," JoJo said as Moira walked
away. "Talk about your razor's edge."

"She was right on the money," David Prince told him. "Motivation. That's why actors keep having sound-stage romances. It's the
motivation that puts them over the top."

Byron Clement, groggy from the painkiller injection the doctor
had given him, stared up at his bedroom ceiling. Rafaela was holding his hand, the one that wasn't bandaged.

"Want anything?" she asked.

"Certainly," said Clement. "But I'm in no shape for it now."

"You'll soon be better. Then I want you to make love with me.
I'm not afraid any longer."

"Left off worrying about your future husband, have you?"

"I will never marry," said Rafaela.

"Of course you will."

"I will never find the right man."

"Why not?"

"Because he won't be you. It is you I love, Clement, whether you have a wife or not, whether you stay or leave. I will always love only you."

"I hope so," said the actor, pulling her on top of him. "Because you belong to me. No one will ever make love to you but me if I can help it. Don't you know I adore you, Rafaela? Do you think I could leave you now? When I've done with all my scenes here, I'll have to go back to England to sort things out with Sylvia. Then I'll come back. Can you wait that long, darling?"

"Yes, yes," replied the girl, planting wild kisses on his face.

Clement ran his hand over the curve of her breast. "Do I get a look at these now or must I wait until the wedding?" He gave a little cry as Rafaela jostled him while opening her blouse.

"Easy there," Clement gasped. "Rafaela, take it easy."

★ ★ ★

Clement, would you like some tea?" offered Lady St. Giles. "I make it right here in my bedroom. I spend a great deal of time up here— reading, watching the telly. It was you who got me liking tea, you know." Rafaela poured the actor a cup.

"And Englishmen?"

"Oh, yes, of course. One needn't be a Dr. Freud to understand why I married Alec. Also, I made my foster parents very happy. A man with a title—even if he was involved with films and the theater. You see, they reasoned it was only a hobby with Alec, a rich man's whim. They had no idea how keen he really was, that it was actually his profession."

"In any event," said Clement dourly, "I'm sure your parents preferred him to the old Jew."

Rafaela's cup never made it to her lips. "What do you mean, Clement?" she asked, nearly whispering.

"Why couldn't you wait for me, Rafaela? I begged you to have faith in me, to understand. I told you I'd be free in time, but you didn't believe me. I suppose no one could blame you. But I did. I blamed you for a long, long time."

Rafaela's eyes filled with tears. "I believe you loved me. Oh, not twenty years ago. I wasn't altogether sure then. But somehow over the years I did come to believe it. Anyway, that isn't why I didn't come to Hollywood."

★ ★ ★

The voice on the other end sounded pinched and metallic, not at all like Clement's usual silk-lined instrument.

"Rafaela, darling, I've been trying like mad to reach you. Something's happened. When I got back here, my wife told me she's been seeing the doctor. She had a growth in her breast. They operated this week and hopefully removed everything."

"How terrible! Oh, Clement!"

"Sweetheart, listen to me. I love you more than anything on earth, but I'm not a monster. I can't ask Sylvia for a divorce now. At least not yet. Don't hate me, Rafaela."

The long-distance connection roared in Rafaela's ear. Or perhaps it was her own head that was making the noise. She felt dizzy, faint.

"Stop that talk," she managed to say. "I know you are doing the right thing. I could never hate you. I love you."

"Then come to me," urged the strange voice. "When Sylvia's feeling better, I'm going to Hollywood. Prince has told me they're talking about a new picture for you and me. Maybe it'll be a decent story. Anyway, I told him I'd do it providing you were willing."

"Clement, you can't!" cried Rafaela. "You tell me you hate Diadem. They will want you to sign the contract again. You are the man of the moment now—I read in the paper you can be nominate for the Academy Award. You will surely have better offers than another silly Diadem film with me."

"You're funny with your man of the moment. Do you fancy I care about that now? I'm half mad here because I can't be near you. I'm begging you to go to Hollywood, Rafaela."

"I am not under contract with Diadem."

"I know they plan to offer you one. Prince said so. He wants to work with you, again. It won't be the same for you at Diadem as it's been for me. They say I don't photograph well, so I fell into the crack between leading roles and character parts. But Prince assures me you can be another Sophia Loren."

"Prince, Prince, the Jewish man who doesn't like the Jewish face. Well, I, Rafaela, do like the Jewish face—even his!"

"What do you mean?"

"Nothing," said Rafaela. "I am not Sophia Loren. I do no more films for Diadem. *Basta, finito!* Not even with you, *caro mio*—especially not with you. You are the great actor. Go and be great. For this you will thank Rafaela who adores you. No more Via Appia for you. No more the no-good rubbish."

"Darling, have I seen the last of Rafaela? Are you running the credits now? Can you do that?" The voice sounded smaller, infinitely sad.

"*Addio, mi amore*," said Rafaela, who hung up the phone and burst into tears.

★ ★ ★

"It was all in vain," said Clement. "Nothing got better for me. I didn't win the Oscar and the great parts never came. I remained the man who didn't fit the mold. Oh, I made many more pictures, but none of them were especially memorable. My scenes with you in *The Appian Way* were the last thing I did on the screen that I'm truly proud of. I was a man in love and you were the spark that caused me to burn so brightly—if briefly.

"I tried to phone you, hoping you'd changed your mind, but you'd moved from your flat. That was when I got it through my head you didn't want me to find you. But I never stopped thinking about you. Once I saw Luchino Visconti, the director, at the opera. I cornered him and asked him if he knew anything about Rafaela Livi. 'Disappeared,' he told me. 'Never made another film as far as I know. Somewhere I heard she went to live with an old Jewish man, a millionaire.'

"I couldn't believe it. I mean, after you'd defied your parents to go into pictures it didn't make sense for you to suddenly give it all up to become the mistress of an old man, however rich he might be. Still, Visconti wouldn't invent such a rumor. Then I blamed myself. You were pure and chaste before I came along, Rafaela. I remembered your telling me how much virtue meant in Italy. But all that had nothing to do with acting. You must have had offers, you, the girl of the moment in your own words."

"Moments pass very quickly," Rafaela said. "Yes, I had offers, but I couldn't face them. I felt vulnerable, without defenses. Don't think it didn't occur to me that, should I do another movie, I might meet another man like you, handsome and bursting with charm and self-assurance, trying to make me fall for him because he was bored between takes. How did I know I would be sensible? I only knew how easily I fell in love with you."

Clement stood up. "Perhaps now you can comprehend that you weren't the only one with feelings. The truth is, I began to hate you after what Visconti told me. You made me feel shabby. How long would you have waited had I been a wealthy man, Rafaela?"

"What are you talking about?" Rafaela demanded angrily. "I've explained everything to you and still you don't understand. I never cared about money, in spite of how things look. Yes, I lived with an old Jew. He was my uncle, Claudio Giordano, a wonderful writer but hardly a millionaire. So much for rumors."

Clement studied Rafaela as though he were seeing her for the first time. "You, Rafaela? You're Jewish? I had no idea."

"I never told you because I was a little coward at twenty-three. I was afraid it might make a difference between us. David Prince knew and he practically demanded I tell nobody. He was worried it might damage my career." Rafaela gave a throaty chuckle. "My career!"

"Prince had a ghetto mentality—even though I suppose he meant well. He liked you, you know. He thought you could go places—so did I. You had talent, Rafaela, a lot of it."

"But not enough heart. That you took away with you, Byron

Clement. And so I turned to my uncle, the only person I could talk to about you. He was kind and wise, full of witty remarks that made me laugh and took my mind off the pain of losing you—or of never having you in the first place. One day, his secretary, upon whom he relied very much, left him to get married. I simply took her place and lived with my uncle until my own marriage."

"You became a secretary!" marveled Clement. "You, the most beautiful girl in Italy—to me the most beautiful girl in the world. You were on your way to becoming an international star. Was your uncle's work more important to you than our own career?"

Rafaela, Lady St. Giles, the chatelaine of one of England's greatest country houses laughed ironically. "I never thought of it that way. But, yes, now that you mention it, his work was infinitely more important than mine. Even at twenty-three I had the sense to realize that."

Clement put his hands on Rafaela's shoulders. "Oh, Rafaela, there was no reason in the world for you to keep such secrets from me. You'll laugh when I tell you just how foolish you were. Look at me, my face! Is this the map of Great Britain, I ask you? I am a Jew myself. I never mentioned it because I thought it was obvious enough in my case. Dear God, is it possible we knew so little about one another?"

The actor sat down with Rafaela on her bed. He took her hand. They resembled a long-married couple, stunned by some tragedy in their life, comforting each other in silence.

Finally, Clement said, "Until I joined the Royal Academy of Dramatic Arts, my name was Nathan Abarbanel. Half the people I know still call me Nate to this day. The Abarbanels come from Spain—Sephardic Jews. Well, now do you at last believe that I'm the fellow you ought to have married? Even your uncle would have agreed. But I already had a wife. And Alec St. Giles had none."

"Clement, I'm afraid that's what it came down to. You never did divorce your wife."

"There seemed no need," said the actor. "My dreams of romance faded, and Sylvia and I grew apathetic together. I became preoccupied with my work, and she with her health. We made the adjustment."

"Never mind," Rafaela told him gently. "You needn't go into detail. I'm not as ignorant as I used to be. I know what marriage can become. If it's any comfort to you, there weren't any happy endings for me either. I have reason to believe that my husband is in love with someone else."

"Do you mind terribly?"

"No," replied Rafaela. "That's the trouble. I don't mind at all."

"Where are your children? Surely you must have children."

"Two. A boy and a girl. Both grown and away at school. It was far better when they were here, but—" Rafaela shrugged. "Clement, you don't know how much good it's done me to see you again. I used to think sometimes I'd dreamt you, made you up. Well, we've reminisced enough, don't you agree? Time to go downstairs and join the party."

Clement clasped his hands decisively. "Wait a moment. There are happy endings. It's only a matter of changing the script. Rafaela, tell me the truth: how do I look to you now?"

"If you had come to Rome just as you are, I would have loved you no less."

"That's all I need to know. As *you* know, I'm an out-of-work old actor with not much money in the bank, but I have a comfortable flat in the city and some prospect of getting jobs in television on the strength of my worn-but-familiar face. Added to that, I don't run after young actresses any longer. Can you live without that party downstairs?"

"If you mean Alec, the answer is yes!"

"How long will it take you to pack a bag?"

"I'm already packed."

"Rafaela!" said Clement, astounded. But he quickly recovered the pace, just as he would have done had this been a play instead of real life, where the cues are less predictable. "Come on then!"

Byron Clement took Rafaela by the hand. They retrieved his own overnight bag and began to walk very fast. Downstairs they came into the room with the assembled guests, heading at once for Lord St. Giles and Rosamund Peters.

"There you are, Clement," said the peer heartily. "We were wondering where you'd gone. I see you've found my wife."

"Found her and mean to keep her," replied the actor. "Rosamund, dear, please give me the keys to the car. Rafaela and I are leaving. St. Giles, I'm in love with your wife. You may have her things sent to my flat."

Lord St. Giles laughed, but when he saw the look on Rafaela's face, he stopped at once. "You're not joking, are you."

"I don't do comedy," Clement informed him. "The keys, Rosamund."

"Now see here," St. Giles began, but Rosamund had already taken the keys from her purse.

"You promised to do me a good turn," Clement told her, "and by God you have. Good-bye."

Exeunt Byron Clement and Rafaela Livi, surely older and perhaps wiser but definitely star-crossed no longer.

John Drummer, momentarily forgetting his aversion to Rosamund, came over and demanded, "Where's Clement going with that pretty lady? I thought I heard him say good-bye."

"The blighter's stolen my wife!" croaked St. Giles. "What in the devil did he say to her?"

"Something you forgot to say, I should imagine," drawled Rosamund, very posh indeed, her confidence restored now that her rival had been spirited away.

Drummer stared at the door. "Good heavens! Now that's what I call a dramatic gesture."